ESCAPE FROM RUNWAY TWO SIX

Michael Harris

MINERVA PRESS
LONDON
MONTREUX   LOS ANGELES   SYDNEY

ESCAPE FROM RUNWAY TWO SIX
Copyright © Michael Harris 1997

All Rights Reserved

ISBN 1 86106 231 1

First Published 1997 by
MINERVA PRESS
195 Knightsbridge
LONDON SW7 1RE

Printed in Great Britain by
Antony Rowe Ltd, Chippenham, Wiltshire

ESCAPE FROM
RUNWAY TWO SIX

To Diana
In an effort to bury the past

Prologue

14 March 1980

"Norwich approach. Golf India Papa. I've a rough running engine and intend putting down at Little Snoring. I'm not declaring an emergency."

"Roger India Papa, that's copied." The air traffic controller made a note and continued with his routine shift responsibilities.

Barry smiled nervously as he circled the light aeroplane over the old Norfolk RAF base and glanced down at the short strip, still just serviceable. Under the crops it was possible to make out the shadows of the three old runways, and some of the concrete bases of the mess huts. He thought about the Lancasters that must have returned after their sorties deep into Germany, and those that had crashed due to flack damage or tired and injured crews. 'And I'm doing this deliberately?' He shivered.

Last time it had been an accident and he tried to remember clearly the moment just before the wing touched. Could he pull that off again? Would the result be the same? He went over the calculations. Stall speed, left wing down, forty-five knots. Approach the airfield at fifty-two but nose high. Check the fuel, good, nearly empty. Left tyre pressure low, yes he'd checked that just before take-off.

He was suddenly frightened at the thought of fire and the pain of injury and death by burning fuel. He remembered the horrific pictures from the guinea pig club and those brave crews who had been disfigured for life.

"Sandy, are we expecting any visitors today?" The farmer heard the engine drone from the kitchen garden, where he was drinking a well-earned coffee after his early morning start.

"No one rang, John," she told her husband.

The farmer strolled out of the back gate. "Someone's up there. Sounds rough to me."

'Keep altering the power,' Barry instructed himself. 'Make it cough. If anyone's around it must sound like engine problems.'

He spotted the wind sock. Fair crosswind, and it was starting to drizzle. Finally the time had come. 'This is it.' He banked the aeroplane toward the runway and set it up for a controlled crash. 'Damn! If I was trying for real she would have dropped a wing anyway in this wind. Now I want it she won't go!' Suddenly the sound of the stall warning buzzer filled the cockpit as Barry forced the left wing into the ground.

The noise of metal reshaping itself filled his ears for what seemed several minutes, and then there was silence. He sniffed for any fuel smell and judging it safe his mouth pursed into a small grin, before he slumped back in his seat to await what would follow.

Chapter One

Eighteen months earlier

"Tonight then, love. Don't forget we're going over to Tom and Margaret's. Have a comfortable flight."

Barry waved to Sybil from the car and wound up the driver's window. He set off for the airport, near the Bournemouth coast, where he flew regular trips to all parts of Europe for Marvel Air.

The company had been in operation for five years and was owned by Patrick Clancy, a likeable Irishman from County Cork, who'd made his money in property and other deals. No one really knew the truth about Pat, but somewhere along the way he'd learnt to fly, and the small airline was his latest love affair. There was talk of drug running in the Caribbean and deals in the United States, but none of the staff gave it much thought, because Pat was a super boss, had played rugby for his country, and was a great character to know.

Barry parked in his reserved spot and made his way up to the flight planning section and through to the Met office.

"Morning Sue. You're looking very haveable today." Sue smiled at the comment which she would only have taken from Barry, knowing his sense of humour and how much he loved his wife.

"That's a compliment after last night's party. Too much Merridown!"

"God! That stuff's lethal. I should stick to the gin. So what's the verdict?" Barry shuffled the weather faxes which Sue placed before him.

"Not bad going. Should be clear after the mist has lifted, then CAVOK. There's a front coming in over the Bay of Biscay, expected mainland at fifteen hundred. It'll probably give overcast and low stratas on your return."

Barry admired Sue and her meteorological knowledge. He trusted her analysis, even though the responsibility still lay with him.

"Sound. Should give Norman something to think about." Barry was flying with a new co-pilot on the trip to Nice today. "I think I'll set him up for a check on the return leg."

"See you. Must go. Got to give a briefing to some student pilots."

As she left he made his way back to the operations room to file a flight plan, and then wandered to the aircraft service area .

"Watch the port engine fuel-flow readings," said Mike Swift. An ex-RAF fitter he could remember back to the days when the most critical job was swinging the wooden props of old Tiger Moths. With upgraded training, he was regarded as one of the best for the post-war jet engines.

Marvel Air was kitted out with four BAC One Elevens, which had seen better days with a holiday travel business that had gone into liquidation. Patrick had snapped them up for a 'few good punts' as he liked to put it. 'A lick of paint and you'll not know the difference' he joked. But in fact he'd had them checked out thoroughly, giving them engine overhauls, installing some uprated avionics and very smart, modern fire-proof seating.

The external livery incorporated discreet Irish green tones, and the fleet looked very attractive on the apron. Patrick acted casual but was also careful to protect himself. 'Always leave yourself an escape route.' It was a philosophy he'd learnt from bitter experience.

"Norman. Can you do the pre-flight checks? I just want to confirm the fuel upgrade, Mike says one of the gauges is not checking out."

"Wilco."

"Weather's going to close in later, so I suggest you fly the return. I can give you an instrument check, if that's okay?"

"Fine. You're the boss." Norman had the confidence of youth, having qualified within the minimum regulation hours. "Are we full?"

"About three-quarters outbound, but maximum coming back; end of holidays, probably," Barry volunteered his reasons for the return journey.

With all the checks done and the engine gauges reading normal, he taxied out to the runway for a departure to the west.

"Golf Oscar Mike is cleared for take off, left hand turn out, heading one six zero, not above two thousand feet, contact approach one two..."

"One two two decimal four..." The crew carried out their standard procedures and Barry set course for a direct flight to Nice.

"Sorry Sybil but we've got a small mechanical problem which will delay departure by a couple of hours. I suggest you go round to Margaret's and I'll join you later." He rehooked the wall phone.

They both enjoyed the bridge evenings and relaxing with a few drinks. Tom was a insurance broker and Barry was always pleased to get away from flying talk and delve into the mysteries of high finance. The girls were happy to let them argue stockmarket jargon 'bulls and bears', while they contented themselves with the latest gossip of who was befriending whom.

"Can't service it today. I've checked with maintenance and they say there's no problem with you going. You're checked out with the correct load." The engineer seemed casual about the problem.

Barry cursed. The fuel gauge had packed up completely. "I'd better get permission otherwise we'll be stuck in Nice over night."

"Tim, Barry here. It's a lousy line... Listen, the port engine fuel gauge is US. They say it's okay to go. Can you authorise for me."

"Stand by."

Barry looked out of the window to see the rain steadily turning the tarmac darker. 'That front's come in earlier,' he thought. 'Going to be a dirty flight home.'

"You there Barry? ... Got you a clearance, but you must do a physical check. Can you choose the minimum fuel burn flight level?"

"I'll try. Will probably depend on the weather; it's clamping in here."

"Okay, up to you. Safe journey."

"We're cleared," he told Norman. "Let's go. I'm supposed to be visiting friends tonight."

Once they were airborne Norman trimmed the aeroplane at the economic flight height and settled back to monitor the instruments. Barry handed him control and he was in charge unless instructed otherwise.

"I'm going back to chat with the passengers. Request from Chairman Clancy, part of the company's new public relations policy. Who do I concentrate on, the ladies?"

"They're more likely to be impressed, so yes, but don't make it too obvious, and don't just favour the young ones," Norman grinned.

Barry moved quietly through the plane carrying out this latest duty. 'Makes sense,' he thought. 'Flying is becoming very competitive and we need satisfied customers.' He enjoyed meeting people and this made a relaxing break from being up front. He answered questions on safety and service, plastic food, knee room, turbulence. 'Pretty standard,' he thought 'what else can they ask? Daren't discuss their love lives.'

He noticed the small movements as he walked the aisle, and decided to return to the flight deck.

"Just spoken to Brest control. They're forecasting lows over the Channel. Might be down to five hundred feet."

"Looks like an ILS for you. Happy?"

"No problem. Ninety-five per cent last check."

"One hundred is the only score for me son. I like to walk away."

They continued with aviation talk, and Barry looked for any signs of pressure from his co-pilot. The landing would not be easy for an experienced captain, and he was concerned as to whether he should take over.

The lightning hit without warning and the aeroplane lurched through the deteriorating weather. Barry switched on the safety lights and reached for the intercom.

"This is Captain Johnston. We've run into thunderstorms over Northern France and I would request that all passengers return to their seats and fasten seatbelts. We'll try to work round the storms, and I'll keep you informed of any changes."

"What's it like back there?" Barry directed his question to Sally the senior air hostess as she entered the flight deck.

"Okay. Lost a few cups of coffee on that last bump, and a lady fell in the gangway and cut her head slightly. The girls have things under control. Shall I offer them free drinks?"

"Sounds like a good idea. Wouldn't mind one meself," he joked.

"On me when we get back."

"Done."

"So what's the verdict?" she asked.

"Don't know. The storms are obviously stronger than forecast, and we've run into headwinds. Could turn back or divert but I'm not happy with no measure on the fuel burn. We don't want to be stewing around in these conditions longer than necessary. I'll try Southampton."

Sally nodded in approval and made her way back to the passenger cabin.

"Southampton approach, Golf Oscar Mike, could you give me the latest weather, your field and Bournemouth."

"Stand by Oscar Mike."

"Look Norman, I don't think this is ideal for your check out. I'm taking over, there'll be enough work for both of us."

"Roger, you're the skipper." He was relieved at the captain's decision, but tried not to register it.

"Oscar Mike, this is Southampton with your weather. We have heavy overcast, base five hundred and lowering, embedded thunderstorms, *vis* two thousand metres, surface wind north-west, thirty-five gusting forty. Bournemouth's the same."

"That's copied." Damn, the ILS is on two-six, wind right across the runway. Barry looked at Norman and knew he was thinking the same.

"Southampton. Could you get me Gatwick and Luton's latest?"

Sally returned and could tell from his face that there was no joy. The bad weather was concentrated on the London area and Southern England.

'Well here you go Barry, that's what all the training was about.' Most of his career had been on short-haul flights in some of Europe's worst winter conditions, and he was well experienced in coping with storms. Why did he feel uneasy? This year had been very busy for Marvel Air and Barry had flown a lot of hours. The holiday season nearly over, he was looking forward to a break. Sybil and he loved walking and had rented a small cottage in Devon. He suddenly wished they were there, breathing the sea-sprayed air off the cliff tops.

"Oscar Mike is cleared to flight level six zero. Turn onto heading two six zero, and report established localiser."

"Two six zero. Oscar Mike."

Something's wrong. They were still eight miles out and nearly on course but the auto pilot was suggesting a heading fifty degrees off. He studied the screen.

"Established." Norman cut through his concentration. So they were. The navigation instruments were all lined up. 'Funny. Maybe I'm tired?'

"Oscar Mike. We have you, seven miles to roll left of centre. The base is three hundred, visibility eight hundred metres in mist and heavy rain. You're number two to a Jetstream on short finals."

Barry started to worry again. The autopilot was tracking the apparent runway centre line and was also locked onto the glide path. But radar saw it differently, and so did the wet compass.

"Oscar Mike you're left of course. You need two seven five. Be warned that some of the approach landing lights have been damaged by an earlier storm." Barry needed that like a hole in the head. He was suspicious. Maybe the autopilot was affected. Suddenly the headings were swinging all over the place.

"What's that crazy instrument doing?" He saw the concern register on Norman's face.

"I don't know, I don't believe it!"

Properly programmed the autopilot should have sensed the radio beams, calculated wind drift, speed, and any other variables, nailed the ILS and tracked the plane to the ground. Barry could still see the blackboard and the diagrams of his ground school instruction days.

"Seems okay now."

Barry was still not happy. "I reckon it's hemstitching." It was jargon for an instrument trundling back and forth like a wallowing boat in heavy seas, or a bloodhound following a scent.

"Turn left at the intersection." The Jetstream was down. "Oscar Mike is cleared to land, surface wind northerly, forty-five knots. Pass your message Foxtrot Echo." The controller was obviously busy and Oscar Mike was one and half miles out, and on its own.

"Passing eight hundred." Barry nodded as Norman carried out the landing check list and read off the heights from the radio altimeter.

"Still playing up. I'm taking it out at five hundred." He continued with the aircraft's descent as his co-pilot relayed the height readings.

"One mile to..." The words died on his lips as Norman saw the high rise building loom into the windscreen! "...Bloody hell!"

"Full power!" Barry screamed the instruction as they both rammed the throttle levers full forward. They just saw some frightened faces through the top windows as the port wing snapped off a large aerial on top of the building. Oscar Mike seem to crawl into the air as Barry threw out the autopilot and struggled with air speed before he could raise the undercarriage and trim the flaps.

"Jesus, where were we?" Barry felt the sweat soaking into his shirt as he concentrated on controlling the labouring One Eleven.

"Tower, this is Oscar Mike. We're overshooting, problem with ILS. Request Radar vectoring for two six for a precision approach."

"Roger Oscar Mike. Did you reach your decision height? We didn't get your call or see you."

"Yes, but we were left of the runway due to autopilot failure."

Paul Egerton was senior controller at Bournemouth, and he shivered on hearing the explanation. He knew the One Eleven was on finals and he suspected that approach control had cleared the plane for landing just before he'd come on duty. Still, he should have made contact.

In order to cut costs the council-owned airport only budgeted for one controller when they weren't busy. Bad weather increased the workload and it was left to the senior controller to decide on more personnel as necessary. He'd registered the forecast that day and had intended that two controllers would be on duty. Mary his wife had seen it differently and hence he was late.

"You're pathetic. God knows why those pilots put their trust in you! Can't drive the car without banging it."

"It's your fault, you're the one who winds me up."

"I'm moving in with Harry and that's it."

Paul studied his plump wife and thought how ridiculous she looked in a short skirt with that silly gold ankle bracelet. Trying to be a teenager again. He'd loved her once but now the nagging and taunting were too much, and he felt relieved that she was leaving. She'd done it before, mind you, but she wasn't going to come back this time. No way.

"Be nice to feel the depth of a real man." She wouldn't leave it alone. He didn't mean to hit her so hard but the blood had poured from her ear and lips. "See if Harry likes kissing that!" he shouted, boiling with anger and shaking at the same time. Calming down he felt guilty. Maybe he'd ignored her needs over the last few years. But things weren't easy. The council's cost-cutting exercises worried him, and he wasn't getting any younger. He was finding it difficult to cope with the stress of the job.

"Harry you'd better come over. Mary's had an accident. Cut her face, might need stitches. She's told me about you so the best of luck. I don't want to see either of you again. Got to go now, I'm on duty."

"Oscar Mike turn onto a heading of zero six two and report at the Hotel Romeo." Paul returned to focus on the problem out there in the strong winds and rain. "You said left of runway. How far?"

"One and a half miles maybe." Barry didn't like this conversation going out for all to hear.

"I suggest you report to the tower after landing." He realised this could be serious. One and a half miles, that would put the aircraft over a highly-populated area. The captain said he'd reached decision height, but with the base down to two hundred he must have been lower. The high-rise flats were about one fifty feet. Paul closed his eyes at the thought. 'Concentrate, I need to get them down.' Through the misty window he could see the rain blowing across the runway and the windsock nearly horizontal.

"Met what's the base now?" he buzzed their open line.

"Last reported one seven five occasional two."

"One seven five Oscar Mike, are you legal at that?"

"I am today. No fuel readings. I'm coming in." The voice sounded taut.

"Roger, Oscar Mike, turn to two five zero you have radar approach to half a mile and one fifty."

Chapter Two

Patrick's face was grim and his expression was mirrored by Tim Mitchell, Senior Captain of Marvel Air, as he handed the letter to Barry Johnston. The pilot took the envelope nervously, knowing it would contain confirmation that he was to be grounded pending an investigation. He read it slowly and nodded an acknowledgement to the other two. Patrick showed him to the door with no further explanation.

The courtroom was busy with everyone engrossed in their papers, and he felt his presence was redundant. Sybil smiled encouragement, for which he was grateful. She looked tired and he supposed these proceedings where a strain on her also. He remembered their wedding and the good times and laughs, and felt guilty for the worry she was having to endure. 'When this is over we'll take that holiday to New Zealand that we always promised ourselves.'

His mind wandered as he tried to recall the display screen and the information it was giving. Runway two six, yet his heading was fifty degrees off.

"Oscar Mike is cleared to flight level six zero. Turn onto heading two six zero and report established localiser."

"Two six zero. Oscar Mike."

"Would you explain in simple terms to this hearing the exact operation of the instrument landing procedure." Judge Newall was already bored with the technicalities of flying and the boffins sitting around in the stuffy courtroom. He hated aeroplanes and wished he hadn't been briefed for this one.

He'd seen it all, from those early article days to official referee, and finally circuit judge. Frankly all he wanted now was to retire to a Scottish island and waste the rest of his life painting and enjoying the company of the locals over fine malt whiskies.

He studied the defendant and glanced at his notes. Barry Johnston, forty-seven, married, no children, that's all they gave.

"What else?"

His mentor had once told him that he could spot a criminal a mile away, and whatever the evidence, respecting his duty to judge on that alone of course, he'd often had to convict or release knowing deep down that the public, or the Crown, were not getting justice. Newall didn't go by that, but thought he might put it to the test today.

He was just getting into the airline captain's psychology of dress, appearance and stature, when he was brought back to the proceeding to listen to his question being answered.

"The instrument landing system, or ILS for short, is a navigation aid which can be selected by the pilot to guide him to the airfield and the runway." Stephen Oaks was a typical civil servant who had worked for the Civil Aviation Authority for as long as he could remember. Precise in detail, he was not going to make any mistakes at this time in his career, for he was looking forward to retirement within the next four years. "The system comes in various categories, but category one, cat. 1 as it's known, is the appropriate approach for this case."

Judge Newall studied the expert and his smart grey suit over the top of his half-moon reading glasses, and then glanced at his notes. "Mr Oaks, so that there is no misunderstanding, I must advise you that the proceedings are that this Court will decide what is appropriate," he paused, "and for your purposes today, you may take that as meaning myself." He smiled briefly with the authority of a schoolmaster. "Please continue."

"Yes, your Honour." Stephen seemed unruffled by being put in his place. "Well, there are three categories of approaches which depend on the weather minimums, the training of the flight crew, the electronic systems available on the airfield, and..."

The Judge interrupted. "I see..." but he didn't. Why couldn't this be a medical trial? The last one with the drugs doctor had been fascinating. A few naughties in it as well. He chuckled at the thought.

"So what was the category – is that how you describe it? – that was in use in this instance? Cat. 1 you said?" The Judge was writing and didn't even look for acknowledgement, but glanced at the wall clock and then nodded to the benches. "I suggest a ten-minute break."

The chairs shuffled as the attendants stood up and a quiet babel of conversation broke out within the small groups.

"Phew! This is going to be longwinded?" Tim Mitchell turned to his solicitor for an opinion.

"Yes, old Newall can drag things out a bit. Depends on whether he's interested in the subject. He's playing with the witnesses for amusement at the moment."

"But surely this is only a preliminary hearing to decide whether there's a case to be heard?"

"I'm sure that's right. But the Judge must be reasonably certain of the facts before he comes to a decision. You'll have to sweat this one out a bit longer."

Tim Mitchell sighed. As senior captain of Marvel Air he was responsible for the conduct and training of the flight crews. Barry Johnston was a good pilot, well qualified with over eleven thousand hours, and a clean accident record, till now. He was well liked at the aero-club where he still flew the trainers and did some instructing. His friendship with Barry and his charming wife Sybil, went back to the early days of the airline. Now he'd been instructed by the owner to mount a legal action.

"Why not an internal disciplinary board procedure?" The question had been asked.

"Members of the public were put at risk. We've a duty to them and the good name of the airline to uphold." It was a powerful argument from the chairman, and Tim had not been able to counter it in any way.

The proceedings dragged on and Judge Newall was soon looking at the clock again, and indicating the need for a luncheon break.

Barry was not hungry, and they left him sitting alone with his wife and his thoughts in the cold court corridor as the others breezed off to take some lunch.

"Two six zero. Oscar Mike." Barry was trying to concentrate on the words and the court evidence, but his mind kept going back to that disastrous day last September.

"The court will stand."

Judge Newall, with a good lunch comforting his stomach, made his way to the bench and adjusted his glasses to read the notes.

"I find some difficulty with this preliminary hearing in that there appear to be errors and circumstances which may or may not be linked. We have heard from several experts about the procedures required to ensure safe flying conditions, and it has been shown that these did not work entirely satisfactorily on this occasion – however it is unclear whether this was due to technical faults or human error and I consider that this requires more investigation." Barry felt his heartbeat rising as he waited for the Judge to continue "...with that in mind, and in view of the fact that some of the public where put at risk, albeit without injury thank God, I am minded to rule that this case should be set aside for trial in the High Court. So that is my decision. I leave the officers of this Court and the legal representatives to make the necessary arrangements." The Court rose and Newall made his way back to his chambers.

"I'm free to go, what now?" Barry questioned his lawyer. He gathered later that it would depend on the airline's decision on whether to continue with the charges, or even extend them.

"What do you mean extend them?"

"Well the Judge was indicating that there might be a case for criminal charges."

Barry slumped in his chair. "Jesus no. There's no way I was at fault. The instruments were on the blink. They all know that. They're trying to stitch me up."

The lawyers said nothing and gathered their papers.

"Damn you then! I'm not taking the rap, you see?"

Chapter Three

"So you see, Miss Marshall, it makes a lot of sense to produce an affidavit, otherwise you might have to face the stress of the witness box."

"But you will be asking the questions?"

He loved the apparent innocence. So attractive to still come across it, even if it was not all genuine. So many of his cases these days involved streetwise girls, who would bite your bollocks off without question. He loved a touch of femininity, seeing himself as a softy at heart. Mind you, some of his colleagues had found it tough going in court.

Donald Opperman QC was a force to be reckoned with. Gentle as he was, he had a very decisive legal brain. In his early career he'd produced some stunning cross-examinations and was very respected by his learned friends.

"Brilliant defence Donald." A junior had flattered him during one of his trials. "It was so beautiful I felt I had to write it down."

"I'm pleased you did. Perhaps I could have a transcript, as I've completely forgotten what I said." He chuckled, loving the play-acting. What other profession allows you on the stage, even if you get the script wrong, and still pays you handsome money. I'm a lucky man.

Some said he was a people's lawyer. Maybe. But Donald did not want to be typecast. Any brief, maximise your earnings, you're a long time dead. That was the *modus operandi*. Not sure he meant it, but a good enough philosophy until he found something different to fill his easily bored mind.

"How do I say it?"

"My dear, just put down in your own words exactly what happened. You're not on trial, and no one has yet been found guilty. All we are trying to find out is what actually happened. You achieve nothing by holding back. In fact you could do Mr Johnston more harm by being evasive, for the judge might read something into your evidence that isn't there."

Donald was a passive flying passenger, although intrigued by the technology. He enjoyed the excitement of airports. When Patrick Clancy rang to ask his advice he'd listened more intensely than usual, as Pat had been at university with him. Donald was godfather to the Clancy family and felt an allegiance there, although he was not totally sure about some of Pat's activities.

"Patrick, long time eh?" They shook hands. "What can I do for you?"

"One of my pilots might have screwed up a landing which could have been disastrous. I think he was at fault. He's blaming other factors. We've had a preliminary hearing and the judge has given me, or the company the right to go further."

"Criminal action?"

"You might be right. No one was injured. But there's no doubt that the passengers were not put at risk." Donald ignored the double negative for he knew what Patrick meant.

"Have you had any reaction?"

"What, from the passengers?"

"Yes."

"Not much at all you'd say. But it was an awful day. Poor visibility in thunderstorms, so I expect they were being bumped around a lot. Weren't surprised when the pilot overshot."

"I see."

"Mind you the passengers on the port side must have seen something because the wing caught a television aerial on top of a high-rise building."

"Really, so it was a close thing?"

"Closest in my experience." He swallowed as he was reminded. "Anyway to answer your question, I've a letter from a guy who says he's representing some of the passengers and would like a meeting. I think he's a quasi-legal from the tone of his approach." Patrick passed over the paper.

"Okay. I'll need to study that, and I'll need to talk to the rest of the crew. What are their views?"

"Well the co-pilot is standing behind Johnston, but I would expect that, after all he was up front as you might say. As to the others I don't know. Sally Marshall the senior air hostess might be good for starters."

"So what are you asking? You want me to make a case?" Donald raised his eyes in answer to his own question. "Unlike you Patrick, you're normally sympathetic to your staff."

"I give them plenty of rope, yes. Barry's a good pilot. Clean record. But I have the reputation of the airline to consider, and an angry public along with the competition could put me out of business."

Donald managed a smile for himself. 'When would Pat ever go out of business? He might dump it, but he'd come up smelling of roses.'

"Well I can take it. Just winding up on a strip club rape case. The owner has been enjoying his female employees as if they were office perks. One of them had enough and cried rape. Forensic have had some fun. How d'you prove who was last when you're at it every night? Still I..."

The knock on the door interrupted his banter.

"Come in."

"Mr Opperman?" Donald nodded, annoyed at this intrusion to his story. "I'm occupied at..."

"Sorry Donald." Pat took over. "Let me do the introductions. Tim Mitchell, our senior captain. Been with me from the start. Tim's responsible for the training and safety of the flight crews' procedures and type checkouts."

"I see. Unfortunate situation Mr Mitchell."

"Yes, we're all very concerned, but thank God no one was hurt."

"You'll have your views no doubt, but your chairman has asked me to take a brief for criminal negligence." He looked to Patrick for confirmation and turned back to catch any reaction from the captain.

Tim showed it in his face. He was dreading this decision although he had feared the worst. He'd gone over the procedures and what happened that late September afternoon until he was exhausted.

"Let's follow the procedures again Barry. You were locked in auto, but the heading was oscillating. Thirty degrees wind correction checked out with the wet compass, ADF was unreliable due to the storms..." The two pilots worked meticulously through all the technical points again.

"It was the crazy auto! I keep telling you! The old ones never gave problems. It's okay to uprate, but I bet the old man picked these up as a job lot at a Dublin car boot sale!" Tim understood the frustration, the man's career was on trial.

"Cool it Barry. Remember you've got a medical tomorrow with the shrink. High blood pressure and anger aren't going to help."

"Sorry, but Sybil's worried out of her mind. She won't take any pills to help herself. Me? It just keeps on going round and round in my mind... Thanks for your help, I appreciate that a lot. But you've got to look after yourself otherwise you'll be sucked into the charges. You're my boss remember. Responsible for my behaviour."

Tim let the words sink in. He was right for sure, but there was something missing , and at the time it wasn't clear what.

"Last question. Forgetting the auto, how come the mile and a half drift and the height? Are you suggesting failure of the gyro compass and radio altimeter as well?"

"Look Tim I'm tired. I don't know. Jesus, I've flown planes with nothing but a wristwatch to guide me. All I can say is that the auto was on the blink and the back-ups misled somehow."

'There's no way the jury will swallow that defence.' Tim was worried. 'I'm not sure I can help him. He's going to need a good lawyer.' He stood up. "I need a drink, care to join me?"

"No thanks. Medics remember? Wouldn't do to turn up half-pissed. Need to get home. I don't like to leave her for too long at the moment."

Back at the briefing in the Opperman chambers Tim had asked, "What will happen to his licence and pension if he's found guilty?"

"That will depend on the verdict. He'll probably lose his commercial licence through the authority of the CAA. Pension? Well that will be up to Marvel Air." He turned to Pat but got no reaction.

"I think that's as far as we can go Patrick. I look forward to your formal instructions. I'll be in touch." Donald showed them the door.

They left the room and Tim hurried past them to get away.

"Tim. One minute." Patrick grabbed his sleeve. "I know you're upset by my decision, but you'll need to understand..."

"Oh, I understand," he replied with feeling. "You're about to ruin a man's career, not to say his life and probably his marriage. I hope you're happy?"

"See here now! I know you and Captain Johnston are friends, but you must divorce that from your mind. I'm *not* happy that you're acting rationally at this time and therefore I'm putting you on stand down until further notice. It'll be for your own good."

Tim said nothing as he stalked away.

Chapter Four

The Queen's Head was a tatty pub on the estuary, away from the smart marina berths. The backwater had collected a mixture of old house boats and wrecks and was home for some who'd dropped out of the rat race. Barry had passed by a few years ago, when he was thinking of investing in a small dinghy. His sailing days never took off however, always too busy. He viewed the washing lines and the flower pots and the beaten up push bikes, and for once felt envious. 'What cares do they have? Probably collecting the dole or working the black economy.' He realised that was hardly fair. 'They've probably got more worries than you. That's why they're here and you have your fancy cottage. Such is life, I'm going to have that drink anyway.'

"Pint of Stella – packet of Winterman and some matches please."

He passed through the veranda to tables overlooking the creek and sat down before lighting a cigar, and stared vacantly out over the water.

"Same again, with a whisky chaser." 'This is crazy, they'll be distilling my blood tomorrow.' He went over the events again and the evidence from the preliminary hearing. 'Was I wrong?' If you're not careful you can easily start believing others. 'Stick with it.' But he wasn't confident.

The voice was quiet and for a moment it didn't register. "Not seen you around. Off the boats? Mind if I sit down?"

He studied his new company and was pleased to be greeted with a warm smile from a young gypsy-looking girl. She had strong cheek bones with a slender swan like neck, and dark almost black hair which hung simply past her shoulders. Her slim, petite body boasted firm breasts which were easily emphasised by a tight fawn-coloured blouse, and Barry guessed she had legs to match her model-type figure, beneath her ankle-length skirt.

She stood shyly holding a cup of coffee.

"Please." He stood up to show her a seat.

"Definitely not from these parts, there's no gentleman left here." She laughed. "Old sea salts yes, but gentlemen no. Some can be good fun." She smiled with an innocence that he suspected was not so naive.

"So come on, what are you celebrating?" She pointed to the tumbler and whisky glass.

Maybe it was the alcohol or the relaxing unknown surroundings, but Barry suddenly needed to talk, and this stranger was available. He'd tried to discuss it with Sybil, but somehow they were almost too close, and he couldn't find the words. Tim had helped, but only on the technical side. He needed more; someone to understand his emotional feelings, a simple listener and here she was. He looked into her inquisitive eyes and decided to talk.

"I'm an airline pilot. Work up the road at Bournemouth."

"Hey, that's interesting. I've got a friend who lives on the estate up there. Sez one of those airliners nearly took their roof off. Few months back as I remember."

The blank reminder made him jump, and he stared vacantly into her eyes as if he needed time to assimilate her statement.

"Have I said something I shouldn't have? You've gone pale."

He focused his eyes. "Would you believe me if I said I was flying that aeroplane?"

"Look, it's none of my business." Somehow she sensed a deeper problem. "Would you like another drink?"

"I'll get them."

He returned from the bar and poured out the whole story as if she'd been a life long friend. He ordered the whisky bottle to the table and persuaded her to lace the coffees. Nothing was held back, even the intimacies of his marriage, as he unloaded the frustrations lodged in his brain. By the time he stopped talking the bottle was empty and he was ordering again. She didn't stop him. 'I'm not his wife.' She felt thankful.

"I think I've said enough. I'm sorry, I had no right."

"No, I'm very interested. They can be a bit boring round here. It's all marine stories or big fishing catches which nobody believes."

"Thanks for listening. I've probably said too much. Last coffee and I must go."

26

She reached over and put her hand gently on his arm. "I can't
help you with your case, and maybe you'll lose, but so what. Don't
let it eat into your soul. Your life is flying and you'll always be able
to do that. Someone will hire you, maybe in another country, or you
can buy a plane and live in a caravan. Life's for the living and it ain't
always easy – I know. I've had it rough but that's another story."

Suddenly Barry felt ashamed. Here he was off-loading his worries
onto this slip of a girl and he hadn't even asked her name.

"Judy. Just ask for Judy. They all know the pubs I use."

"Well Judy I'm getting drunk. Illegal to drive, not allowed to fly,
but I feel a whole lot better thanks to you. Please don't repeat my
story."

"You're all right. I'm not a talker just a listener. Tell it all to
Judy they say."

He kissed her like a father and walked unsteadily out to the car.
He took the back route home keeping the speed well down. 'Nice
girl. Hope she keeps her mouth shut. Shouldn't have talked so much.
What about her friend in the flats?' He felt guilty, then giggled.
'Haven't drunk that much for ages. Can still take it, eh?' He turned
the radio on full and wound down the window.

"Where the heck have you been?" Sybil was standing on the
doorstep as the music-filled vehicle turned into the drive. "Barlows
have been trying to contact you."

"Barlows? Who the hell are they?" Barry was finding it difficult
to focus his mind.

"The lawyers we were recommended by Tom, you remember the
other night?"

"Yes... yes... of course, silly of me, did you get their number?"
She handed the note to him and he kissed her and staggered down to
the toilet to relieve himself. The cold water helped a bit as his
unsteady fingers punched out the code. "Universal holdings PLC.
How can we help you?"

"Sorry. Damn! Got the wrong number." Sybil stifled a giggle
with her hand over her mouth. She pulled up a chair and made him
sit down.

"Zero... two... eight..." He concentrated on pushing the right
keys, and listened for the dialling tone. "Barry Johnston. I was given
your name by Tom Goff. Returning your call."

"'Tom – yes. I remember. Spoke to me the other day, so I have the gist of your dilemma. What can I do for you?"

"I'd like to arrange a meeting as soon as possible. I believe – that is my airline is going to bring criminal charges."

"I'm sorry to hear that Mr Johnston, I can fit you in tomorrow"

"Fine. I have... um... a medical in the morning. Three o'clock suitable?"

"Ask for David Jenkins, and bring any papers you might have."

"Thank you Mr Jenkins, thank you very much, see you at three." He misplaced the handset to watch it fall and spin as the wire unwound from its dangling position.

"Did you have a good lunch, darling?" She said it with a teasing tone, but relieved that he looked more relaxed than he'd been for several weeks.

"I'm feeling a lot better, how about going out for a meal?"

Sybil smiled with consent and brushed his lips with hers. What ever it was, it must have been strong. "I'd like that. Why don't you come upstairs and help me choose a dress. Perhaps we could both take a shower?"

Their sex life had never been adventurous and Sybil had lived a narrow childhood as an only child of doting but well-meaning protective parents. She knew that Barry was more experienced, and she was certain that he'd strayed during their marriage. She accepted that, as long as he showed her some love and came home. She worried about his problem, mostly because she couldn't relate to the situation. She sometimes wished her parents had kicked her out at an earlier age to fend for herself. Streetwise. That's the training she needed.

It was good. Better than ever before. She wondered if it was due to the tension, but what the hell! She stroked his hair as he slept and wondered what fate had decided for their future.

Chapter Five

The courts were a second home to Judge Norman Teal-Jones, and he robed in his favourite room, taking in again the splendid pictures of his favourite mentors which adorned the walls. He always enjoyed a new challenge and likened a fresh case to the anticipation of a starting a new term at university. He was an unashamed academic and should have been a professor of English, his favourite subject. Still the legal profession had given him ample opportunity to use his language to advantage, and he was not too displeased with the outcome. He lived in a splendid house with a frontage onto the River Thames and also farmed in the rolling hills of Devon. Always privileged, his father had given him an excellent education and left enough money for him to have chosen not to work at all.

"The Court will stand."

Judge Teal-Jones surveyed the benches before him and glanced at his notes. 'Aha, Mr Donald Opperman QC, I might have guessed. Surprised anyone can afford him these days. Lost his last case before me I recall. Have to be on my toes, he'll be looking for a win... Mr David Jenkins for the defence. New to me.' He looked through his brief. 'Recently appointed to the bar. Now that might be interesting!'

"Mr Opperman if you please."

"My Lord, I do not propose to waste the Court's time with a lengthy opening. You have before you a transcript of the preliminary hearing under Judge Newall which summarises the basics of this unfortunate incident. You will see in the summing up that Mr Newall was unable to decide whether this unsatisfactory flying situation was caused by a technical fault or faults, or simple human error. My task is to show, that is to show the jury that..."

Barry listened to the lawyer labouring over his opening address for the prosecution. 'Save time? Well this wasn't a good start. When did lawyers ever save time? Surely it's in their interest to drag it out.'

Weeks back he'd fidgeted about on an old chair in the cramped offices of Barlows solicitors. "Frankly Mr Jenkins, I can't afford that sort of money for counsel. As it is I've had to sign a personal guarantee with the bank to pay for your estimated fees."

"Well, I can take it. I've just been called to the Bar. I'm not an expert in advocacy, and we are up against Donald Opperman. It's your choice."

"So you see my Lord," David was on his feet. "We do not see this case as one that might require recourse to the finer points of law," Donald raised his eyebrows, "more a case of facts, that is, was Captain Johnston guilty of endangering the passengers due to errors on his part, or did technical failures override the pilot's control?"

"Mr Oaks would you please take the book in your left hand and say after me...?" The proceedings dragged on with no new evidence over that of the preliminary hearing. Stephen Oaks was true to form being even more careful this time, as he gave a very comprehensive account of the skills and techniques of instrument flying.

Sally was very nervous and scared by the proceedings. She'd woken that morning feeling tired after a restless night. She felt sorry for Barry but she was not happy that he'd been in total control that day. There was an anxiousness which she'd not seen before, and he also seemed worried about the co-pilot. Of course Donald sensed her vulnerability, and prised it all out.

"So Miss Marshall, in your opinion Captain Johnston was unable to cope with the workload in the deteriorating weather conditions?"

"Now come Mr Opperman, you know better than to lead the witness. Members of the jury please strike out those remarks by counsel. In your own time Miss Marshall." The judge used his charm and smiled benevolently. A smart girl, watching her career I suspect.

"Well sir. I... that is..."

"Please address the jury." Donald, acting hard today, was giving her little chance, and however carefully she tried he finally got to her.

She broke down and stated that she thought the captain was at fault. Although hearsay, the co-pilot had confided to her that Mr Johnston had ignored the radio altimeter readings and was too low even if they had been centred on the glide path. 'I should have called the co-pilot after all,' he reassessed, but then Donald had felt he might have been a hostile witness, and agreed with the defence solicitors that neither of them would take evidence.

Tim Mitchell's performance was professional; he advised that a oscillating, or wandering autopilot was a fault that all his flying staff were trained to cope with. The weather that day was appalling but the Captain had sufficient back-up aids to make a safe landing.

"As I understand it, after overshooting as you phrase it, Captain Johnston was able to make a safe landing with the assistance of radar?"

"That is correct, my Lord."

"If he was having difficulties why did he not request this service in the first place?"

"I don't know." 'Ask him,' Tim thought.

"But you would agree that was an option?" Tim nodded. "No further questions."

"How much does it cost for fuel if an aircraft has to abort a landing and overshoot?" David in cross-examination was struggling to win any points in his favour.

"It depends on the aeroplane," he delayed, "this type, I would say two thousand pounds." The jury murmured at this piece of information.

"So it is not a procedure that an airline would encourage, presumably in the interest of keeping down costs?"

"No, providing there's not a safety risk."

"Quite. Are your crews briefed on their duty to save costs?"

"Yes indeed."

"So a captain would require a very serious situation to make a decision to go round, and could face disciplinary action if he was found to be wrong?"

"Yes, that is so." Tim was not unhappy with this line of questioning which he could see might help Barry.

"One final question. The captain can divert to another airfield if weather conditions are below the safety minimums?"

"That is correct."

"Again I assume that a large cost would be involved and that this is therefore discouraged by the airline?"

"Yes, but in such a situation the pilot can ask for permission to divert, so to some extent he can share that responsibility."

"I see... I have no further questions."

"On that last point," Donald was back on re-examination, "was any request for diversion made in this instance?"

Tim hesitated before he replied. "Not to my knowledge my Lord."

"I suggest we break there. Two o'clock?" Both lawyers nodded their approval.

Barry massaged his head with his fingers. 'I've no chance! They're going to murder me!' He sat in the Pig and Whistle over a dry cider and tried to make some sense to it all.

"Barry? It is isn't it? The vaguely familiar face was a study of concentration as the eyes asked the question.

"Sorry, do I know you?"

"Julian, you remember? The Manor Club. I used to play piano down there.

"Julian, of course, I'm sorry, some time ago. So how're you making out?"

"Great I..." He droned on with the minimum of attention from Barry; it wasn't really what he needed, just someone to talk to. Didn't matter if they listened. His music had been the same, background, never too inspiring. "So Lucinda left me because of Frederick, she just couldn't understand..." He hardly heard the stories; his head had no room for other people's problems.

"Julian, got to go." He was desperate to be left alone.

"So pleased to meet you after all this time, and so pleased it's all worked out well. Playing at the Sugar Club, back of Park Lane, call in some time. Lanson on the house."

Barry made his way to the toilets and slipped into the upstairs bar. He downed a few large gins and tried to relate to the trial. Scapegoat was that their game? Patrick would be protecting his investment, and Tim and Sally their careers. He couldn't blame them for that. The rest, ten per-centers, in for the fees.

He felt very lonely. He couldn't share this with Sybil. Of course he knew she supported him, but how could she know he was right. She must have her doubts deep down. What did that pub girl say – "Life's for living." Easy words, not so easy to follow.

"Will you address the jury and explain briefly your experience in the aviation business, and your employment position with Marvel Air."

Barry replied noticing that Patrick Clancy had decided to attend the afternoon session.

"In your many hours of flying have you encountered a situation similar to that which occurred at Bournemouth last September?"

"No, my Lord."

"Are you asking this Court to accept that over some..." Donald checked with his notes, "eleven thousand hours of flying you have not had bad weather or instrumentation problems?"

"No I didn't mean that."

"So perhaps you could explain what you do mean?"

"I have flown in all weather conditions including thunderstorms, and I've flown with instruments not working properly. This time it was different. I cannot explain why, but there must have been a major fault with the landing aids."

"You heard Mr Mitchell's evidence?" Barry confirmed. "Do you recall that he told the Court that no malfunction of the relevant flight deck instruments was detected after a thorough inspection?"

"Yes."

"Yes. I understand there was an aircraft ahead of you?"

"A Jetstream."

"And that aeroplane landed safely?"

"I believe so... Yes, I remember hearing taxi instructions."

"Would the pilot have been using the ILS system?"

"Yes... at least I heard no other service being requested."

"Quite. So does that not indicate there were no problems with the ground electronic installation?"

"It would seem so, at least for that landing." Barry added.

"Yes or no is all I need."

"Well, yes, I suppose."

"Yes?" Donald repeated the answer.

"So what have we got? If the ground installations were functioning correctly and there was no malfunction of the aeroplane's instruments, we need to find another explanation... Would you not agree Mr Johnston?"

Barry felt the trap like a fish in a net, and knew he wouldn't escape. He watched Patrick leave the courtroom as he looked despairingly around for help.

"My Lord, that concludes the plaintiff's case."

David Jenkins was good. Even Donald was impressed with his skill. 'I must remember to add him to my list. Would make a good junior on some of those very technical cases that come up from time to time.'

David had only one card to play, and that was to try and impress the Court with Barry's experience and knowledge of aeroplanes and the equipment needed to fly them safely. He went over these points *ad nauseam*, until he felt the jury were almost pleading to let the accused go.

Judge Teal-Jones was getting bored. David could see that by the fact that he'd stopped making notes. The Judge kept glancing at the clock and David realised if they didn't close soon, the case would run over it's allocation and that might not benefit his client.

He closed with as much sympathy as he could risk, asking the jury to return a verdict of not guilty based on the evidence that, no one could be sure why the instruments that afternoon gave misleading readings.

Donald Opperman had a field day with a superb summing of the evidence, skilfully cross-referencing his argument and ending with a strong statement to the jury that they had no choice but to find the defendant guilty.

The jury were thanked and asked to return the following afternoon to give their decision.

Barry couldn't go home and he wandered into the West End looking aimlessly at shop windows. He stopped at a sandwich bar but found the food stuck in his throat. He walked out with a ham roll in his hand to find a ragged down and out sitting on the pavement. He gave him the roll and the look on the dosser's face was like a child being given his first toy from Father Christmas.

It made him feel better to realise there were people worse off than himself, but it didn't help him with the injustice of it all.

He made for home and crept into the spare bedroom to avoid disturbing his wife, hoping, but not really believing, that tomorrow would end the misery of the last six months and allow him to escape from the memories of runway two six.

"Members of the jury, have you reached a decision?"
The foreman nodded and the Judge despatched the usher to collect the paper.
"Will the accused please stand."
Barry vaguely heard the Judge telling him that he was criminally guilty of negligently endangering his aircraft and passengers. "... and I sentence you to a fine of five thousand... or sixty days... costs will be assessed at..."
"Please let us through." David Jenkins guided his client past the reporters and flashing cameras, and hurried him to a taxi.

"You can appeal."
"What's the point? They needed a head! If it hadn't been me they would have gone for Tim or even air traffic. They know I can't afford to fight."
"I'm very sorry. That was a farce in there. The idea of taking an incident like this to a court of law is nonsense. You can never get to the truth this way." David was cross with his own profession and the lack of support it afforded to the likes of Barry.
"You did your best. I'm not grumbling, just very tired."
"I would like to know what happened to the work and maintenance sheets for the replacement autopilots. Very convenient that they were missing!"
"Leave it David. Take me home." He'd had enough.
'I think I might do a little fishing on my own. That Tim Mitchell knew something which he never volunteered, and I didn't like Miss Marshall's evidence. No, maybe I could get the CAA to instigate an enquiry on the airline, license check or something.' David let his thoughts mull around until they arrived at the cottage.
"I don't know what to say." She was frightened to touch him. David had rung Sybil from the City and given her the verdict, for Barry had not wanted her to be present in court.
"Don't say anything... Get me a very large scotch. Won't have to watch my alcohol level now will I?" He felt defeated and rejected and longed to be up above the clouds, away from the tension that was

gripping his chest like a vice. He walked into the garden and kicked a flowerpot in his frustration.

"Give him some time. Try and find some other interests for him... I must go, another client. I'll keep in touch."

"Thank you David. You've been very understanding. I hear what you say but flying is his life. I'm frightened that he might do something stupid."

"If you need any help or advice you know where to get me?"

"Yes. Thanks again." She shook his hand. "Goodbye."

The letter came two mornings later.

"The bastard hasn't even got the guts to tell me to my face."

He read the words. *...due to the verdict, I have no other choice but to ask for your resignation.* 'Hasn't got the balls to sack me!' *...your pension contributions can be...* He didn't need to read on and handed the letter to his wife.

"I know how you feel, but at least you haven't had your licence revoked."

"Not yet, but I bet the CAA will remove my commercial rating. In any case who'd employ me?"

The official letter arrived the next day.

Chapter Six

"Two hundred a month plus services. Rent is payable in advance."

"Who's responsible for maintenance?" The colour scheme was awful and needed some cheering up.

"Outside is up to the owner, inside you can do your own thing, subject to reason."

Barry was hustled around the small bungalow by the bored estate agent, and broadly took in the main features. 'At least it's got a decent kitchen,' he thought.

"Okay, I'll take it. It's back to your office for signing the lease?"

"No that's all right, I'll pop it in the post. If I could just have a cheque for the first month?"

He collected the pictures and other bric-a-brac from the car and thought about the rows. The last nine months had been hell. At first the drink had dulled his mind, but then its effect wore off, and he became so aggressive as he drunk more and more. Social security, how he hated those visits. "Are you really looking for work?" Pompous idiot. Then the headaches and dreams. Patrick, Tim, Sally and the others clawing at him through the iron railings and tearing off parts of his clothing. "You need something to help you, please see the doctor!" Sybil had pleaded so often. "I'm not going to take drugs and that's final," and yet he was, straight out of the whisky bottle.

He looked at their photographs again, taken in Devon. Why had it come to this?

"I'm sorry I can't help you any more, I want you to go." The words came back to him like a knife in the shoulder blades. He didn't fight. What was the point, the blame lay with him. They put the house on the market and sold it very quickly. Sybil went back to Mum, and he bummed around cheap hotels until deciding to rent something. They left the divorce question alone. "We both need time."

Margaret took sides and her sympathies went totally to Sybil.
Tom sat on the fence. "You've not been easy to live with, I bet.
Still, I thought Sybil was stronger than that."

"Thanks for your words of wisdom." They were facing each other
in Tom's office. "I need your insurance advice, not your counselling
skills." He managed a grin. 'First signs' Tom thought, 'maybe he's
on the mend.'

"Fire away."

"You know we got a fair price for the cottage?"

"Yes, I'm not surprised. You did a lot on that place and bought it
cheap as I remember."

"Anyhow, we only had a small mortgage, so we've both got some
spare cash. I've decided to buy a small plane and go back to
instructing."

"Can you do that, I thought you'd lost your licence?"

"Only my commercial. They didn't take my private or instructor's
away."

"I see. So what are you getting?"

"Well I've seen a few single-engine that could be suitable, that's
all I need. I wondered if you could get me some quotes?"

"Not really my field, but I'll ask around. What value d'you
reckon?"

"Forty thousand."

"That's for the plane I assume. What about third parties?"

"Don't know. Would have thought half a million. Yes?"

Barry left his office feeling a little brighter. At least something
was happening. He drove out to the grass airfield which was close to
the Welsh border and not far from his newly-rented bungalow.

"Is Darell Brown around?"

"You'll find him over in the hangar."

"Barry Johnston." They shook hands, "I came over the other
weekend to look at the Cessna, you remember. Is it still for sale?"

"Hi. No it's gone, but I have a nice two-seater just come in. A
repossess job I believe. Like to see it?"

They walked over to the second hangar and Darell pointed out the
very smart white and blue striped aeroplane.

"How many hours?"

"Only five hundred I believe."

"And price?"

"Looking for twenty thousand."

"Really?" Barry could hardly contain his surprise.

She flew beautifully, and it was a joy to be behind the controls again. He circled the field and tried three landings before taxiing the craft back to the hangar.

"I'll give you the deposit now and the rest when I've sorted out the insurance. Can you do a fifty hour on her?"

"Sure thing Mr Johnston, I'll throw that in."

He drove back whistling to the latest number one. 'Actually got a tune you can hum to,' he thought.

The rain started as the clouds came in over the hills. He had to see Tom on the insurance, so he decided to drive down to Bournemouth and stay at a small hotel he'd been using on and off since leaving Sybil. The weather got worse with the rain beating down on the windscreen, almost too much for the wipers. He briefly noticed the sign for the Queen's Head as he passed it and braked hard to skid to a halt, and then backed up. 'It was the Queen's Head wasn't it? Yes, I wonder if she's still around?' He drove down the lane and pulled into the pub car park.

Ordering a drink he dropped into casual conversation with the barman. "Last time I was this way, I chatted to a girl called Judy. She still come here?"

"Not seen her for some time. I'll see if anyone knows."

He sipped the brandy and relaxed after the concentration of driving in the rain. The place was even worse than he remembered, and he'd drunk a lot that day. Funny they'd never mentioned anything at the medical, for his blood and liver must have been well tanked-up. Drank a lot of wine with Sybil that night as well. He remembered their lovemaking and the release they both had needed. 'Do I miss her? I don't know?' Circumstances change people and time fades.

"King's Head."

"Sorry, not with you."

"King's Head, that's where she hangs out these days."

"Oh right, got it. Where's the King's Head?"

"Out of here, turn right, about a mile and half, left and immediate right, another half mile on your left. Lies back from the road."

He followed the instructions and was pleased the rain was easing. The King's Head was a vast improvement on its female counterpart and Barry settled easily for another brandy. He turned around and there she was. She was wearing a long green skirt with a red off the shoulder blouse which complimented her black-haired gypsy beauty. He thought she was just as attractive this time, and liked what he saw.

The slanging match got worse and he realised that her friend, a fat balding guy in sailing gear, was giving plenty of hassle.

"I wouldn't take your miserable twenty. You owe me one, you bloody bitch!"

Giving it no thought he walked calmly across the boarded pub floor, and took hold of her arm. "Come on Judy, time we went. Mustn't miss the party." She obeyed like a lamb, as he quickly bundled her into the car and accelerated out of the car park, heading off fast in case they were followed.

"Do you always pick up your girlfriends that way?"

"I remember you were pretty forward the last time we met."

They each laughed and smiled with the obvious pleasure of meeting again, which showed on both their faces.

"Who was that slob?"

"Oh, a guy who did some work on my houseboat. Reckoned I owed him payment in kind. Thanks for rescuing me, but I could have handled it."

"I feel a fool."

"No. It was nice. The perfect gentleman again."

"I don't feel like being a gentleman with you dressed like that."

She smiled at the compliment. "I read the reports in the local *Advertiser*. I'm sorry you lost."

"Thanks, I'm getting over it. You hungry? Can we stop for a meal?"

They dined simply at a small bistro, whose owner had a wine cellar out of class with his culinary efforts. They talked little, but both seemed hungry to explore the mutual comfort of each other's presence.

"I never thanked you for your words of wisdom that day. I'm planning to fly again. Bought a small plane." He touched her warm hand.

It had that inevitability of the romantic film, although the hotel room could have been grander and the champagne cooler. He watched her sleeping peacefully and marvelled at the ability of a human body, that was so active a short while ago, to now be so silent. He touched her smooth skin again as if to check it was real, and felt her purr as she slumbered. He was not inexperienced, years in the flying industry had given its opportunities, but with Sybil he'd found contentment and not needed the chase any longer. Still it had been nine frustrating months since the High Court judgement, and he felt justified at this turn of events, and the need for comfort that his head wouldn't yet release. He poured the dregs from the champagne bottle and dropped it by accident on the floor.

"I woke you. You okay?"

"Come back to bed." She curled her body in invitation. "If there's any more of you I want it all." Their lovemaking this time was uncontrollable and Barry knew she needed this as much as he did.

They breakfasted in the tiny dining room and tried to hide from the knowing looks of the other residents. Commercial travellers to a tee, Barry could see they were slightly jealous. Judy was having to wear yesterday's clothes, and the shoulder blouse was hardly everyday workwear. 'Probably is in their eyes,' Barry thought 'I expect they think she's a working girl.'

"Waiter, would you mind if we skipped the breakfast. I'd like a bottle of your house champagne, a small glass of Cointreau, and some cold ham and cheese with biscuits."

"What are you doing?" Judy started to giggle.

"I'm having some fun, the best I've had for ages, bollocks to them all."

She collapsed in laughter, and hooked the sleeve of her blouse even lower off her shoulder.

"I think the little guy in the corner is about to have an orgasm." "Certainly gone off his eggs." They giggled on like a couple of schoolkids. Later in the car, they cried until their stomachs felt like falling out, and finally sobered to the realities of life and the day ahead.

"Can I see you again?"

"I'll kill if you don't."

"I loved it, but I'm not right yet, you understand?"

"Go fly your aeroplane Biggles, and when it gives you no thrill, come see sexy Judy."

He drove back to her houseboat, but she wouldn't let him in. "Maybe one day, 'bye, I love you."

He waved from the car and saw her running down the gangway. She stopped him as he was reversing. "By the way I forgot to tell you. That girlfriend in the flats. You remember? She told me some funny things about an Arab who was living in one of the top rooms."

"Funny what?"

"Well apparently he was an Iraqi. There was talk of his being involved in spying or something like that."

"So what's funny?"

"Well, his flat was raided by the police, or some security boys, and they found it full of drugs, traces of diamond dust and a lot of electrical gear."

"Electrical gear? What sort?"

"I don't know. Radio equipment for sending messages. That's what my friend said."

"So why did she tell you this?"

"I don't know, but after your flying incident I gather the occupants of the flats were planning to take action against Bournemouth Airport. However, so my friend says, they were advised by the owners not to worry, as they were looking into any concern with the airport themselves. There was talk of compensation, I'm not sure for what."

"Do you know who owns the flats?"

"No, but I believe they're Middle-Eastern gentlemen, certainly not English."

The information struck no chords for Barry, but he locked it away with the intention of giving it further consideration. 'Perhaps I'll have a word with Tim.'

"Thanks for a lovely time, I'll be in touch." He kissed her again.

"I hope so, don't let me down." He saw her fighting back a small tear.

He felt for her hurt. He was damaged, but someone had hurt her more. 'One day I'll find out the truth, but not yet.' He drove away with his mind full of action and questions.

Chapter Seven

"Tim it's Barry, how's it going?"

"A voice from the past, good to hear you. Never been the same since you left."

"How's the boss? Same old cheerful Paddy?"

"Not really, I think your case still worries him."

"And so it should. Bastard never rated me. His loss. I'm coping. Just."

"I hear your lawyer's still sniffing around. You going for an appeal or something?"

"That's a thought. Get right up Pat's nose if I did that."

"So you flying at all?"

"Yes. I've invested in a light single. Might go back to instructing."

"Good for you. You need to keep your hand in."

"No thanks to Marvel Air."

"You know my feelings Barry. I'm doing my best."

He ignored the comment. "I rang you because I wanted to ask a favour." Barry related the facts that Judy had unloaded, without revealing his source. "No idea whether it's relevant, but any information might be of interest. You never know, but if something emerged I think I owe it to myself and Sybil."

"Any clues? What's on your mind?"

"I don't know. Something threw me that day and as sure as eggs is eggs, it wasn't me. Maybe something to do... No I can't figure it out."

"Leave it with me, I'll make some enquiries." He thought back to his doubts. Something missing?

"Sorry to hear about you and Sybil."

"The way it goes. I'm not very proud. Our women put up with a lot."

"Glad I never got too involved. Had my challenges but they saw through the true bachelor."

"Nice to talk. Contact me if you find anything interesting. You can get me on..." The conversation drifted on, but Barry was anxious to ring off. What support has that 'friend', he emphasised the word, really given me over the years? Tim liked to be seen as a caring man with a heart of gold, but he'd a way of using people for his own ends. If there was any mud around it never stuck to Mitchell. He'd probably forgotten the Munich flight. They never found the alcohol factor but Barry had. 'Don't open up old sores, you've got enough on your plate. The past has happened and you can't go back.' He smiled with the scent of Judy still caressing his body, and was feeling excited at getting airborne again.

Still in thought, he rang Tom to fix an appointment for tomorrow. 'I need a good night's sleep. This Rambo stuff's for the youngsters.' Still, he felt younger than he'd done for ages.

He woke early to the sound of the birds singing outside the window. The view from the hotel bedroom was limited, but the early sunshine was heralding the likelihood of a warm June day.

Barry was anxious to sort out the paper work so that he could fly his new toy, and arrived at Tom's office far too early. He bought a paper from the nearby newsagent, and popped into the cafe next door.

"Airline Investigation" the headlines where on the second page. He read on "Yesterday the Civil Aviation Authority served an injunction on Marvel Airlines, who operate out of Bournemouth, grounding the entire operational fleet whilst safety checks are carried out."

The article went on "A spokesman for the airline stated that no details of the injunction where known, and the owner, Irishman Patrick Clancy, was meeting his lawyers in London today. Angry holidaymakers stranded in the departure lounge at Bournemouth were demanding alternative flights, and some were threatening to sue the airline."

There followed photographs of Patrick alongside his fleet of One Elevens, making a Churchillian victory sign. Barry remembered the occasion, a sort of topping-out day to celebrate the launch of the new cheap fares airline for the discerning customer. A lot of water had flown under the bridge since then.

He continued reading and came to a paragraph which made him sit up with more attention. "Some fifteen months ago one of the company's jets was involved in a low approach over an housing estate which endangered the passengers on board. A High Court action was brought by the airlines owners against the captain of the aeroplane, who was found guilty and fined for negligence. The pilot, Mr Johnston, maintained in his defence that the instrument landing aids in the aeroplane where at fault."

The final words made Barry think. "...after the verdict several of the Marvel Air staff stated that the captain had had a raw deal." 'They never told me that,' he mused. 'I wonder if David Jenkins's behind this? Must give him a call.'

Glancing at his watch he realised he was now late for his appointment and hurried back to Tom's office.

"See you've already read about it," he said as Barry placed the paper on Tom's desk. "Doesn't help you, all these safety scares only put up the premiums on flying and you're looking for cheap rates."

"Don't the underwriters separate commercial business from private?"

"No chance. You're all bundled together, and there aren't many who will write cover in any case. Risky old market."

"So what've you got?"

"Well on the information you gave me we can do the hull for two and a half and... "

"Cut the jargon Tom, how much?"

"On forty thousand. Two grand, with Francis Aviation Insurance."

"How soon can you put me on cover?"

"Straight away."

They sorted the details and shook hands on the deal.

"We must have a jar sometime. Bit difficult with Margaret at the moment, perhaps in London. Have you ever been round the Lloyds building?" Barry shook his head. "Right then I'll give you a ring and we'll take in a meal. You'll find it interesting."

"Sounds good. Thanks for arranging the insurance. I'll await your call."

The drive back to Wales was uneventful and Barry was eager to finalise the aeroplane purchase and also to sort out some furnishings

for the bungalow. 'I wonder if Judy likes flying? ... Odd about
Patrick's scene... That premium was based on forty... plane's only
cost twenty but looks more. I suppose it doesn't matter.' The various
questions rattled round and within no time he was driving up the lane
to his new base.

Barry helped himself to a scotch as he listened to the answer phone
messages.

"Darell Brown calling, just to say the plane's been checked out and
ready whenever you are."

"Tim Mitchell. There's a few problems coming out of the
woodwork. Can you give me a call when you're free? Home number
if you could."

He pressed the play/pause switch and refreshed his glass.

"You have one message." The answerphone hadn't finished.

"Oh, shut up." Barry cursed the machine.

"You bastard! You've got under my skin. I thought I was over all
that." Judy's voice filled the room. "Love me soon." She meant it.

"You have no more messages."

He slumped onto the settee and started to feel the anger coming
back. He'd had it all mapped out and that disastrous day had screwed
everything. The depression hit him again, like sudden waves crashing
on the rocks, and he cried and cried with deep uncontrollable sobs.
Perhaps if they could have had children? He knew how disappointed
Sybil had been when the doctor told her. He wished Judy could be
with him, but he knew the time was not yet right. He finished his
drink and then, wiping his eyes, spent the rest of the day sorting out
the house before he rang Darell.

"You okay for the morning?"

"See you about ten."

Chapter Eight

"Tim, for Christ's sake, how long have we known each other?"

"I'm sorry Patrick but I'm not going to lie again to save your neck."

"What d'you mean by that?"

"Barry? You put one hell of a pressure on me at that time. I wish now I hadn't listened."

"I know I can be hard sometimes. It stems from me being a kid in Ireland. My mother had it rough with so many mouths to feed and Dad in the pub all day. She earned eighteen shillings a day from the milk, and we pulled in another five from the peat farm. Not a lot for a family of our size." Patrick held up the fingers of both his hands. "I promised meself that I'd make it, and provide her with some luxury and grace in her old age." For once Tim felt he was being honest.

"So you made it?"

"Too late. I bought her a beautiful house in Connemara. Six bedrooms, lovely gardens, with fantastic views to the Atlantic Ocean. She died the night after I signed the contract."

"Sorry Pat, I didn't know that. What happened to your father?"

"Gone. Never heard where. He befriended a lot of women I was told. If I ever found him I'd kill him. That's a promise. Then you'd really have something to defend, eh?" Patrick smiled grimly at his words. "Let's discuss this elsewhere where we can relax. Have you been to the Sugar Club?"

Patrick had been with the lawyers all morning and he was pretty concerned. He'd asked Tim to come along to give some technical backing to his arguments, but Tim had not been too helpful. The facts were that he was skating on thin ice with the maintenance checks, and was using an unlicensed outfit to service the planes. They were relying on some old signatories to check off the schedules, but on the latest batch some bright spark from the CAA had queried the paperwork.

He knew he was in deep water, but sales were down and cash flow was hurting. "Let's get over this hump and then I can afford to get back on stream." But Dianne didn't help. She'd got used to the lifestyle and she also had the photographs. How had he been so stupid? He would never be able to face the children.

"Sugar Club."

They taxied from the City to the West End both deep in their personal thoughts. Patrick was wondering whether he could buy Tim's allegiance, and Tim was toying with his conscience against bending the rules in his favour. 'You never make any money by being honest.' Least he hadn't so far.

"A bottle of the seventy-nine to my account."

"Certainly Mr Clancy , would you like some girls to join you?"

"Maybe later. Got some business first. You understand?"

He waited until the wine had been served and then looked quizzically at Tim. "Who set us up with the CAA? That's what I want to know."

"I reckon it was that lawyer Barry hired, he's been sniffing around and asking questions."

"I didn't know that, who's he been talking to?"

"Well, Norman for one, but also Mike Swift."

"Mike. Jesus! He wouldn't get much truck from him."

"I'm not so sure. Mike hasn't been too happy since your pay freeze, and I know there is discontentment in maintenance."

"I bet you Barry's behind this. Never could give in gracefully. Well he isn't going to mess me around. I'll put the heavies in if necessary."

Tim felt worried. He knew Pat could be moody, but he'd never seen him like this. There were rumours from the past and he decided to warn Barry about this turn of events.

"I want those checks countersigned before the CAA get me into court. There's a company in Dallas called Redwing Servicing, run by a Chuck Alston. Has a subsidiary over in Belfast who service helicopters for the North Sea operations. Least that's a cover for some other doubtful work with some Third World outlets."

Tim was listening intently, wondering what was next.

"Chuck owes me a favour, one he has to honour. I didn't think I'd ever need it, but there doesn't seem to be any alternative."

"Why are you telling me this?" Tim poured out some more wine and braced himself for the worst to come.

"Because you'll be going to Dallas to arrange for Chuck to sign off the maintenance forms. Simple eh?"

"Is that legal?"

"Sure, Northern Ireland comes under CAA regulations, not a problem."

Tim took in the implications of Pat's intentions. "I'm sorry Pat, as I said before I'm not going to lie any more."

He fished the envelope from his inside jacket pocket and placed it in front of Tim. "There's more to come, I'm going for a leak."

Tim stared at the brown package on the table. He knew it would be a lot and he was scared. Pat would never do things by half, so he must be worried to go this far. Tim was fifty-five and this was the best job left for him in flying for sure. He'd moved around a lot and the transferred pension would not go far. If he refused then that would be curtains for the rest of his career. No illusions that Pat would see to that. He knew the canny Irishman had deliberately frightened him with the heavy mob chat, and was certain it could be served for real.

"Helen this is Tim. Tim meet Comfort. You girls thirsty?" Patrick returned with two dark-skinned beauties in tow and made the introductions.

The Jamaican hostesses slipped into the tiny seats and Helen placed her hand on Tim's thigh. "Haven't seen you in here before, enjoying yourself?"

Tim tried to listen to Patrick's jokes which started to flow, over the mixed sounds of the piano and the silly giggles from the girls. Helen's hand and the champagne were making it difficult for him to concentrate on reality, and he could feel the pocketed envelope pressing against his shirt.

They danced on the tiny floor and she asked Julian to play the blues, whilst forcing her thigh into his hardened groin. He was mesmerised by the silkiness of bare shoulders as he caressed her back, running his hands down to the crease of her bottom sensually exposed by a backless dress. Later, at the flat, as he experienced Helen's mouth imitating the pictures on the video, he knew he'd been bought, but accepted it without a care.

"Have a rest love, I'm going to take a shower."
He slipped out quietly, leaving enough for her taxi fare back.

Chapter Nine

The Farnborough airfield had many memories for Dennis Hopkins and he took in the familiar buildings as he drove through the security entrance that morning. He sensed again the thrill of those post-war airshows, when the technology advanced each year toward reaching the sound barrier. Suddenly it was there, and the bang was followed by the air pressure in the ears as the Hunter fighter flashed along the runway at three hundred feet, with the shock waves flickering in a water haze around the wings. His first assignment had been here, after the tragic crash of a prototype, and he'd been fascinated ever since.

Dennis now worked as an independent insurance assessor, having reached the limit of promotion within a large corporation. Although accepting varied briefs, his first love was the aero industry and he already felt the buzz of this latest investigation.

"First left, just passed the black sheds," the gate man directed Dennis to the investigation hangers.

"I'm looking for Gill Francis, Francis Aviation Insurance. Name's Hopkins."

"Hangar number two sir." The man pointed to the office door.

She greeted him with a warm smile. "Morning Mr Hopkins, we've never met, but your reputation precedes you."

"You're very kind ma'am, not unknown yourself."

Gill was fairly new to the aviation business, but had already built up quite a substantial client portfolio, and was gaining considerable respect from some of her competitors. Daddy financed the company, but she'd had to fight for recognition in what was mostly a man's domain.

"Gill please. Have you seen the set up?"

"No, this is my first visit to the new sheds."

She guided Dennis through to the next section where a twin-engined plane lay in pieces like an Airfix model, which someone had forgotten to glue together.

"I gather there was only one death, the air hostess wasn't it?"

"Amazing really, you look at this and you'd think – no chance."

Dennis studied the wreckage to get a general feel of the situation.

"Fill me in on the full story."

"Coffee first?" He nodded. "I don't have everything, but I gather the owners had leased the Fokker to Niger Travel and the plane was scheduled for a flight to Bahrain with some Arab diplomats on board."

"You cover for leasing?"

"Yes. I've found a niche market there, especially with the more obscure African companies. The big boys don't seem to want it, and have left them out."

'Maybe you should,' Dennis thought.

He watched her sifting through the paperwork and was not unattracted by the view. A brunette, with a trim figure, early thirties he guessed. She was wearing a grey trouser suit which gave her a formal look, and he wondered if that was deliberate, to be more 'one of the boys' perhaps?

"D'you suspect foul play?"

"The plane came down in the Niger desert area, that's why we've been able to recover so much of it. If it had been an explosion I doubt the bits would have been so close, and we wouldn't have the survivors. Can't rule out a shooting, but there's no evidence from the crew or passengers."

"Would they volunteer if there had been? What about the black box?"

"No box, no help there."

"What was the compliment?"

"Two flight crew. Two air hostesses. Four diplomats and two rich-looking Middle-Eastern females. There was also a fair amount of diamonds found in a suitcase that was hidden in the wreckage. There were probably more, the other cases weren't checked."

"Who found them?"

"Luckily there was a Red Cross convoy on route to the capital, Lagunda, and so they were picked up almost immediately."

'Fortuitous perhaps,' Dennis thought. 'I wonder whether any real vultures were waiting?'

"You have the names?"

"Yes, that's routine from air traffic. D'you want them?"

"I'd like to check. Computer sometimes throws out oddities."

He spent the rest of the day poking over the remains of the aircraft to see if there were any clues to the accident. All seemed in order, although he found some electronic parts which weren't related. He removed some small bits for checking with Jim, an avionics expert who had a workshop on the business estate. The only other clue was two small holes in the main and back-up fuel lines. 'I wonder?'

"What do you make of it?" He'd left Jim studying the pieces for long enough and was anxious for an opinion.

"Nothing to do with the plane, that's for sure. Some sort of electronic locking device, you know the type of circuitry used to isolate car radios. This is quite complicated though. There are also small bits of a jamming circuit which seems familiar."

"Like what?"

"I need more time to evaluate," he paused, "maybe part of a radar set."

"I think you'd better have a closer look."

"Sure, love to. Can we say next week, I'm very busy at the moment."

Dennis was disappointed. It was always the same. Once he got his teeth into the problem, he was like a bloodhound chasing the scent, and always felt deflated if he lost the momentum, and had to delay.

Chapter Ten

The caretaker was bored with his job, bored with his wife, bored with the porno books, bored with himself, in fact just plain bored. So when Tim Mitchell walked into his scruffy security office he was more than ready to enjoy some company.

"You the caretaker?"

"Bloody am. I'm sick of this place, you can fire me if you like, I'm just pissed off with life and everyone."

"Picked a bad day have I?"

"You try this sodding job. I've been here for three years and no one has ever thanked me for anything. I sort out their problems, carry their shopping, fix plumbers and electricians, sort out their garbage, listen to their moans, protect them from their unwanted friends. I don't know why I don't just wipe their arses and wank their pricks."

Tim had to laugh. "Best job description I've heard for a long time, you should go down to social and file it."

"So what sodding service d'you want?" He sank back in his chair and glared at Tim.

"Advice."

"Is that it, bloody advice? I'm not yer citizens' bureau you know."

"No, I appreciate that. I want some advice on this place. I'm not your boss so I can't sack you. Also I'm prepared to pay for the right advice, and... I'm also prepared to thank you. Now isn't that the best offer you've had all day?"

The caretaker started to show interest. "Sorry guv,. You know how it is? Lost a few bob on the races yesterday. Her indoors went bananas. How can I assist?"

"You said you'd been here three years." He stuck his thumb up. "D'you remember an incident when an aeroplane got very close to this building in bad weather, about eh... fifteen months ago?"

"Yes and no. I know about it, but I wasn't on duty. I swap shifts with me mate, but he couldn't help you, 'cos he was off sick at that time."

"Okay, that doesn't matter, I just wanted to know that you were around at that time. Now d'you recall a Middle-Eastern gentleman who had a flat on the top floor?"

"You mean Azif the Arab? Hardly a flat. More the penthouse suite. You should have seen the gear he had up there. Sotheby's would have paid a fortune for some of his stuff!"

'He's not so stupid as he makes out, so watch your questions.' Tim held back for a bit. "Haven't got any water have you? And I could do with the toilets."

"Cup of tea do you?" Tim nodded. "First door on the left."

"So tell me about Azif."

"What's to tell? Smooth looking fellow, expensive suits, fancy girlfriends, parties, one Arab's much like the rest. Too much money. We should have never found the oil for them. Flipping act of geography that was. If they weren't sitting on that black gold they'd still be sewing up tents, and riding their camels."

Tim ignored the doorman's précis of the Middle East's fortunes. "Funny place, with respect, for such a guy as you describe, to set up base. It's all right, but these flats are hardly Park Lane?"

"I thought that. But they sometimes fall out with each other, don't they? Also they don't all have rich sheiks for dads, so some of them have to resort to crime or dodgy dealing to keep face. Isn't that right?"

"So what dodgy dealings was Azif into?"

"Can't help you there."

"Come on, just think."

He paused a while and started to pick his nose. "The only thing I didn't understand was a delivery marked fragile which came slightly damaged."

"For Azif?"

"Yes, well addressed for his flat. I took it up and let meself in with the pass key. We 'ave to have one for fire risks," he explained the need. "I was curious, thought it might be another antique, so I had a peep through the torn wrapping."

"And?"

"Looked like some electrical parts to me, radio, or sex aids maybe, that's more his line." He paused again. "Anyhow, nothing of interest to me?"

"One last question." Tim counted out three twenties from his wallet. "Is there a common television aerial on the roof of the building?"

"There is, except Azif's."

"Sorry, are you saying Azif had a separate aerial?"

"In one sir, you should be on Mastermind. Not only a separate aerial, but a big disk. I reckon it was an early satellite receiver. That's the one that was knocked off by the plane... I've got it now! That's what you wanted to know, I suppose you rented him the gear?"

"Thanks for the chat. Forgotten it haven't we?" Tim shoved the notes into his hand.

"Cheerio guv. Not such a boring day after all. I think I'll have a flutter on the three thirty."

Back in his office Tim went over the facts and realised he was getting out of his depth. He was floundering somewhat aimlessly with very few clues and not much of a plan. All he had was a colleague who was convinced he'd been misled when landing, and now some information relating to electrical equipment in a flat nearly hit by the airliner.

Was there a connection? No idea. Also there was the mystery Arab and talk of police raids, drugs and diamonds. Not really his scene.

'Should I get involved anyhow?' he posed the question. Things hadn't always been right between him and Barry, but there'd been an occasion when Tim had broken a few rules, and he'd been grateful for Barry's support at the time. He wasn't satisfied with the judgement and felt embarrassed with the evidence the lawyers had dragged out. 'No, I'll stick with it, but I need some help.'

He reached for the Yellow Pages and scanned through the index for private investigators. They were listed under detective agencies. He thumbed through the various adverts and was confused by the choice and amused by some of the services on offer. Personal and High Risk escorts. What did that mean? De-bugging sweeps? There was an all female agency specialising in matrimonial and other surveillance work. 'Not for this one' he thought. Then he spotted it. Hogan Investigations. "Any place, any time."

Charles Anthony Hogan sat in the Southampton office with his feet on the battered desk and surveyed the post in front of him. Three bills, four 'make you a million' offers, one demand from his ex-wife's solicitor, a bank statement and a travel brochure with some beautiful bronzed bodies temptingly smiling a 'wish you were here'. He threw the letters into the bin, picked up the glossy brochure and flicked through the pages.

'Finish this one and I'm definitely going' – that was a promise. An ex-policeman, he'd been in Special Branch until a badly broken leg gained in a Soho raid had left no choice but to take the early retirement offer. The ex-wife took most of that, so he'd no option but to eke out a miserable income prying into other people's business. He hated Charles and the shortened Tony or 'Tone', so his colleagues ended up calling him Hogan.

He moved to the tiny kitchen and plugged in the kettle. Back in the office Hogan browsed round the bookcase seeking some inspiration for the next move on a stolen property case he was pursuing. He poured the coffee and hobbled back to his desk.

He was staring at the glass door with the black letters NAGOH glaring back, when the phone rang. He answered automatically, "Hogan Investigations. Hogan speaking."

"Mr Hogan, my name's Tim Mitchell. I need some help to find someone and check out what they were doing fifteen months ago?"

'A nutter. Why do I always get nutters?' He shrugged his shoulders.

"Not a lot to go on... Mr Mitchell you said?"

"Perhaps we could meet? Then I can explain better?"

Having promised himself a good lunch today, for at last some cheques had been paid in, he didn't want to work. The leg was playing up and he wished there was a way of getting under the skin and massaging the bones themselves.

"Where are you?"

"Bournemouth. I could be at your offices within an hour."

"No sweat. I've got to meet a client at Ferndown," he lied. "There's a hotel down there, forgotten the name, just on the roundabout. Could be there by twelve."

"I know it, thank you. I'll buy you some lunch." Hogan grinned at that.

Tim turned up Barry's number and dialled out.

"Barry, said I'd keep in touch. How goes the battle?"

"Okay, settling in. Got your message the other day. Sorry I haven't been back."

"Have you heard the latest on Marvels?"

"Yes. Read it in the paper. What's going on?"

"Don't know. Pat's being hassled by the CAA. Wondered if you had anything to do with it?"

"Not guilty. Why is that a problem?"

"Pat thinks you're involved and he's acting pretty angry."

"Sod Pat. Serves him right. The CAA can close him down for all I care."

"Be careful. I've not seen him like this before."

"What's he gonna do, send in his buddies?"

"You know Pat. Blows hot and cold. Apparently your legal guy, David Jenkins isn't it, has been sniffing around."

"Not on my instructions I can assure you. I can't afford the bugger."

"Thought I'd let you know. That's all."

"Thanks for the warning. Sorry for yourself. Take care." They rang off.

Tim thought about the other matter regarding the flats and the action he was going to take, but decided it was too early to involve Barry. He collected his keys and walked out to the car park.

From a vantage position of the corner seat Tim was able to survey customers as they went to the bar. He was curious to guess which would be Hogan when he felt the hand on his shoulder.

"Mr Mitchell?"

He spun round to greet a stocky man of about five foot ten in height. The guy sported short brown hair and wore a baggy grey stained suit, with a blue-spotted tie loosely hanging around the unbuttoned shirt-neck.

Hogan was amused inside by the look of surprise on Tim's face. He'd been there an hour before, and already enjoyed a couple of beers. He'd spotted Tim as he got out of the car, and guessed this was his future client by the way Tim was watching everyone.

"Mr Hogan?"

"Hogan will do."

"I didn't see you come in."

"Is that a compliment?" he begged the question.

"I suppose it is. The unseen surveillance. Your profession's trademark?"

"Well I was here before you , it's not that clever."

Tim called the waiter over and they ordered some food before settling down with drinks. Hogan studied his client and tried to guess the occupation. 'Smartly dressed – banker? Service industry maybe? No, he's some sort of manager, can tell that by the way he organised the food. Car business...'

Tim interrupted his guessing. "I'm senior captain for Marvel Air. We're based at Bournemouth Airport just down the road." 'No, I wouldn't have got that for all my boasting that I can judge most people.' "Some time back we had a near miss during a landing approach..." Tim went through the whole business, the court case, his concern over justice, the unanswered questions in his mind, and the initial investigation he'd carried out.

Hogan listened with increasing interest. They were not usually as intriguing as this. Motor offences, petty theft, or the odd divorce were his normal bread and butter. He enjoyed another swig of the rye whisky, savouring the warmth it gave, and admiring the golden colour as he twisted the glass around in his hand.

"So before I go any further – one, are you interested? – and two, what d'you charge?"

Hogan's eyes moved from the glass to study the man sitting waiting for an answer. He leaned back in his chair and held out the empty tumbler. Tim called over the waiter and spoke again. "Well?"

"Yes to one. One seventy a day plus expenses, and no air travel to two."

Tim absorbed this. "But you may have to go to the Middle East?"

Hogan explained about his leg and how the pressurisation affected it and the cramped seats. He laid it on a bit.

"I can probably arrange special air fares, so you'd go Club class. That should give you the room."

He thought about it. Seemed all right. Could get some pain killers for the leg. Maybe see some of those bronzed beauties. No, they cover up over there. His face dropped a little. Why couldn't it have been a West Indies show. He nodded a thanks to the waiter and swallowed carefully before replying further. Mustn't seem too keen, or he might try to knock me down.

"Club class... agreed... and five hundred up front?"

"Three hundred."

"Okay, you're on. Tell me exactly what you want."

Chapter Eleven

The sun was already biting into the early morning mist as the last of the packing was finished. The shorts were his favourites and he put in three pairs. 'Answerphone off, no point while I'm away. Main switch off. Calor gas,' he ran through all the checks and shut and locked the front door. 'If I've forgotten anything, too bad.'

"Customs form and flight plan. Weather looks great. See you next week."

"Thanks." Barry collected the papers from the tower and made his way out to the aeroplane. He stood awhile to admire the simple beauty of the machine and then stowed the last pieces of luggage before carrying out the final ground checks. With the seat belt clicked he started the engine.

He was disappointed that Judy wouldn't come. "Not this time," she said. "I think you need a break on your own." In a way that was right as he loved flying alone. You could look down from the sky and everything was like a toytown model. Above the clouds of fluffy cotton wool you felt closer to heaven. Still, he would miss her in the evenings.

He set course for Exeter with a plan to cross the coast and fly into France, first stop Quiberon. After that he had decided to fly down to Biarritz, stopping at various small airfields on the way.

"Brest Control this is Golf Echo Tango reporting south of Deauville, requesting a flight information service..." Not that it was needed. The visibility was sixty kilometres, and there was nothing around in this vast country to spoil the flight.

He switched in the wing leveller and relaxed to admire the scenery. In no time he was talking to Quiberon approach and cleared for a landing on runway three zero. Coming in over the sea there were perfect views of the small town and the sandy beaches.

"*Centre ville.*" The unpolished French was good enough for the taxi driver, and he sat back to take in the ambience of the sea-washed peninsular.

Booked in the Bellevue, Barry settled down to enjoy an enormous plate of oysters followed by a lightly-baked skate, with a bottle of well-chilled Muscadet to enhance the meal. Relaxing still further with a cognac, the pressures and stresses of the past year seemed to melt away, and he retired to bed feeling better than in a long time.

The nightmare came without warning and Barry woke with perspiration drenching the thin sheets covering the bed. He was trapped behind the iron railings again, but this time there was a way out through a hinged gate. The catch to the gate was in the shape of the steering yoke of an aircraft, but however hard Barry tried to turn it, it wouldn't budge. Patrick was laughing and Sally was caressing her bare breasts as if in invitation. Only Tim seemed to care as he held out an unreachable hand in help. Patrick laughed again and walked away with his arm around Judy.

He slumped into the bathroom and wiped the sweat away feeling sick at the visions of the dream. The oysters joined the French sewerage system as special guests that night.

Barry rose tired after a disturbed sleep and tried to clear his head over some strong coffee. He booked out and decided to walk back to the airfield, and work out a plan for La Baule-Escoublac which was only a short trip down the coast. He didn't feel like flying, but felt a need to escape as if the nightmare could be left behind.

The sky was cloudy and there was a hint of rain. Barry took off and set course across the bay noting the white waves and the leaning boats on beam. Good wind for sailing today.

The depression hit again and suddenly he was frightened. The nightmare, the oysters, marriage, it was all welling up. He felt sick again. Hyperventilation – try to remember the training – brought on by anxiety and apprehension, causes loss of carbon dioxide; breathe slowly. He felt dizzy and faint while trying desperately to concentrate on flying.

Slowly Barry regained his senses only to realise the closeness of La Baule. He circled the bay and gave out a radio call. The garbled French reply made no sense, and Barry realised it probably wasn't for him. This was a club airfield and although the international language in the air was English, the local clubs often only communicated in their own idiom.

Barry circled the field and set up for landing. The dizziness was still there and he struggled to read the dials. He started to panic with the realisation that the air speed was too low. "Forty five knots, nose high, I can't hold it. We're going..."

The plane stalled at fifty feet off the ground with the left wing dipping into the runway. The hull spun right around as the wing detached itself and the undercarriage collapsed. The propeller dug into the tarmac as the engine broke free, and the plane skidded to silence, with the tail sticking up like a squashed scorpion still hanging in for its last sting before dying.

For ten seconds nothing happened, and then the sirens went like hell. Although a small field, it was well equipped and the safety services swung into action. Luckily for Barry the plane did not catch fire, and even better he was not injured, apart from some severe cuts to his head and badly bruised arms.

"*Mon Dieu! Tu as eu de la chance!*"

They took him to the hospital but Barry was keen to book out before they could run up a large bill. He was still feeling sore but anxious to survey the damage to the aircraft.

'How did I survive that?' he shivered. The plane was a write-off. Barry rescued his small luggage with some difficulty from the badly bent fuselage, and then took some photographs with a disposable camera.

He taxied to Nantes and caught a flight back to England. His head hurt and there was still a dizziness which seemed to affect the vision. What was happening? He felt scared for the first time ever, and his hands shook recalling the loss of control of the aeroplane.

As soon as possible he put a call through to Tom's office.

"I've got a problem. Crashed Echo Tango in France."

"Seriously? Are you hurt?"

"No I'm fine... few scratches that's all."

"But you've only just bought it." It was a silly remark, but the first that came into his head.

"I know, that's the way it goes. Just my luck lately."

"What was the problem?"

He nearly said pilot error. It was on the tip of the tongue, but something made him hold back. "Not sure, could have been fuel starvation, or mag failure. She died on finals... So what's the procedure?"

"How much damage?"

"Write-off I guess."

"They'll want to see it. I'd better get someone onto it..." Tom jotted down the details.

Dennis got the call as he came out of the shower. Francis Aviation, Gill Francis would like a word.

"You've caught me naked." He couldn't resist the test.

"Hope it's a pretty sight," she bounced back.

"Better shape than some of those wrecks you show me." He heard her laugh. Maybe she's taking the bait? Or maybe she's game anyway? "So what's brewing?"

"Get yourself respectable and I'll tell you."

"Dinner?"

"Why not? I don't relax enough these days."

"Pick you up. Where?"

He drove to the mansion in Richmond which stood high above the River Thames, thinking there was obviously money in this game. Then he remembered that Father was behind her, and this was probably his domain.

"Miss Francis will be with you shortly sir, she's asked me to serve some drinks while you're waiting."

He sipped the Famous Grouse and admired the view from the large bay window which gave a panoramic vista of the river winding through the valley below. The lounge was decorated in Georgian style and complimented the setting of the estate. The walls were adorned with original oils which wouldn't have gone amiss in the Tate Gallery. "Ah, those elegant days, I can almost hear the coach and horses coming up the carriageway..." He spoke the words out loud.

"You disappoint my Lord, I thought the dress was to be that of the flesh?" She'd combed her hair long and was wearing a light-coloured silk dress that wouldn't have left much change out of a thousand from Harrods. The transformation from the efficient businesswoman he'd met at Farnborough was dramatic, and he felt a twinge in the groin as he gently kissed her cheek.

"How come your old man's got all this? It is his isn't it?"

64

"What endearing words you do find for such occasions! Yes, the old man, as you put it, is filthy rich. Made it in property in the States. Any other questions or may we dine? I'm hungry."
"So insurance is just a plaything?"
"Mr Hopkins I am beginning to go off you. Do I detect a touch of jealousy?"
"You win. Always wanted to be born a lord. Silver platters and the like. I can spend it beautifully, but I'm buggered if I can accumulate it."
"Maybe you should court a rich bitch like me?" She took her glass to the settee and sat down, deliberately letting her dress fall open to show off smooth bronzed legs.
"Where d'you want to go then?"
"My bed any good?"

He caught the Gatwick flight to Nantes International feeling a million dollars. Some said rich bitches were the best. Either that or the cuddly ones who were sometimes very grateful. He couldn't believe last night. Her idea of hunger certainly hadn't been gastronomic, although she'd probably eaten most of his body as if near starvation.
He felt sore in places he was happy to be sore. Butchers are supposed to have strong sex drives. All that handling and cutting up of meat was the theory. Maybe she gets her kick out of the accidents, like people who go to Grands Prix hoping to see a crash.
Returning in the afternoon, he studied the accident report. Two-seat Cessna, piled up on finals, weather not bad, moderate cross wind, pilot eleven thousand hours. He made a note of that. Stalled and dipped a wing on finals. Maybe fuel or mag but no positive evidence. Airfield subject to windshear. Possible pilot error. Complete write-off.
He visited the hospital and obtained a medical report, noting that the pilot, a Mr Johnston, had sustained a badly gashed head. Discharged himself straight away, so it couldn't have been that bad.
Pretty routine. Shouldn't take long to write. He chewed the tasteless omelette, and washed it down with some warm champagne. He inclined the seat and settled back with a contented Cheshire cat grin on his face. 'I still can't believe it, she was fantastic.'

The air hostess noticed him grinning to himself and asked, "A penny for your thoughts?"

"I'd love to tell you but I daren't. Anyhow you'd never believe me."

"It must have been good," she smiled. "Another drink?"

"Gill, I'm back." He avoided any reference to the previous night. "Plane's a mess, I found nothing. Probably was fuel, but the pipes are so buggered I couldn't be certain. Pilot was well-qualified, so I'm surprised he lost it. Maybe some wind shear at the failure moment or a sudden gust. Can happen to anyone however experienced. It's the hour you're flying, not the hours you've flown. Isn't that the saying?"

"Send your written report and I'll deal with it." She sounded professional and frosty, and he wondered if she was regretting last night.

Barry arrived home feeling stupid. All those years of experience and in less than eighteen months he'd fouled up two landings. There was nothing on the answerphone and that made him cross. 'But you turned it off didn't you? What d'you expect?'

While breaking out ice cubes from the freezer Barry wondered about getting some medical help, and then realised something wasn't quite right. Subtle but he felt the presence. The hairs rose on the back of his neck with the realisation that he might not be alone. The answer phone was on. 'Check it again. But I left it off.' He moved quietly around the house trying to rack his memory on the lay out. It was all so new. 'I haven't been here long enough.' Then he spotted it.

The cat was only a stray, or maybe she'd been abandoned by the previous tenant. He'd left out the food. Barry liked animals even though they'd never been accepted by Sybil. To her they where second best to the children she couldn't have.

He sniffed the plate carefully. Paraquat weed killer. Barry knew it, as he'd always been fussy with the weeds on the drive to the cottage, and he'd always disliked the distinctive smell. Whoever was responsible they were leaving an uncomfortable message that they'd been visiting. He shivered for a moment.

After burying the poor creature he went back gratefully to the iced whisky. It was only as the liquid touched his lips that he thought again. Tim's warning about Patrick. Surely not. Not Pat's style. But who though? It made no sense. Barry checked the rest of the bungalow before unwinding to ponder on the latest events in his life.

Chapter Twelve

The Holiday Inn should have been acceptable, but was run by profiteers in a country of corrupt politicians. Even Azif recognised that. Give them their independence and what do they do? Screw it up. The only thing they know is how to screw.

He took the lift and heard it die as it left the thirteenth floor. "Jesus, I hate this country!" Even with his background he was nervous. You don't get cooped up with strangers like this if you can help it, anywhere. The emergency bell gave no help, and Azif had to sweat out twenty minutes in the stuffy atmosphere before the lift suddenly started.

He hastened to the room and turned on the shower. The rush of hot air and sand hissing from the nozzle that greeted him was enough, and he flopped onto the bed feeling cheesed off and angry.

Time's a healer, and Azif grabbed at its help. 'Hang in' he told himself, this will be your revenge, be patient.

He recalled the initial approach in his years as a teenager. Not long out of college with a degree in electronics, the messengers had made it quite clear. Your father's life is in his son's hands, the President has made his decision. Azif hadn't appreciated that the easy comforts of his youth, with the luxurious apartments, the horse riding, the holidays in Europe and the young girls, were pre-planned, as a cruel plot to blackmail a repayment from him, for the 'mistakes' of his family.

The knowledge that his father's sentence had been drummed up to that of a rapist had shocked him enough. He didn't believe the charges and suspected they were a barbaric penalty to pay for favours withdrawn from his beautiful mother, who'd worked for the military in her younger years, when the President had been a colonel. The fact that it was alleged that his father had been involved with the President's favourite mistress was frightening enough. He knew his father could never love again, and any remaining life he might have lay in Azif's hands. They'd made it so clear. He was unable to contemplate the hideous torture and murder of his mother, and he feared for his sister, of whom he'd heard nothing in five long years. "I'll attend to their requests, but I will take my revenge," he promised his family in a silent prayer by the bedside.

The long-distance call from the States came through. "Chuck, thank God I've got you. Taken four hours."

"Azif, where the hell are you? You sound rough!"

"I'm stuck in Lagunda." He heard Chuck grunt.

"What in hell's name are you doing there?"

"Chuck, leave it. I'm hot. Thirsty. This place is a dump. You wouldn't believe it. The guests are shaving in the swimming pool and I'm bloody hungry." Chuck listened, waiting for more answers.

"The plane ditched in the desert."

"How come?"

"No idea."

"Accident?"

"Search me. I doubt it."

'I don't believe this. You'd better believe it.'

"So what's on?"

"Half the diamonds missing, Wasp 200 destroyed or stolen, bits left around. It's a bloody mess."

"You'd better stay put, I'll get one of my boys over. This needs some thought." They rang off.

Azif brushed past the scruffy guy at the reception desk, mopping the perspiration from his face, and hardly noticed the slight limp as the man picked up the holdall and made his way to the lift. Lounging back with a warm beer he decided to take stock of the situation. Delivery had been planned for tomorrow and someone was going to go berserk. He shuddered at the thought. The crash was no accident, or was it? He didn't know. He was sure that his protection gang were on the wrong track. They'd been told that someone had been sniffing round the flat he'd rented, and asking odd questions.

"There's nothing there," he'd told them, but they had decided to put on some pressure. 'You'll open up a hornet's nest if you're not careful.' But they seemed to think that the investigators were on to them, and had some evidence that might have something to do with Azif, and that he was under surveillance. They said they needed to divert matters otherwise their cover could be blown.

"You're mad," he told them. They're not the CIA. Heard that they were from the local airline investigating procedures. 'We'll see. Muddy the water, cause a little internal confusion. Divert the scent.' Then they'd bungled a search of one of the pilot's homes and poisoned a cat. Divert the scent? The idiots were amateurs!

No, the desert problem was from another source and Azif was scared.

Hogan splashed the sandy water over his body and towelled off the grime from the airport taxi ride. Sod that Mitchell fellow, he'd said the Middle East, not this hole. Still, can't really hold him responsible for the change of plan. He changed his shirt and mulled over the information he'd been given, and his instructions.

This Iraqi – Azif something – had rented a top suite in the high-rise flats near Bournemouth Airport, and apart from girlie parties had taken deliveries of electrical gear, and also rigged up a large aerial on top of the building. Tim reckoned that this gear, whatever it was, might have had something to do with the failure of some instruments that pilots use to navigate.

"Sounds plausible," Hogan had volunteered.

"So go and find out."

Azif had been difficult to trace, but with the help of a lass who worked in Universal Travel, an outfit that organised charter flights, especially around the Arabian and African countries, he'd struck lucky. Apparently there was a private flight from Las Palmas scheduled for Bahrain and the passenger list included an A. Azif. He discovered that Azif was the surname and there was no indication of a name to put to the initial. He'd checked on the day of the flight and had intended to make contact in Bahrain. He got the message of the ditching from the same girl, and that the survivors had been brought back to Lagunda, the capital of a small state in the Niger region that had recently been granted its independence. Luckily Caledonian could re-schedule and now he was holed up in this dump. Further enquiries had led him to the Holiday Inn and he grinned at the contact just made in the foyer. 'there's still life in the old dog.'

He contacted Tim with the latest situation and then settled for an Impala steak which tasted better than the smells coming from the noisy kitchen.

Chapter Thirteen

Chuck Alston's father had left him a ranch and nine hundred square miles of good beef grazing, four shallow oilwells, a garage full of Cadillacs, three completely different aeroplanes and a Harley Davidson. As a kid he'd flown the crop sprayer from the age of twelve, graduating to the twin at sixteen. Flying was like riding a bike to Chuck. With no brothers or sisters, and his mother in a psychiatric ward, he'd got used to being a loner. He'd courted, but the gold diggers after his wealth were too high a price to pay, so he lived alone, except for his black house-servants.

Chuck supported the IRA. Grandfather had been from Belfast, and it suited his purpose. The calls yesterday where still on his mind.

"I'm ringing on behalf of Patrick Clancy." That old dealer, he's still around. He burped as he remembered their drinking sessions. 'Never could take the rye whisky, that Pat.'

"Want's a favour you say. What favour?"

"Not on the telephone."

"Tell the old dog to get his butt over here if he wants my favours."

"It's a delicate matter sir, and Mr Clancy cannot travel at this time."

"Don't give me that crap. Dying is he?"

"Not exactly." Tim went on to explain about the injunction and that Patrick's hands were full at the moment. Couldn't leave the country.

"Poor old shit. Okay, when d'you want to see me?"

He knew Patrick would call the favour one day and he couldn't really grumble. Now he was running for governor he needed a clean sheet, and that business with Sheila must never come out. Pat had taken the blame, and the money was still transferred through Pat's account in Ireland. If she ever guessed that he was the father it would cost him a fortune. 'No, I still owe Patrick one.'

Then Azif. What the hell was he playing at? The Iranians know where the help is originating, and Azif needs all the promises he can get for his family. Let's face it, he's running one hell of a risk dealing with his country's enemy. He wondered. Who else would know?

He rang Hal. "Got a problem with the two hundred. I'm coming over." Chuck climbed into the open Eldorado which he still loved driving and trucked it over to Hal's place.

"Sure I can fix another, but these modifications don't grow on trees." Hal handed Chuck a cold Coors.

"D'you reckon anyone else has gotten wind of our deal? No leaks in your organisation?"

"Maybe. Doubt it. I need eight days and that's without testing."

"Four, and another quarter a million."

"You're a soft touch today. You need this badly?"

Chuck nodded. "With favours in both countries I'll hold the negotiating power. It's all I want Hal. Father had financial dreams, but I can't have those with the fortune he left. So it's political power. That's all that's left."

He drove back and stopped at the Redbird Motel which had been the inspiration for the name of one of his companies. Molly fixed his usual Jim Beam and studied the lined face, which was looking more tired than of late.

"You keeping well?" she asked with concern.

"Yeah. Fair I suppose. You know Molly, there're moments when you ask, what's it all about?"

"Not like you Chuck." She felt a small ache in her breast. There'd been a time when she might have become Mrs Alston but it was not to be. She didn't want his money or kids, just to be something better than a barmaid. She thought about their fun time in California, but she was only thirty then and raunchy with it. Fifteen years on and double that in weight, she could feel her thigh fat wobbling as she walked to the bar. Not much of a catch now.

"Take the bottle, might cheer you up." She slid it cowboy style along the polished bar as she passed to serve a couple of truckers.

"Mr Alston isn't it?"

Chuck looked over to one of the drivers. "I know you?" It was a half-hearted question from the farmer.

"Delivered some gear to your place last month. Work for Hal. Got a rush on for more he tells me. You shifting drugs or something?" The comment was in sport, Chuck realised that, but he felt like throttling the nosy bastard.

"Just a money press to print lousy dollars to pay off loud-mouthed yids like you, so look after it with care." Molly heard the words in surprise. She'd seen Chuck angry but not often with his tongue. A fist occasionally. He must have worries.

"Hold on. We was only joking."

Chuck threw back the dregs and dumped a hundred dollar bill on the bar.

"Give 'em one. Sorry, tired." He shuffled out to the car.

The drive back was uneventful except for the dust storms building and blocking out the sun. Whirlwind, he reckoned, better get straight back. The wind increased as he neared the ranch, but he could see from the distant electric sky that the storm would pass a few miles south of the house.

The black Buick was unfamiliar and it didn't connect, for his mind was still on that crap in the Motel. 'Whatever came over me?' He found no answers, apart from feeling old and foolish.

"A Mr Mitchell is waiting, Boss," the Southern drawl of his Negro housekeeper greeted him on the wooden porch of the grand ranchhouse.

Of course, he'd forgotten. Jesus! How'd the guy got here so quick?

"Mitchell, hi there. I wasn't expecting you so soon."

"I understand sir. Forgot to tell you I was ringing from Miami while I was waiting for a connecting flight."

"So how's Pat? Gotten himself in trouble?" he smiled knowingly.

"Not exactly. Things are a bit tough in the UK these days. Lot of competition, new safety regulations coming in, passengers demanding better service. Puts a strain on the cash."

"He after money then?" Chuck retorted.

"Not quite." Tim was finding the direct approach difficult to handle.

"Don't tell me he want's to sell the airline? No, I've got it. He want's me to take up some stock. That right?"

Tim started to feel put down by this large, brusque, straight-talking Texan. He'd experienced the directness of Americans during his career, but this man had an overpowering presence.

"No stock, you buzz Patrick now and tell him no stock."

The lighting crash heralded the storm which hit with a ferocity that tested the foundations of the timber and brick-built ranchhouse. The hailstones rained down like golf balls, and Tim watched them bouncing off the stone-lined driveway with an unreal fascination. Chuck had left and he could be heard bellowing out instructions to someone. The wind followed the hail and suddenly the whole building was surrounded by dust and sand which screeched on the glass windows. It was over as fast as it started and suddenly everywhere was quiet.

"Big twister." Chuck returned with a coil of rope which he tossed in the corner. "We don't often get 'em right on top. Not good for flying." Tim agreed with that statement.

The phonecall took Chuck away again and Tim was left to observe his surroundings. He took them in with increasing disbelief. The lounge was over sixty feet long and stocked more than ten leather-covered chairs and settees. A huge bar took up most of one end, and the Steinway grand was almost lost in one of the corners. Large Chinese rugs covered the solid teak floor, and ornate antiques tried to fill the rest of the room. A couple of pearl-embossed guitars were slung casually on a large pecan sideboard. Tim looked at some of the paintings and then spotted the shotgun rack which would have made a proud collection for a cowboy film. The French doors led out to vast patio and he watched the dying raindrops splashing into the Olympic-sized swimming pool. 'How d'you accumulate such wealth?' He shook his head with the silent question.

"Like the place?" Chuck followed him onto the terrace. "I've organised some food, real steak burgers, Budweiser okay? So how d'you say we slow down, eh? Let's hear the whole story."

Without interruption Tim was able to fill Chuck in with the problems of Marvel Air and the CAA pressures on the service records.

"So if I'm reading you upside, the servicing's legit – it's just that the company's not registered?"

"Right."

"And Pat wants my Belfast boys to sign off?"

"Right again."

Chuck tapped his boots on the paving slabs as he chewed on the cheroot in his teeth. "Can't see a problem. Probably need a tie-up or the like with this maintenance outfit. What's their name?" Tim couldn't remember.

"No matter. Detail... Tell Patrick I'll fix it. Food?"

Chapter Fourteen

He tried to comprehend, but something in his mind wouldn't accept the words being spoken. He held the phone away from his ear and heard Tom's blurred voice as if trying to understand the conversation in a crowded room or listening against a background of motorway traffic. The news was unreal like a radio play, and he waited to hear other characters join in the dialogue, and for the scene to change cheerfully.

"I'm desperately sorry. Anything I can do let me know. Margaret's still being difficult but she's a bit shocked at the moment. She'll come round, don't worry."

Barry replaced the handset in slow motion and walked through the kitchen into the garden with its soft views over the Welsh hills. He opened the back gate and drifted toward the distant Fells as if he was already late for an important meeting and didn't care. He tried to rationalise his thoughts but the news clung too deeply as he stumbled aimlessly along the lanes and through the fields. The screech from the car tyres broke into his numbness as he crossed the country road without a glance to traffic. 'Better he hit me.' It didn't seem to matter.

Hours later with the sun nearly set, he was back in the kitchen sitting at the scrubbed-pine table with a steadying glass in his hand. He started to draw up a list of phone numbers and found Judy's in his diary.

"My wife... she's dead." He blurted out the flat statement.

"How, why, when?" The questions came out as an instant reaction, but with concern in her voice.

"Late last night. Collapsed after returning from a meal with friends. No reasons as yet... heart maybe."

"What are you going to do?"

"I don't know. I feel screwed up these days. Crashed my plane... life's all shit at the moment."

She felt for his bad luck and sensed the little boy lost, and his need for comfort. "Come and see me soon. It's all I can offer."

He longed for her body again to take away the hurt in his mind, yet he felt a conscience for Sybil, and the duty he needed to perform for their love in the past. Barry took the prescription to the local chemist with the casual words of the doctor still in his ears. "Valium. Take one a day. Best I can do." 'You need to be dying these days before they take any real interest,' he thought, 'nutters like me come pretty low down their priority list.' He carried on with the funeral preparations.

The tiny chapel was full and Barry had forgotten how many friends they'd made. He met relations only remembered in photographs and some he'd never seen. The service reached commitment time and the priest nodded to Barry. Slipping a pill into his mouth he made his way to the lectern.

He felt the dryness of his throat and tried to control the notes in his shaking hands. 'I'm not sure I can handle this, but I must.' He looked at the congregation but everyone was a blur. He stared at the coffin, almost longing to be inside where no problems existed, in place of his wife. He'd decided to give the address rather than leave it to some unknown priest. Who really knew the woman who lay with them today better than her husband of many years?

"I hope you'll bear with me, for this is the hardest thing I've ever done, but I need to say what I feel." His voice shook with a nervousness deep in his stomach, and moisture glazed his eyes. He breathed in hard.

Time seemed to stand alone in that crematorium with Barry's memory of idyllic moments in their marriage, of the simplicity of young living, the challenge of flying, the holidays in the sun, the cottage, the rows. Why had it all gone wrong? It was over, history, and he needed to put it decently to ash for life to go forward. He focused the waiting congregation.

"Why does one have to hurt the person you love, and leave it too late to say I'm sorry...?" Barry waited to let the thoughts sink in... "Why are we so selfish as not to see the pain we inflict on our partner, when all they're trying to do is help and understand our problem?" Barry poured his heart out that day as if he was a genie who'd been released from a magic lamp to air his last wishes. His words were felt by everyone, and the uncomfortable shuffles and wet faces reflected the truth many others recognised in his heart-searching apology. He finished exhausted, but with a relief that he hadn't experienced for a long time.

It was then that he saw her standing at the back of the chapel. As they focused on each other he felt her dark eyes penetrating right into his soul, and he knew in his heart that their lovemaking later would be both gentle and wild. She was gone as quickly as she'd appeared, and he was grateful for her understanding of his tasks that special day.

Later, with only a few mourners left and the wake over, Tom decided to take Barry's mind of the funeral and went over the insurance details of his claim and the findings of Francis Aviation.

"So they're paying in full?"

"No reason not too. Plane's a write-off."

In the early morning hours as he lay quietly with Judy, wondering about the fate of life, a plan started to form in his mind. 'Forty thousand and Echo Tango only cost twenty. Insurers never checked the value, they just accepted my figure. A tidy little profit. What if I could make that happen again? Have to be with a different insurance company or someone would smell a rat.' He considered the various possibilities and looked to see if Judy was awake.

'What if the ownership was different in each case? Yes, that would work, but the pilot would need a disguise. Crashes need to be write-offs. How can I pull that off every time? Go for five and make a hundred grand and then off abroad with Judy. We can do it again in another country. I'm fed up with trying to be Mr Nice.'

He mulled over other questions and felt the adrenalin flowing through his blood. 'I need this drive otherwise I'll vegetate.' Judy moaned with a sleepy pleasure as she received the full demanding effect of the new excitement which suddenly flooded his body.

"What brought that on? What's so good?"

She sat by the window brushing her long black hair and Barry still wanted more of her nakedness with a desire he'd not felt since his youth. She saw the passion in his eyes and slowly stepped into her high-heeled shoes and then let him crawl over every inch of her body, smiling teasingly as she watched him slowly lose all control. Her hands skilfully guided him to a closeness and climax which left them both shivering and exhausted, perspiring with satisfaction. After a magical peace which seemed timeless, they eased apart and Judy returned to her hairbrush.

"So what's good? You haven't said?" her voice had the throaty huskiness of a woman fully in control of her sensuality.

"How can I, when you dress like that?"

He outlined his scheme with its risks and rewards, laughing at its boldness.

"But that's illegal and dangerous, not your scene, surely?"

"Wasn't. Is now... Bonnie meet Mr Clyde."

"You really mean it?"

"You'd better believe it, as the Yanks say."

"Well if it's going to keep you performing like now, you have your Bonnie."

She moved to sit on his lap and made him fondle and kiss each of her firm breasts in turn. As she became aroused again, he sensed her still-demanding lust and unselfishly stroked her body which wriggled in excitement until she needed no more. She slowly slipped down till her head was between his thighs, to gently mouth him as a silent act of thanks and love. He had no choice but to give in to the perfection of her performance and desire.

The cheque arrived unannounced and Barry banked it straight away. He settled the small fee from La Baule for dumping the remains and picked up a copy of the latest flight magazine to look for a suitable replacement. 'Better change type, foreign this time?' he thought. He found the answer on the last page. It was perfect, small French four-seater, recon engine, body in need of attention, price by negotiation. Barry dialled immediately and listened to the grateful seller.

"Looking for fifteen grand, worth more but I've little choice."

They drove to Gloucestershire like a couple of doves who couldn't keep apart. Judy's wandering hands made it difficult for Barry to concentrate, and at one stage he pulled into a side lane so that she could sort him out.

"I owe you one," he volunteered.

"You do, and I'll hold you to it Mr Clyde."

"Fancy the thousand foot club?" He chuckled at the thought. 'What's happening? A few days ago I was ready to leave this earth, now I'm acting like a teenager.'

"Fourteen and a half, we've a deal." Barry shook hands with the youthful man who was selling him India Papa.

"You've got a bargain there you know." Barry smiled. 'A bargain yes, but not the way you're thinking lad.'

"Small point. Does it matter to you what the invoice figure is?"

"No problem. No VAT. Why?"

"Well, I'm buying it as a company asset and the larger the apparent value, the more I can offset against investment tax."

"Sound to me. Screw those tax parasites for as much as you can. That's why I'm having to sell. Got their knife into me."

They left with paper work showing a sale at forty grand and a new ownership and Barry arranged to collect the plane within the next few days.

"Right, you're my broker now."

Barry explained to Judy the rudiments of insurance and instructed her to sort out a new company and to get cover based on the false figures. "Wear something sexy," he told her. "And make sure you're dealing with a man. I suggest we take a photo of the plane with you standing in front, in one of your off-the-shoulder gypsy outfits. Lunch as necessary but no more."

"Possessive are we?" She giggled. "If I'm your moll, I should be allowed to play all my cards." He felt a silly jealousy, far beneath her years, but she kissed his cheek in reassurance. "If I had to give one there would be two for you," she teased.

"Molls are two a penny. So you watch your place."

"Do I get a spanking tonight?" She was enjoying the banter.

They'd been again. He noticed small items that had been moved, especially as the tidy-up from the funeral was still clear in his mind. 'I must contact Tim,' he reminded himself.

Barry settled down with the flight manual for his new 'short to live' aeroplane to work out the details for a controlled disaster. As he studied the figures his mind wandered around the events of the last year, from the flying mishaps to Sybil's death, to Judy, and now the beginning of a criminal career. Relaxing in front of the fire a contented tiredness took over, and he fell into a deep sleep.

Chapter Fifteen

Hogan was bushed. He'd spent a week trailing Azif and nothing had happened. He'd tried bugging the room but mostly the phones didn't work and he suspected that the regular electrical failures set up surges that damaged the sensitive electronic equipment.

Azif spent most of his time at 'clubs' and there was no way this limping white limey could get to enter those. 'Reverse apartheid', he rued. Still tonight he might have struck lucky. She wasn't pretty but available, and in the rest room at this time of a small night club in the basement of the hotel. Not pretty was being kind. His face grimaced. 'Still, look at me, hardly good material for *Vogue*. Anyhow, it's business.'

She returned and looked a bit better this time, although he wondered if it was just the effect of the champagne. Ought to do something at these prices.

"Sonya yea." She puckered her nose.

"It's not what you think, but I need someone to show me around. Get me into places. You understand?" She nodded but clearly didn't.

"Only take US dollars." Jesus this is hard work.

As he refilled the glass she grinned and presented a mouth empty of most of its teeth, with those left blacker than her skin. "Toilet. I'll be back."

He washed the sweat off his face and wished he was home in the offices at Southampton instead of this hell hole. 'Money's a bastard. Sod the old man, he could have left something! Fuck Tim and Azif and Sonya.' He wandered back to the table to find her dancing with a guy uglier than her.

He slipped a note into the waiter's hand. "Tell that arsehole to piss off and leave my women alone."

She sat down and grinned again and Hogan nearly wished he was wearing coloured underpants. "You know the Chi-Chi club?"

"Fifty dollars."

"Your father a financier or something? You only converse in money."

"No father... fifty dollars to go to club."

Shit, slow it down. Losing your rag, Hogan.

"So can you and I go there?" She shrugged.

"Tomorrow night. Ten thirty. We're going to Chi-Chi's. Okay?"

"Your room key."

"No thanks Sonya. Some other time."

The late night porno movie was about as exciting as watching two dogs on heat and Hogan reached for the mini bar. The beer was hot as usual and he finally gave up and settled for another sleepless night in unbearable humidity. 'This's it. My last assignment for sure.'

Dozing with no sense of time Hogan heard the door fall open rather than being eased, and found himself staring into the barrel of an unknown gun, held by an aggressive guy also unknown.

Ugly, from the club, was sitting in the back of a battered black Mercedes whose mileage clock must have wound round several times during its chequered life. Hogan, having woken with a thumping head from the poor champagne, paid more attention to the man this time, and noticed especially the scar through the right ear and the two fingers missing from the left hand. He was bundled alongside his host and was greeted with the combination of bad beer, and the smell of sweat which Ugly had tried to disguise with a cheap talc.

"You stink." It worked in the films. Showed you weren't an easy pushover. Trouble is they don't simulate pain on the screen other than by sight. Maybe a lot of money to be made here. Todd AO was a success with three-dimensional colour, why not Realadrama with pain simulators in the seats. Hogan tried to distract himself from the pain of the crushing blow to his leg, which took him back to the agony of that Soho night. They'd done their homework and it hurt.

"You like Sonya?" Ugly gave him a hideous grin.

"Fuck off."

The second round was worse, and Hogan voted to pack in the Clint Eastwood act and try to earn his money more comfortably.

"You guys got a problem?"

The silence volunteered nothing and Hogan decided to take stock of the situation and collect his thoughts. He was obviously into something bigger than Tim Mitchell had guessed and this lot, whoever they were, reckoned he knew more than he did. So play it along, find out as much as possible, and then leave them realising he was only a small fish who'd jumped into the wrong pond. Trouble was that if this was a big deal, they might not put him back in the water. So an escape plan was required.

The dawn drive out of Lagunda did nothing for his confidence. Maybe it hadn't focused so clearly before, but the dross in the centre of the freeway seemed dirtier than usual. He'd been told that executions still took place on the beaches. The favourite was to hang the 'culprit' from a gallows-type structure, and to lessen his agony by using the body for target practice with the latest anti-personnel firearms.

Several hours later the driver turned off the dusty road and through security gates which lead to a long palm tree-lined avenue, ending at a brilliant white Spanish-styled villa.

Hogan was escorted through the cool entrance to a large open lounge furnished with exotic antiques and large flower-patterned settees. He shuffled over the beautiful Italian floor tiles through to the pool area, and was shown to a sunlounger table occupied by two other female guests.

Azif arrived and announced himself by fondling one of the beautiful Eurasian girls, sunning herself in little more than a G-string.

"You may go now Kobaf." Hogan felt easier after Azif's dismissal of Ugly and his gunbutting colleagues. 'I won't invite them to my retirement party,' he thought. The drink tasted of his favourite Jack Daniels, and he sipped it with a muted pleasure after the bumpy car trip.

"Enough ice?" Azif was smiling at him with a sense of achievement and Hogan guessed why.

"So when?"

"Gatwick. You were spotted buying similar in the duty free." He held up the rye whisky bottle. "Kobaf's been tailing your every movement since."

"A giveaway," he shrugged. "Still, at least I get to talk."

Azif indicated that the girls should leave and they sidled off tossing their hair like a couple of racing fillies. He drew on his cocktail straw and sat down opposite Hogan.

"You first." It was said with authority and Hogan suspected that the villa bodyguards weren't far away.

He studied his captor who was wearing an immaculate Italian cut white suit over a pale green open-neck shirt, and guessed that the buckled shoes had originated from Tuscany. Azif didn't strike him as aggressive, but then many Arabs don't, he told himself. Let someone else do the dirty work. 'So do I come clean or fish around?' The answer was given for him.

"I know about Mitchell; the doorman of the Bournemouth flat was most cooperative. Your Mr Johnston has been warned and we're in contact with our American friends. So don't be shy." He waited in amusement.

"Okay, it's not a problem and not as sinister as you may think. All I've been instructed to do is to find some evidence that might help a guy whose job's been screwed. My client wants to see if your activities have any relevance."

"Go on."

"Any more of this?" Hogan held up his glass. Azif clicked fingers and a black maid topped up the glass.

"It all starts with an airmiss at Bournemouth..." He went through the details as he remembered them from Tim's meeting in the hotel, filling in with some of the court's findings, and then laying on fairly heavily the queries to the technical side.

Azif listened attentively to Hogan's story. 'So that's it! He knew this was a blind alley. Nothing to do with the desert crash! Get a replacement from Texas and I can let them know we're back on course. I'm in the clear but I need something to divert the others whoever they are. Maybe I could use this detective.' A plan was beginning to form itself.

"I see. Why the cloak and dagger stuff? Why not a direct approach?"

"Dunno really. Mr Mitchell thought your gear might be secret in some way and he wouldn't be able to test his theory."

Azif said, "It is, and there's no way you'll get details. They're top secret with my government, and I don't intend to make the mistake of becoming an unfortunate guest of one of my country's safe houses."

Hogan could see he meant it and sympathised with Azif's fears. 'I wouldn't risk being taken hostage, not in that godforsaken country.'

He sat back to consider his next move. Nothing seemed appropriate and he felt a bit useless. Might as well get out of this hole, but he didn't like coming away empty-handed.

Azif hung onto the moment as he gauged his timing. He could offer the girls, but he doubted that Hogan would be interested. The guy's been around too long. Looks tired, probably only motivated by cash, booze and a good meal. Maybe enjoys a bit of sport. Wouldn't like to mess up though. Pride and fair play probably. Terrible British failure in this modern corrupt world.

"I feel I owe you an apology."

"You what?"

"I feel an injustice. You will realise that my religion does not favour mistakes and we can be very generous in such circumstances."

Hogan got his ears together and started listening. A couple of hours ago he was worried about his chances of becoming a permanent cripple. Now he was drinking his favourite brew, and this smooth-talking arab was apologising. 'Where's the catch,' there had to be one?

"Look Azif, I may have got in deeper than I should have, but I'm not stupid. You could get rid of me right now. So what's the deal?"

"Patience my friend. Pleasure should never be hurried and now we understand each other you're my guest. I believe your leg still pains you. We'll attend to that first, and then we'll dine in comfort and maybe enjoy some Eastern relaxation. Business is for later."

The Jack Daniels was taking over, and Hogan was more than happy to be escorted to the suite overlooking the pool area where the girls were still enjoying their freedom in the setting sun. He knew there'd be further checks so he set the tiny recording device, realising that his drinks had probably been laced. He left his wallet with the dummy information as an easy find, before he flopped out on the queen-size bed for the welcome release of his tired brain and aching body.

Chapter Sixteen

Barry checked the paperwork again and was pleased with the results. Judy had done a great job and the French prototype was nicely insured for forty grand, with an ownership in the name of Tony Hastings.

She flew well, and for a few days he thought about cancelling the whole idea. But he was still angry with the events of the last eighteen months and wanted revenge. 'They took my career – I'm taking their money.' It was illogical, but it suited his purpose.

He rang Judy with final instructions. "Should be there 'bout midday. All being well I'll give you a call to come and collect me. Stay by that pub phone in King's Lynn as we agreed. You can be with me in half an hour."

"Right Clyde, don't cock it up."

"I thought that was the idea?"

"You know what I mean. Yourself not the plane."

"I'll give it my best."

"Frightened?"

"Mixed feelings. Scared I suppose. Stomach's rumbling."

"Good luck. Wait for your call."

With the plane airborne, he set course for Norfolk and his planned destination.

"Norwich approach. Golf India Papa. I've a rough-running engine and intend putting down at Little Snoring. I'm not declaring an emergency."

"Roger India Papa, that's copied." The air traffic controller made a note and continued with his routine shift responsibilities.

Barry smiled nervously as he circled the light aeroplane over the old Norfolk RAF base and glanced down at the short strip still just serviceable. Under the crops it was possible to make out the shadows of the three old runways, and some of the concrete bases of the mess huts. He thought about the Lancasters that must have returned after their sorties deep into Germany, and those that had crashed due to flack damage or tired and injured crews. 'And I'm doing this deliberately?' He shivered.

Last time it had been an accident and he tried to remember clearly the moment just before the wing touched. Could he simulate that again? Would the result be the same? He went over the calculations. Stall speed left wing down, forty five knots. Approach the airfield at fifty two but nose high. Check the fuel, good nearly empty. Left tyre pressure low, yes he'd done that just before takeoff.

He was suddenly frightened at the thought of fire and the pain of Injury and death that burning fuel could inflict. He remembered the horrific pictures from the guinea pig club and those brave crews who had been disfigured for life.

"Sandy. Are we expecting any visitors today?" The farmer heard the engine drone from the kitchen garden, where he was drinking a well-earned coffee after his early morning start.

"No one rang John," she told her husband.

The farmer strolled out of the back gate. "Someone's up there. Sounds rough to me."

'Keep altering the power,' Barry instructed himself, 'make it cough. If anyone's around it must sound like engine problems.'

He spotted the wind sock. Fair crosswind, and it was starting to drizzle. Finally the time had come. 'This is it.' He banked the aeroplane toward the runway and set it up for a controlled crash. 'Damn! If I was trying for real she would have dropped a wing anyway in this wind. Now I want it she won't go.' Suddenly the sound of the stall-warning buzzer filled the cockpit as Barry forced the left wing into the ground.

The noise of metal reshaping itself filled his ears for what seemed several minutes, and then there was silence. He sniffed for any fuel smell and judging it safe his mouth pursed into a small grin, before he slumped back in his seat to await events ahead.

The farmer heard the crunch and fearing the worst shouted to his wife "Quick Sandy they've crashed! Ring for an ambulance! I'll take the tractor!"

The small aeroplane was lying on its side halfway down the old tarmac and concrete runway, and John could see that one of the wings had broken away. As he got nearer he focused on the bent propeller and the engine which had been torn off its mountings.

A write-off he guessed, but what of the occupants? There was no sign of fire and no sign of the pilot. He forced the tractor to a skidding halt and ran to the plane having grabbed the fire extinguisher.

He found the pilot in his seat with a lot of blood running down his face. "You all right?" He received a shaky nod. "Let's get you to the house. Nothing broken?" Again the pilot shook his head.

John helped him into a spare seat that he'd fixed for taking the children round the farm, and drove back to the farmhouse.

Barry looked at the aircraft as they bumped along the narrow farm track. 'Made it. All that planning, stall speeds, worked out, but Jesus, that was too close for comfort,' he thought.

"Got some brandy in the house. 'Spect we could both use a slug or two?"

"I'm all right really."

The phial of blood which he'd squeezed down his face was drying and the smell made him feel sick. 'Twenty-five grand,' he smiled slyly and then gritted his teeth as he noticed the farmer looking at him quizzically.

"You sure you're okay?"

"Yes thanks. A little dazed."

"Name's Bakewell, John Bakewell." The farmer decided he ought to keep talking. He'd read somewhere that you mustn't let the patient fall asleep if you suspect concussion.

"Tony Hastings." He and Judy had drawn up a list of pseudonyms for the insurers, and had decided to use surnames based on old aeroplanes. They'd had a laugh sitting on the rug in front of the fire making up the combinations, "What about Burt Lancaster?" Silly how you can be when you're in love.

"I was on my way to Norwich."

"What happened?"

"Not sure, engine died on me."

"Fuel?"

'Careful, this guy's a shade too inquisitive, I'll have to watch what I say.' They rounded the farm shed and Barry saw the reason why, in the form of the Jodel parked outside a small hangar. A fellow flyer?

Inside the warm kitchen Sandy, the farmer's wife, had brewed some tea, and Barry sipped it with helpings from the Bakewell brandy bottle.

"The ambulance's on its way. Another twenty minutes they said."

"I don't need to bother them. It's very kind of you but I think you ought to cancel the call. I've only had a shaking."

"That cut look's bad." Sandy was fussing like any mother would.

"I'm okay really. Look I've been flying a long time and I've had plenty of training on medical matters. Divert the ambulance in case they're required elsewhere."

"You sure?" she looked to her husband for help.

"Give them a ring." John made the decision and Barry drew a breath of air in relief.

"Let's treat that cut."

Although Barry tried to stop her she insisted and he was forced to visit the bathroom. He could see she was puzzled and he kept using his handkerchief and moving his head to try and confuse her. Grabbing a plaster he turned away and asked if he could go back to the warm kitchen.

"May I use your phone?" Barry rang Judy and manufactured a pretty good disaster story with lots of "don't worry darling"; "I'm all right really"; "I'll get a taxi... well okay if you insist."

"My wife'll pick me up." He appeared puzzled for a moment then said. "I need a favour, and that's to ask you if the plane can be left alone until the insurers have had a view."

"Sure, I'll fence it off and paint a white cross on the runway."

The farmer wanted to talk technicalities and Barry was not pleased to hear that he'd been an aircraft-fitter in the last war. He listened politely and said little himself.

"Like to look around myself if that's all right."

"Of course. I'd be grateful if you didn't touch anything," he asked again. "You know these insurance boys. Find any reason for not paying."

"You crashed before?" It was a throwaway question and it caught Barry on the hop.

"No, I eh... well no," he stuttered. "I read the accident reports in the flight magazines." Barry could see the farmer was not too convinced.

"My head's hurting, do you mind if I lie down for a while? My wife should be here soon."

Judy arrived wearing a blond wig which made her look very tarty with her dusky skin. Barry had only vaguely disguised himself by leaving on a week's stubble. Between them they made a scruffy couple, and he was already questioning arrangements for the next one.

Farewells and thanks over, John decided to wander over to the airfield.

"Back shortly love. Just going to nose around."

Careful thanks to his training, John looked for fuel leaks; a latent fire was always a danger. The detached wing lying someway from the fuselage was bone dry and he couldn't see any sign of fuel on the runway. A closer look at the other wing still attached, showed virtually no Avgas. 'Norwich he'd said. Good sixty miles plus reserve. There's no way he'd have made that.' He continued to fish around and although the engine had broken away there was no obvious external failure to his skilled eye. 'Maybe he just ran out of fuel? But the guy said he was an experienced pilot... still it happens."

He started to walk back and caught the flash in the sunlight. Bending down he picked up a plastic tube that was lying near the bent door. It didn't mean anything to him and certainly wasn't an aircraft component in his knowledge. He tucked it in his pocket and turned as he heard the farmhand calling him from the sheds.

"Trouble with them sheep fences again. They're roaming out on the road." John busied himself with farming matters and forgot about the crash.

Sandy's Lancashire hotpots where the talk of the village and John smelt the flavour as he dumped his boots by the back door. His Guinness was poured with a perfect head and he smiled at his wife with that glowing comfort that they'd given each other over the years.

Content after the meal they settled by the fire to review the day. A long time ago they'd agreed that this time of the day would be given over to chatting, for running the farm left them apart for long periods. They talked on farm matters, and how the family were doing for a while, then Sandy changed the subject.

"Find anything out there?"

"Nothing obvious. Seemed low on fuel but maybe it's drained away. Very volatile that stuff."

"Funny about that blood."

"What blood?"

"You know, you picked him up. He was covered on his face, and it had drained down to his shirt."

"Yes. Must've banged his head in the cockpit."

"But there was no cut!"

"Sorry, I'm not with you?"

"I tried to dress it, but when I washed his face there was no cut, at least nothing that could have caused so much bleeding. There was a scar on his head but that was well healed. So where'd it come from?"

"No cut? What about the plaster?"

"Got that from the cabinet. He snatched it and stuck it on himself." John listened to his wife's words with increasing interest. What was going on? He suddenly remembered the tube he'd found out on the runway and got up from his chair. "Hang on love, I've got something to show you." He found the item in his jacket pocket and handed it to Sandy. "It was lying by the aircraft."

"What's this?" She studied the tube, turned it around, and then gave it a sniff. She looked up at her husband and he could see the surprise dawning in her eyes.

"Come on then, what d'you think?"

"It's a phial."

"File, what d'you mean a file?"

"Not the file you're probably thinking of. A phial for holding liquids."

"Such as?"

"Blood."

John let this information sink in as he reached for another Guinness. A tube of blood, why? Sandy sat staring at the piece of plastic with no answers in her mind.

"Why a tube of blood or a phial, whatever you call it? Is it some form of medication?"

"Maybe. Perhaps he was carrying it for some reason and it broke and squirted over him. Perhaps that's why he acted funny in the bathroom?"

"I can understand that, but why be so secretive?"

"Embarrassed?"

Neither could come up with any better explanation and after talking about other things they decided to have an early night.

"I might make a few phonecalls tomorrow."

"Like who?"

"Norwich Airport for one."

"Did we get Mr Hastings' address or telephone number?"

"No. He never suggested it."

"Probably forgot. Still shaken I expect."

"Hum, maybe. His wife say anything?" Sandy shook her head.

John rose early and couldn't wait to ring Norwich. He'd slept fitfully with a sort of excitement which he hadn't experienced since the War. 'A sense of adventure I suppose.' Farming was all right, but you couldn't beat the buzz of flying and the fear of the unknown. It brought back memories of his time in the services, and for a moment he looked wistfully at the photograph hanging in the hall of the Squadron, with himself as a young recruit in his first uniform.

"Norwich Airport...? Could I have air traffic...? Air traffic this is John Bakewell. Own a farm at Little Snoring, and run the airstrip out there."

"Mr Bakewell, how can I help you?"

"A light aeroplane crashed on the strip yesterday. I believe it was on route to your field and I wondered if you knew of the circumstances and whether a Mayday was made?"

"Stand by. I wasn't on duty yesterday but I'll make some enquiries... can I ring you back?"

John itched about all morning not wanting to leave the telephone. The call came just after lunch. "Mr Bakewell. I believe you've been enquiring about an aeroplane in distress yesterday?" It was a different voice than before.

"That's correct."

"Can you give me the call sign?"

"Golf Charlie Hotel India Papa."

"I understand this aircraft crashed on your airstrip?"

"Affirm." John slipped into air traffic jargon.

"Will you be requiring to make an official report?"

"No, I'm just collecting the facts for insurance purposes."

"I see... I'm not sure I should be giving you this information, but an India Papa did call us yesterday and reported a rough-running engine, with the intention of putting down at Little Snoring."

"Any Mayday?"

"No. The pilot stated he wasn't declaring an emergency."

John thanked the controller and thought about this information. Rough-running engine but no Mayday. Must have been confident he could make it. Hadn't bothered to leave his address or telephone number – it was all a bit too casual. 'I'll wait to talk to the insurance assessor.'

Chapter Seventeen

Dennis received the call as he was finishing a breakfast of cornflakes, toast and honey.

"Medway Services, I've a Chris Alton for you."

"Morning Chris. Haven't heard your dulcet voice for yonks. What's brings you out of the woodwork? Keeping well?"

"Fine, same old diplomatic Hopkins I hear. Sorry to get you so early but I've a meeting shortly that'll tie me up all day."

"That's okay, fire away. I'm all ears."

Chris was a director of Medway Services who specialised, amongst other areas, in aviation and maritime insurance. Dennis had represented them on several occasions, although he hadn't done much with them in the last year or two.

Chris outlined the details of the problem at the Norfolk air strip and a claim request from a Mr Tony Hastings. "Sounds pretty terminal from the info I've had so far."

"Little Snoring, that's an old RAF base isn't it? Been there once I think. Someone told me they stage air shows with some very interesting vintage planes. Must go sometime."

"Yes. Look I'd love to chat but I'm a bit pushed. Could you contact the farmer." Chris gave him the telephone number. "Not sure of my programme but I can probably manage tomorrow, if that's okay with you. Otherwise it'll be next week."

Dennis made the call and arranged to visit the next day. On the spur of the moment he found himself dialling Francis Aviation.

"Miss Francis available?"

He twiddled the pad pencil while he waited. She took her time and he guessed that she wasn't hurrying, as a demonstration that she didn't want to be too familiar.

"Dennis. Good morning. Some time eh?"

"Gill, thanks for sparing a moment. Look, it's a bit of a cheek but I've an investigation to carry out in Norfolk for one of your competitors. Wondered if you fancied a day out. Spot of pub lunch?"

"Who for?" She sounded pleased to hear his voice.

"Medway Services."

"Those sharks. You do have a cheek."

"Come on you all fix the prices. Chris isn't a bad old stick."

"He won't be there?"

"Maybe. I've to contact him again."

"Hang on." Dennis continued doodling on the telephone pad as he started to plan the day. Not so frosty as last time he thought. Maybe I'm not reading the signs? Perhaps it had been the wrong time of the month.

"You're on. Can you pick me up from home?"

"At your command." He blew a kiss down the phone and rang off.

Dialling again he was soon talking to Jim. "You never came back on that electronic gear I left you."

"You're right Dennis. Sorry, I've been rather busy."

"So, anything further?"

"Yes, I had it checked out. Waiting for a report actually. Any rate, it seems it's part of a radar jamming device."

Dennis quizzed him for some time and was left with the knowledge that the gear was probably designed to interfere with the control of sophisticated electronic guidance systems.

"Some sort of defence gadgetry," was Jim's final summing up. "No clues as to manufacture or origination."

Dennis replaced the handset thoughtfully and made a few notes for Gill's attention. He'd not been able to find a reason for the ditching in the desert, and none of the crew had been helpful. Engine flame-out was the best they would offer. Dust in the intakes? This information from Jim was interesting; defence gear and diamonds – quite a combination!

Gill was irritated with herself. The phonecall secretly excited her, and she didn't know why. He was nice in a basic sort of way; maybe that was it. She'd a selection of admirers whom she suspected were after Daddy's money, although she was well aware that the 'old man' was shrewd enough to have tied it up to keep it out of the reach of any gold diggers.

"What shall I wear?" Here she was pacing round the office like a caged lioness on heat, when she should be dealing with the mountain of paperwork on her desk.

The phone rang again and she busied herself with business matters before leaving to have an early lunch at Father's favourite bistro. 'Let's hope there're some diversions around to take my mind off Dennis.' She couldn't forget the last time, however, and the memory made her want to change her underclothes.

He drove over to Richmond with the buzz of another investigation exciting his senses. Or was it the thought of seeing Gill again? Pleasure and business don't always mix, but Dennis had acquired a skill, much admired by his colleagues, of combining them in his favour.

As he nosed around the crumpled aircraft he was able to assimilate the technical clues, at the same time as admiring again the slender brown legs that Gill had decided to display in her skilfully designed slit skirt. He fancied she'd dressed both to stimulate him and throw Chris, and he was looking forward to lunch and hopefully some afters.

Chris was a stodgy performer both in business and socially, and at insurance lunches and dinners, which were occasions for the profession to meet each other, he'd attempted some awful chat-up approaches with Gill and others. Dennis produced a wry grin as he recalled some of Chris's drunken failures. He was amused that Gill would seek to tease this way, but she'd obviously decided to have a fun day, and he was pleased to see her fairly relaxed.

He spent some time searching and investigating for possible signs of structural failure, but even to Dennis' keen eye nothing stood out as an obvious cause. He photographed the wreckage from all angles and paced the runway for any items that might have become dislodged.

"Any ideas?" Chris asked.

"Nothing immediate."

The position of the wrecked parts reminded him of the recent trip to France and he remarked on this to Gill. "Probably due to inexperience this one, whereas on the last the pilot was well-qualified." He glanced at the preliminary notes which showed that Mr Hastings had accumulated one hundred and forty hours on single-engine flying.

John wandered over to the party and introduced himself before offering them the use of his house, and coffee if they wished.

"Bit of a mess. Were you here?" Dennis opened the questioning. The farmer filled him in with most of the facts and Dennis added these to his pad notes. "What age d'you reckon? It's not detailed on my report."

"Late forties."

"Really, I got the impression of a younger man, don't know why, maybe because of the low flying hours."

"Oh, he was pretty experienced I guess, that's why I was surprised at the fuel situation."

They listened to the farmer's comments, and the coffee cups were replaced in unison as the three guests all prepared for the same question.

Chris was the first to say anything. "Experienced you said?"

"Yes. He was cut on the face and my wife had organised an ambulance. He asked for it to be cancelled, saying he'd had a lot of training on medical matters and also that he'd been flying a long time."

"The claim form offers one hundred and forty hours."

"Well that must be balls. Sorry ma'am. Someone's got it wrong. I've been flying for a good few years meself, and this guy definitely had more experience than those hours. "

"What was that about the fuel?" Dennis butted in.

The farmer expanded his views on the lack of fuel against the pilot's intention to make it to Norwich. He also told them about his conversation with air traffic and the pilot's apparent lack of concern about declaring a Mayday.

"If he was inexperienced, you'd of thought he'd be edgy for some help. No, he was pretty cool after the crash. In fact I asked him if he'd ever been involved in an incident like this before and he was a bit funny on that."

"Bit funny? How?" Chris was curious.

"Well, he stuttered. Sort of yes/no. Then he said he'd read about accident reports in magazines..." Dennis allowed his eyes to wander around the cosy farmhouse kitchen where they were seated at an old scrubbed-pine table. A suspicion was forming, and he was starting to wonder whether this incident was a bit too cosy also. "... and the insurance." John was still in flow and expounding his theories.

"Go on." Dennis' attention returned to the farmer.

"He was very concerned about anything being touched. Made some snide remarks about you folks and your reluctance to pay-up sometimes. Half with him on that one." John pursed a cheeky smile. "Had some hard fights meself on farm claims."

"So what are you suggesting?" Although it was none of her business Gill felt she should intervene to stop the men waffling round the subject. 'God our sex gets a hell of a lot of flack for talking too much,' she muttered to herself, 'but you men never seem to get to the point.'

"I dunno. Something fishy. Didn't seem natural."

Chris stood up and paced around the room, thinking how he could put this jigsaw of information into some logical order. "I'm going to have another scout around. Anyone coming?" Dennis nodded and the two wandered out of the backdoor.

"More coffee love?"

Sandy had been out feeding the farm fowl and had not been party to the kitchen conference. She poured the beverage and sat down in the large wicker chair which dominated the fireplace.

"What did they think about the phial then?"

John glared warningly at his wife and smiled invitingly to Gill, asking her if she would like to have a quick look round the farm whilst she was here. "Got a new-born calf. Three days old. Like to see her?" Gill agreed with raised eyebrows as the farmer guided her into the yard.

"Hang on. Just going back for my coat. Still that morning chill." He shivered and then quickened his pace back to the farmhouse to catch Sandy going upstairs to make the beds.

"Forget the phial!" he hissed. "We could be in trouble for touching things out there. I've probably said too much already. It's not our problem, just my nosy curiosity."

"Sorry love, I thought it was important."

"It probably is. I'll have to think about it."

They motored away taking in the pleasant, if flat, beauty of the Norfolk countryside. The Jaguar engine purred along in the now brightening sunshine, and Dennis felt the comfortable warmth of Gill relaxing beside him, with the special aroma that only seemed to come from leather car seats. She smiled invitingly as Dennis watched her using the spray, and he became aware of the Chanel overcoming the more manly scents.

"Lunch soon?"

"Leave it to you."

As they drove quietly along their thoughts were elsewhere, but related to the events of this day.

'File. What was that about? Did the farmer find some papers from the plane?' Gill let the questions mull around in her mind. She looked at Dennis and wondered what was on his mind. Hook the skirt a little and maybe there's an answer. The lack of reaction told her that his thoughts were elsewhere. 'Bugger men! They put themselves into little pockets. One thing at a time. Why can't they spread themselves around like we have to?' She sighed in frustration.

'Come on girl, stop being a psychoanalyst of the male species and just accept that their brains are low slung, even when they try to make out they're working.' She chuckled out loud at her analysis.

"Penny for the joke. What's tickling you?"

"Nothing. Just keep your eyes on the road."

Dennis was thinking about the findings back there and the increasing similarity to the previous investigation he'd carried out at La Baule. 'I need to root out more about the pilots of these planes. Maybe there is some connection.'

He knew Gill was teasing again, but he was determined not to be too keen. 'I want her to want me.' He reckoned he knew her Achilles' heel now. She was definitely turned on at the sight of smashed machinery. Why else did she agree to visit this one? Nothing in it business-wise for her. Entrepreneurs are supposed to have strong sex drives. Nothing wrong with that. She's got a kink on disaster. Weird maybe, but whatever turns you on. 'I'll have to invest in some horror videos and see what reaction I get.'

The road ahead was straight but he could see the sharp corner in the distance as the idea formed in his head. He wound up the revs and turned into the corner just fast enough to lose the rear end so that the car spun sideways before he regained control. He cunningly spun the steering as if still out of control and luckily spotted the field entrance lay-by, and drove the Jaguar over the bumpy clay ruts and through the hedge gap into the field before bringing it to a sliding halt.

He lay back quivering for effect but also in anticipation of her reaction.

"My God. How did that happen?"

He watched her shiver in shock, then she moved across to his body and he felt the comfort of her arms as she drew him close.

"Are you all right?"

"Yes..." He tried to simulate a shaky reply.

"You?" He looked at her with concern, and noticed the fire in her eyes.

"I'm fine. Relax. Car's fine. No bones broken. Quite an exciting way to park." She laughed.

"How can you laugh? We could have been killed!"

"Better enjoy it before we die then. This maybe our last chance."

She reached to find him hard in anticipation of her reaction, and he noticed an initial look of surprise. But then maybe she hadn't been fooled after all.

Neither were bothered anyhow, as they gave themselves to the excitement and passion of the moment. The favourite drophead version was not designed for some of Gill's positions, and she had to drag Dennis out into the yellow field to satisfy the need which had welled up in her from the scare.

They tore at each other's clothing and performed with an animal hunger that matched the rawness of the farmland countryside. She was wilder than before and he wondered whether he would be able to keep satisfying her demands. She finally rolled off his body on to her scattered clothes, and Dennis picked his way back to the car to retrieve his.

They lunched in a pretty country pub on ploughman's and cider, and Dennis could tell from her body language that he'd done all right. The skid was not mentioned but they both knew why, and were both secretly planning the next occasion.

Chapter Eighteen

He watched the King Air as it taxied to the apron and liked the subtle green stripes that made the aeroplane seem sleeker than it really was. The two officials descended the steps to be followed by Patrick with hair blowing over his eyes in the light breeze.

Pat took them for a walkabout pointing to parts of the aircraft in explanation. The executive twin was his latest acquisition which he'd purchased for the growing short haul European market. It was also going to be a plaything for Patrick's personal use.

Tim was aware the officials were from the CAA, and wondered whether they'd enjoyed one of the Irishman's special evenings in Paris. He rued that he hadn't been chosen to captain the trip, but then again he was not totally back in Patrick's favour.

He heard them go into the chairman's office and the mumbled laughs over clinks of glass. 'Reminiscing I expect on last night's jollifications.' He was busy at his desk when the door opened and Patrick walked in with a huge grin like a naughty schoolboy.

"Would you be ready then Tim?"

"Successful trip?"

"Wait an' see now..." He tapped his finger to the side of his nose.

Tim was nervous. This was the second time he'd been in a courtroom to give evidence in eighteen months and he vowed it would be his last.

His boss was wearing a light, greenish suit which gave him the mark of a well-heeled businessman, and he looked relaxed in the general bustle of the court proceedings.

"Mr Mitchell, would you please take the stand again."

Tim sat down uncomfortably and stared at the glass of water on the shelf in front of him. Nervous hands never seem to use this facility and he watched the small fly floating idly round the edge as the usher distributed the papers.

"May I just clarify this point once more?" The CAA barrister was short and thin-faced and was wearing a well-creased suit which made him look more like a badly dressed politician than a lawyer.

"You say that the maintenance company", he rustled his papers for reference, "... Mainline Limited, is a subsidiary of Redwing Services and has an arrangement whereby Redwing can sign off their work. Is that correct?"

Tim felt like a criminal and was very conscious of Patrick's latest package in his jacket pocket. Lying didn't come easy and he tried to avoid the Irishman's honest glare as he prepared to answer. Pat must have paid some healthy sums to get out of this one, but Tim had to admire the way he carried things off.

"Yes your Honour."

"And you consider this arrangement to be normal?"

"Yes. It's not unusual."

The barrister grunted. "What puzzles me is why my client couldn't have been given this information when the question of proper documentation was first at issue."

"If that's a question your Honour, I don't know." Patrick allowed himself a stifled smile at Tim's reply and noticed that the judge made no notes.

The proceedings drifted on, but it became obvious to everyone that Marvel Air had scraped clear this time, and the CAA officials started to ease out of the courtroom for some gin and tonic downing. The judge wound up the hearing on grounds of inadequate evidence, and warned the official authorities to try to avoid wasting public money.

"I told you so." Pat was grinning over a pint of Guinness as he patted Tim on the shoulder. "Now did you not enjoy your trip to Dallas? Chuck look after you well?" Tim nodded. "Give the man a drink, barman."

"He wants a favour in return."

"So he does, and what's that to be?"

"I'll tell you later." He was uncertain of the legal hangers-on and other ears around the bar, and he saw that Pat had got the message.

Tim left Dallas with mixed feelings. He liked the hospitality and the straight talking, but he felt that every conversation was angled towards a deal. There was very little small talk even amongst the women.

Chuck invited him to stay a night and organised a barbecue which was noisy and fun. Tim was nearly converted from his bachelor faith as he chatted to the gorgeous Dallas girls, who looked a million dollars in their leather boots with blonde hair escaping from under cowboy hats. He was guested around but later got to talk with a guy called Hal who was obviously a long-standing friend of the Alston family. Hal was well away on a local brew, but seemed somewhat nervous, judging by the way his eyes darted around the guests out on the patio area.

"You over from the UK they tell me. Friend of Pat, eh?"

"You know Pat?"

"Sure do. Pat, Chuck and I done a lot of business together. Don't deal much these days." He fidgeted with his glass.

"Oil?" Tim thought he'd fish around to see what he might catch.

"Oil, a bit. Oiled a few palms." He turned away as if he'd said something by mistake.

"You from these parts?"

"No. Ohio. Spent a lot of time in Florida, trading into the West Indies."

The conversation drifted and Tim was able to piece together some of his boss's background along with the ambitions of one Chuck Alston. Hal was a useful pawn in the set-up, but was obviously not cashing in enough, hence his disillusion in his later years. The more Hal talked the more Tim worried. The scene wasn't unusual, although beyond his depth, as they'd obviously been dealing in drugs and prostitution. Hal suddenly switched to talking about the illegal arms market, and Tom got the feeling that it was the latter that was holding hard and demanding big bucks from the syndicate. Where and how was not obvious to him, and Tim doubted he'd find the answer tonight.

"I'm on a late flight tomorrow, like to see your engineering works, how about me calling in, perhaps we could take in a burger at O'Gradys?"

"Great idea." That fixed he decided to circulate and await developments.

"Tim." Chuck's arm ran around his shoulder. "Meet Christine. Used to be my lover. Now she's shacked up with a hulk of a man, too big for me. I reckon she'd fall for an English captain though, wouldn't you sweetheart?" He pinched her bum and Tim was forced to grin through this garish scene. Christine didn't appear amused, and from Tim's recent probings he supposed she was still on the books, as you might say.

"Don't want to be a bore Chuck, but I'm bushed. Jet lag an' all. Mind if I get some shut eye?"

He left the party for the relaxation of a gigantic bedroom with two queen-size beds which were lost on the expanse of wall to wall carpeting. He undressed and robed in the off-white towelling before fixing himself a cold Coors from the cooler.

Lounging on the bed he went over the events of the last forty-eight hours and realised they'd been quite exhausting. Pat and Chuck, that was obvious. Everyone had had a punt, literally, as to where Patrick got his money to start the airline and most favoured some dubious laundered business deals. But that was in the past. Chuck and Hal had something going and Tim suspected that it involved the Middle East.

He'd promised to call Pat on the servicing problem and, checking his watch, clicked that he could get him at work due to the time difference. He picked up the phone and found himself listening to a conversation in progress on the line. He was about to replace the handset but stopped on hearing the name.

"You screwed it Azif not me." Tim recognised Chuck's drawl. "So don't come the arsehole with me." He could hear a reply but it was faint and out of sequence as if in an echo box, and Tim couldn't take it in.

"I'm flying it out in the next few days. An old Paddy friend of mine is sorting it. I can't beat that. You'd..." The conversation garbled on but Tim was not concentrating for he'd heard enough.

'Chuck and Azif. Bound to be the same. Azif's not a common name. What's going on? ..."old Paddy friend"...' Tim tucked away this latest conversation for further analysis.

Security at Hal's place was tight and Tim wasn't left alone. The works manager chaperoned the tour and Tim found himself visiting a pretty mundane engineering works. A couple of clues registered. He passed one door with a large 'Strictly Private' sign, and noticed that there were three separate coded locks on the door. He climbed into Hal's Chevey and glanced back at the works to spot a very large satellite-type aerial on the roof. As they drove out to O'Gradys', a truck swung through the gate and Hal braked sharply, his hand going for the horn. He jumped out with a "hang on" to Tim and spoke to the driver who handed him a key for the rear doors. After an inspection inside he returned to the driver and seemed engrossed in giving instructions, waving his hands in emphasis. Tim saw the small parcel pass over and then Hal was back in the four by four.

"Sorry. Just checking on some materials."

They were fixed with seats by the bar and Tim settled back to enjoy the clean comfort and the background country and western music.

"You into electronics?" It was a throwaway line.

"Naw." Hal fiddled with his cheeseburger and Tim could feel his presence wasn't wanted and that Hal was itching to get back.

He offered another drink. "No more thanks." It was a polite 'let's go, that's it.'

Tim rang Patrick from the airport lounge and gave him the good news. He studied the sealed letter that Chuck had addressed to Pat and wondered about the favour. Had to be something to do with the Azif call. 'I need to talk to Hogan.'

"Northwest 237 boarding." The tannoy broke his thoughts as he made his way to the departure gate.

Chapter Nineteen

It needed careful handling and Barry was careful not to push too hard. He filled in the documents meticulously and made sure there weren't any mistakes. He phoned on a couple of occasions making certain that he only talked to junior clerks processing the claim.

As loss adjuster, Dennis Hopkins had no option in recommending full reimbursement and Barry established this fact on one of his routine calls. He wasn't to know that Dennis was investigating other concerns.

The cheque arrived second post and he just had time to nip it down to the bank, calling in the off-licence on the way back to buy a gold topped bottle of Krug. The cork marked the ceiling tiles as he flaunted his 'winnings' and turned an Oscar Peterson tape on full.

He rang the travel agent first and then contacted Judy. "We're off Sunday. Pack a bikini. I'm on the bubbly and I feel great."

"You having a party?" She could hear the music.

"On me own. Downing champagne like it's going out of fashion."

"Sod you, what about me?"

"Sunday. You heard. Your turn then. For the moment it's mine."

"See you then. Don't get too plastered."

He wandered round aimlessly for a bit and then started packing.

They sat outside the piano bar sipping the ice cold Martini's and watched the jet set posing with their Italian cars and Monaco gin palaces and as much brown skin as they dared expose.

Marbella had always been a favourite of Barry's and he'd visited it several times on overnight stays for Marvel Air flights to Malaga. He loved the sheer openness of the place with its lack of pretence, and its promise of fun and enjoyment. Mind you the sun and sea helped, and it was a lot better knowing you had cash in your back pocket.

Judy was fascinated. "Smarter than the houseboat creek." She ogled the glittery scene, enjoying every moment and squeezed Barry's hand under the table.

"I bet you've seen more life than some of them?" He meant it kindly, but noticed she winced slightly, and realised he might have struck a raw nerve. He still knew nothing of her background, and promised himself he would find out soon. He could see it needed an opportune moment.

"So come on Mr Clyde, how much d'we make?"

"Twenty-five. They paid the lot."

"Brilliant. Can we do some shopping tomorrow?"

"If you're kind to me," he joked.

"If we go on like this we can buy one of those." She watched the cruiser gliding silently to its berth.

"We may need one for a get away, they asked me some odd questions. I reckon that farmer was very suspicious."

"Need a bit more planning on the next."

"Okay clever clogs, we'll work on it, but let's have some food first. I'm starving."

"Cacassars. Sounds like that, don't know how you spell it." They were picking and cracking some monster crabs at a marina-side restaurant, and Barry was telling her his story from the Seychelles.

"No, serious, they're an aphrodisiac." He went on to tell her about this bar called Greenways, overlooking a beautiful bay which hosted these crabs called cacassars. It was the only place left in the world where the crabs still bred. Anyhow the legend was that if the human male ate them he would get an erection that would last for a week.

"So this honeymoon couple stopped for a drink and the bar owner told this story only to the recent bride who then ordered a double helping for her husband. When I arrived the poor guy was innocently wading through his plateful, whilst the new wife sat watching and gazing with open mouth in anticipation. I didn't realise what was going on until the boss man told me, and then we both collapsed in tears."

"I don't believe you." Judy giggled.

"It's true, honest."

"Well I hope these are as successful. Better have some more!" She passed a couple of claws over to his plate.

"You're my aphrodisiac," he said. "I don't need any other help."

They spent a glorious week exploring the Spanish countryside and the small villages tucked away in the hills. They rented a speedboat and raced along the coast as if they were in a James Bond film. At night they dined in candlelit corners and made love until the dawn light filtered into their bedroom.

Barry was happier than he'd felt for a long time and he suffered no nightmares or depressions. Gently he eased the hurt from Judy's past. She cried in her need for relief, and he was glad that their talking acted like exorcism, such that the pain would eventually go for ever.

Her story was nasty and Barry felt she held back on some of the more unbearable facts to lesson the blows on himself.

It started about the age of five, when she had to watch her mother entertaining and being beaten by many strange men. By the time she was twelve her mother was using her to supplement their meagre earnings and Judy was subjected to abuse that she couldn't understand.

Many times it was older woman and Judy finally ran away when her own mother, high on drugs and drink, tried to join in a sordid session and to interfere with her own daughter.

It didn't end there and Judy was forced to accept a gypsy existence, living and sleeping rough, and finding odd jobs, for she'd no real education. Finally when she was about eighteen she met a man who ran a boatyard business and was married to a crippled woman. He set Judy up with a houseboat on a special favours basis, and used to visit her once or twice a week. She hated herself but at least he was kind and she'd little choice. He died in her bed and the neighbour on the next boat helped her move him to the shore before they called the ambulance. They suggested to the police that he must've been inspecting some of his tenancies and she never heard another word. She read later in the local rag that the coroner's verdict was natural causes.

"Scrubbing. It's very therapeutic."

"Therapeutic. That's a big word for a small girl like you," he joked to ease the tension of her story, "anyhow what d'you mean, scrubbing?"

"Just that, scrubbing. I scrubbed the boat from top to bottom in a desperate need to clear all the dirt out of my life. When I'd finished I did it again and then I painted everything till it smelt brand new. I went to the local baths and soaked myself three times a day for a week until my skin was almost raw with rubbing and brushing. I made a vow that I'd never sell my body again and I haven't." She stared hard into his eyes as if to say "you must believe me."

He didn't ask, and she supplied the answer. "You're the first since."

"Will you invite me to your houseboat one day?"

"I can now. You've helped me bury the past once and for all, and I love you for that."

"Will you help me bury mine?"

She nuzzled up to him like a furry cat. "Let's go and spend some money, and then let's go buy another aeroplane. You've a business to run and I've some insurance acting to practice. We need to forget the past."

Barry hoped she was right but also worried: it was only his past and the inequity of his dismissal that allowed him to justify his present actions. 'It's only money, I'm not hurting anyone,' he told himself, but somehow it didn't quite satisfy his guilt.

They returned bronzed all over and set out on their next venture. Barry bought a nice little high-winger from a crop sprayer who was wanting something bigger. He registered it in the name of Simon Fury and Judy fixed the insurance directly through a Lloyd's broker. She'd been given the contact via a punter from the Queen's Head, and her brown skin and short skirt had done the rest.

Excited with her success she asked: "What d'you pay? You never told me."

"Thirteen."

"Thirteen? I thought you said thirty!"

"What d'you ask to insure it for then?"

"Forty-five."

"Forty-five. There's no way we can justify that."

"Don't blame me. You gave me the bum information."

He smacked her bottom playfully. "Silly girl. Now we've got a real problem."

"How much would a new one cost?"

"Dunno. Sixty-five maybe."

"Well that's okay, we'll make out it's nearly new."

"You can't do that. Manufacturer's date is in the logbook and can be found out from the plane's registration number."

They looked at each other for a solution, then Barry had a brainwave.

"We could produce some false documents to show that it's had a major overhaul. Recon. engine, prop, undercarriage…" He went on naming the parts. "Then if we arrange a respray it'll seem to be worth more."

"Perfect. There you are! No problem. What would you do without me?"

Barry smiled. "Forty-five. That's thirty-two profit, less expenses. Caribbean this time my girl, and then we'll start exploring the American market."

They spent the last night in their favourite restaurant, planning the future and spending of their ill-gotten gains.

Chapter Twenty

"International. I'd like a person to person with a Charles A Hogan, Holiday Inn, Lagunda."

"Bear with me sir, I'll make some enquiries."

Tim waited a short while before she spoke. "There may be some delay. The country's still using outdated services. Can I call you?"

"This number please."

He was attending to some pressing reports and concentrating on filing the latest airworthiness circulars when she came back.

"That was quick."

"Yes. You never know. Your call for Mr Hogan. The hotel says he booked out two days ago."

"Any forwarding address?"

"Apparently not."

"Okay, thanks for your help." Damn Hogan, what's he doing now? Spending my money, I don't doubt, on making himself comfortable.

'The swines.' He searched again knowing it was fruitless. They'd even had the cheek to leave the false documents. His head was still woozy when the telephone by his bed buzzed.

"Breakfast?" He could visualise Azif grinning at his stupidity as he asked the question.

"I'll be down shortly. Need a shower. What d'you use?"

"Special drug made from palm tree sap. It's not addictive but it's tasteless and very concentrated. Works for seven hours and then you're completely clear. No after effects. Supposed to give you an appetite."

Hogan sat at the ornately carved teak dining table and stared at the kidneys and omelette that was placed in front of him by a pitch black Nigerian beauty .

"So what's the game?" He picked at the food, but wasn't hungry and pushed it away in favour of a cool orange juice.

"No game. You chose the rules and got caught. I hold the trumps for the moment and the key to your release."

"So, you've got my passport, visa, medical cards and my money. That looks like a serious game to me."

"No weapons. We couldn't find anything. So where d'you hide them?"

"You genuine? I'm not Mafia or the like, just a simple private Dick."

"Not so simple I guess." Azif chewed his finger nails as they talked.

"I need your help and I felt some pressure would be necessary to guarantee your cooperation. Help me and I can help you. Your possessions will be returned, and then you'll be free to return to England for a welcome pint of real ale."

Even Hogan's lips felt moister at the very thought of leaving this hot, dusty, humid, godforsaken country "Go on then, what's the crack?"

Azif studied his nails. "Before the details I need to explain something." He dismissed the serving girls with a brief hand movement and drew his chair closer to Hogan's.

He started with his early life and the strict upbringing of his family's religion. To Hogan it sounded like fun. Strict maybe in some disciplines, but he got to enjoy the luxuries of money and the advantages of being male in a chauvinistic country.

"You see it was all planned, but I wasn't to know."

He went on to describe the pressures that were applied to his parents, and Hogan heard the emotion that crept into his voice. 'Cruel, even pagan,' he thought. 'Then I suppose it was like that in the Middle Ages back home.' He carried on listening.

"I have no choice. It's destiny."

"Might be yours Azif, and I'm sorry to hear about your parents and sister, but with respect, what the hell's it got to do with me?"

"Destiny, Mr Hogan. I'm trapped and so are you. I have a duty to perform and you're being paid to produce some evidence. It's perfect, a *fait accompli, n'est-ce pas?*"

"Okay, got the message, now you've filled me in..., so get to the point and let's hear your plans."

"The 'gear' – you called it. You know what it's for?" Hogan shook his head.

"Jamming. It jams missiles and deflects them off course." He waited for some reaction but Hogan said nothing.

"We've lost it. Our chartered aeroplane crashed in the desert and the device was lost. I'm not sure whether the crash was an accident or whether we were brought down deliberately. I know others were after the 'gear' and I wonder if the crew was involved. Picked up by the Red Cross who appeared very conveniently after we crash-landed. The device was not to be found and some diamonds required to smooth safe transit disappeared."

"Nothing to deliver. Up for the chop?" Hogan saw his problem.

"You joke. It's no joke. You don't know our military and the cost of failure."

"I can guess. I read the papers."

"I have a replacement, but I can't deliver myself. I'm too exposed."

"Right, I have the scenario. Now let's see." He paused. "First I get to collect the replacement. Then I get to disguise myself as an Iraqi businessman, then I drive to Baghdad in an Aston Martin like bloody agent 007. Who's joking now?" Hogan stood up and stared straight into Azif's eyes. "No chance. You're barking up the wrong tree here."

Azif was amused by a picture of this stocky, awkward, slightly balding ex-cop, cast in the role of 007 'licensed to kill', who was now staring at him as if he wanted to kill him. "Iran, not Iraq."

"Are you telling me that you're dealing with the other side?"

"They come from the States." It was a statement.

"What comes from the States?" Hogan was getting cross with the situation and this smooth Arab and his sodding family problems. If he was settling his debts via the neighbours no wonder he was scared.

"Wasp 200."

"What are you on about now?" He could feel the pitch of his voice rising. "I thought this was all top secret?"

Azif ignored him. "That's the code name. Wasp 200."

"Are you telling me that the Yanks make these fancy missiles and also make a gadget to override them?"

"Yes, but only for emergency conditions if anything goes wrong when they're testing. They don't provide them as defence material.

We've had them adapted and tested to work as a true military device."

"So these Wasps, how come you found out?"

"Texan. Multi-millionaire oilman. He has a mission about spreading the odds so that no international country can ever obtain total power. Likes to act as a mediator."

"Sounds like he's acting God."

"Yes, that's not a bad parallel."

"And you're buying from him?"

"Partly. He's running for Governor and the Senate, and considers that special relations with Iran will go down well with the electorate. I suspect he's planning to play one nation off against another, and then move in like Red Adair to defuse any conflict, and 'put out the fire' metaphorically speaking. Although the intermediaries are being compensated, Chuck's payment is being granted special visiting rights and diplomatic status with direct access to the President."

"Chuck?"

"Chuck Alston. He's a nice man. You may get to meet him."

Hogan listened to the story and thought how well Azif spoke. He rarely went colloquial, and had presence from an obviously good education. He went on to outline the set-up that had been organised to replace the Wasp 200. Alston had arranged through a UK airline to fly the device direct to an old Army/Airforce field north of Lagunda. From there it was to be transported by chartered flight to Libya, and then by road to Egypt. A sea trip would deliver it in and out of Cyprus, and through Turkey to Tehran.

"Sounds tortuous," Hogan remarked.

"Diversion is the plan. We're not certain of the opposition."

"And I come in where?"

"South Africa."

"Now you've really lost me."

"Decoy. Simple my friend."

"Decoy." Hogan repeated the word.

"You will leave shortly after delivery to Lagunda with some electrical goods which you'll take through Zaire and Botswana to South Africa. With luck our competitors will follow you instead of us, because of some deliberate mistakes on the way."

"Great. So I go gallivanting through the Kalahari Desert with a bunch of murdering fanatics on my tail, to assist some other fanatics playing soldiers with the rest of the world... forget it. Go play your politics elsewhere."

Hogan strode out on to the pool area and collared a servant who was watering the exotic flower beds that surrounded the area. "Get me a cold beer and a towel." He demanded.

With that he stripped off to his underpants and dived in the deep end. 'Sod that Mitchell again, this is not working out at all. He'll have to come and rescue me.' He splashed around like a madman, shooting water over the sunloungers encircling the pool. Slowly his anger tempered and he drifted about until he was just floating comfortably on his back. Azif, standing in the shade, came into focus as the water dried from his eyes. He didn't recognise them at first, and then he grasped that he was waving passports and travel tickets.

"Go fuck yourself."

"I'll see you later. Have a good swim. I can get the girls to join you if you wish."

"Sod off Azif! You can dispose of me if you like but I ain't joining your plans."

"We will see. You'll feel better when we next chat and you've enjoyed a beer. Have several, it may ease your worries."

He wasn't sure whether it was the beer or the massage that had done the trick, but when Azif returned he felt a calmness that hadn't been present that morning. The cotton robe was cool after the dual attention from the house girls who'd raised his temperature to the peak of relief. 'Maybe I should relax more and just cash in on what's going. What the hell, you've got to die sometime. Why not with a smile on your face.' He looked over to where they were sorting out another guest and decided he might go again before he left.

"You've given it some thought?"

"Help each other, that's what you said. So I understand my role, if so minded. How're you going to help me?"

"Evidence. You want evidence that something happened to affect the instruments on that airliner when it was landing. Is that right?"

"That's my brief. Yes."

"You've got it. I'll give you the evidence."

"How come?"

"You know, it was probably right."

"What was probably right?"

"The effect."

Hogan took on a professional look. "Let's get this clear. Are you saying that your device Wasp... what was it?"

"Wasp 200."

"...Wasp 200. Are you saying that it might have caused problems for the instruments, given false readings?"

"Yes."

"Certain?"

"Pretty sure."

"So if you knew that, why were you using it? Putting lives at risk? Surely you're not that callous?"

"We had a helicopter in the location and we were testing signals from ground to air. It was necessary to tweak the power due to the poor weather, and I reckon we exceeded our test radius."

"So you'd give this as evidence?" Hogan couldn't believe it.

"No way. No, our experiments are secret. I told you that before."

"So what's on offer?"

Azlf helped himself to some chopped coconut from a bowl on the white side-tables before he spoke. "You know I'm qualified in electronics?"

"I didn't, but go on."

"I can produce an expert report of an electronic box which would have been capable of having the same affect. This box however will be associated to the television business. You can drum up a story about the goings on in the flat, and the element of doubt should be enough to reopen the case."

"Interesting, but how's your report to be presented?"

"Well I suggest a false name of course. No connection to myself. I'll get an 'assistant' to present it. At the last moment he'll be unavailable, so the report should stand on its own merits."

"Suppose it's challenged?"

"No problem. Any other expert reading my theories will have to agree in principle."

"And this is quite feasible?"

"Yes."

"Why would someone be testing this... TV equipment?"

"Piracy. Illegal transmitting of pornographic programmes from the continent. Goes on all the time. That 'bastard Arab' can be blamed, but he'll have disappeared. The courts won't be looking for a culprit, just establishment of the facts and the cause."

Hogan listened and asked more questions until he was convinced that they could get away with it. There was nothing wrong because Azif had already said that he reckoned his gear had been to blame. So Tim wouldn't be lying just bending the truth a little. Using a different story.

"So that's the cost of my freedom?"

Azif smiled. "It has class."

"One favour?"

"Of course."

Hogan signalled toward the darker of the two Eurasian girls who was allowing a young boy to oil her firm breasts. "Your African trip sounds full of holes to me. I was planning an early retirement but not this way. Like the condemned murderer, I'd rather go with a smile on my face."

Azif called her across, and Hogan was obliged to take over the boys unfinished work.

Chapter Twenty-One

"La Baule Aéroport."

"Oui, Monsieur."

"Je voudrais parler avec le Directeur de l'Aéroport."

"D'accord, un moment."

Dennis was feeling very happy with his life at this time. Gill with the 'hots', the recent light aeroplane crashes and Arab intrigues in the arms and diamond business. Not everyone's hype for a grotty day. It was still raining as he viewed the scenery from the flat window over-looking the Thames at Putney. He'd been lucky with the buy. In between house price wars, and large enough to have the children at the weekends. He wondered about re-marriage and Gill featured heavily. 'Bit lusty at this stage. I think I'll give it more time.' Love again, he doubted it.

"Bonjour Monsieur?"

"Bonjour. Est-ce-que vous pouvez m'aider, s'il vous plait? Je ne parle pas francais. Un peu, n'est-ce pas?"

"Je comprends. How can I 'elp you?"

Dennis recalled the accident with Echo Tango and explained that he was the investigating loss adjuster for the insurance company.

"But I understand that matter, it 'as been done, 'ow you say..., dealt with?"

"That's correct, but I would like your help on one matter."

"Monsieur, vous êtes...?"

"Hopkins, Dennis Hopkins."

"Monsieur 'opkins, I am a busy man. I do not 'ave ze time to open up old investigations that 'ave been completed."

'Typical,' Dennis thought. He glanced at his watch and realised with the time difference that it was encroaching on the sacred French lunchtime. 'The bugger's more focused on his wine choice today than my problems.'

"Just a small favour Monsieur. Do you take photographs when you have such incidents?"

"But of course. It is standard procedure."

"I don't have a photograph of the pilot involved. If you have such a print, would it be possible to let me have a copy?"

"Everything is possible Mr 'opkins," the *directeur* laboured the point, "but I will need a written request from the insurance company."

'Jesus, these Frogs! Are they deliberately difficult? Do they enjoy making life hard, or is it just their upbringing?' Dennis was getting frustrated, especially as he watched the rain pouring down the window frames.

"I really don't have time to go through such a procedure. Is there no other way?"

"Perhaps, *mon ami*." He offered nothing.

Dennis had an idea. "L'Escale, you know it? My cousin is *le maître*. Why don't you lunch there today on my account to cover the procedures for the photographs? He tells me the *moules* are the best on the coast and he cellars a Chablis that is second to none."

Dennis heard the grunt of approval. "My friend. *Merci bien*. I may be able to 'elp you this time. Leave it with me."

"*Vous êtes très gentil. Au revoir. A bientôt.*"

He replaced the receiver and dialled out the next number. "Medway Services, how can I help you?"

She sounded vulnerably innocent, but Dennis avoided his flippant mood and tried to act business like. "Is Mr Alton available?"

"I'll check sir." The phone played irritating classics which seemed to keep in time with the rivulets of water dripping down his windowpanes.

Sorry sir, Mr Alton is not in the office at the moment." However she didn't sound too convincing.

"If he comes in today, could you tell him that Dennis Hopkins rang, and advise him that I'm about to save him a few thousand pounds."

"Eh... hold on a moment sir..., Mr Alton, has just walked into the office, I'll put you through."

Dennis smiled. Probably standing by the telephonist listening to every word. He pressed the key to disconnect the line and then left the handset off the base. "Let him sweat. Teach him not to be so shifty."

A coffee later he rang Gill to let her in on his research into his theories.

"Up at Norfolk the other day, did you find anything else. You were alone with the farmer I recall?"

"Not a lot. He rather clammed up. Showed me round the farm. There was one thing though."

"Tell me."

"Well his wife mentioned something about a file, but I reckon he shut her up, changed the subject you might say."

"To do with the crash?"

"Dunno, what's suspicious about a file?"

"Look I know it's nothing to do with your company, but I'm getting vibrations on this one, and they may link back to the prang in France."

"Prang? Where've you been all your life. Prangs went out with moustaches!"

Dennis ignored her and fired back. "Can you do me a favour and get back there for a chat with the farmer's wife? Sandy isn't it?"

With Gill organised he gave Chris another call. This time he was put through immediately. "Sorted out your personal problems, ready for business now?"

"Sorry Dennis, I was tied up when you rang earlier."

"Really, kinky." He laughed at the thought.

"No seriously, it's very busy at the moment. Couple of shipping disasters off Japan with possible oil pollution."

Dennis decided to cut the joking and get down to detail. "I know you've paid out on the India Papa job, but I'm having second thoughts."

"Now you tell me. You're the assessor. If you've got it wrong I hope your professional indemnity premiums have been paid."

"Let's not get our wires crossed, I'm not altering my report, no way. But I intend to investigate further for other reasons. My choice, my expense. But I need your help."

"Go on."

"Photo. I need a photograph of Tony Hastings. Got one?"

"No can do. We don't file such records." The word 'file' diverted his questions for a moment. 'File. What's the significance of a file?'

"You still alive?"

"Yes sorry Chris, mind elsewhere for a moment. Can you get one?"

"How?"

"Search me. Can't you get Mr Hastings back to sign some papers or something, and fix a camera in the interview room."

"Bit devious. What's in it for me?"

"Do it Chris and I'll show you."

The conversation dried up and Dennis waited for Chris to answer. 'Stodgie's right; not the quickest thinker on his feet.'

"Okay we'll give it a run. Not our usual scene. We'll need your assurance that it's ethical and required for sound commercial reasons."

What's with the 'we'? he thought. Off-loading the responsibility. Typical for the insurance boys. Like the money, don't like the risk. He remembered farmer John's words: "You have my assurance..."

"In writing please," he fired back. "Dennis apologies, I really must go. Give my love to Gill." The phone went dead.

'"Love to Gill"; getting his own back for my "kinky" comment I suppose.' He composed his thoughts and moved over to the desk. 'So what have we got?'

He opened a pad and ruled a piece of double foolscap graph paper. On one side he marked Echo Tango and India Papa, and on the other Fokker Friendship. He couldn't remember the registration number of the Farnborough aeroplane, but it didn't matter for this exercise.

He worked away on the details using a sort of question and answer basis, with headings of type of aircraft, performance, condition after crash, fuel uprate... The pages soon filled and he decided to put a master spreadsheet onto his small computer. He processed the information for several hours, and then broke to ease the messages coming from his stomach.

The scrambled eggs went down a treat, but he was anxious to get back to the screen as darkness took over from the incessant rain. 'We're in for a storm later' he surmised as the humidity forced him to undo his shirt.

It came slowly with a certain logic. The desert scene was on its own, an isolated case. Reason for suspicion, but no evidence. Echo Tango, India Papa; eighty-five per cent crash similarities. Information required for cross-reference: pilots, insurance, owners.

121

He relaxed and started to plan the next move. Deep in thought the ringing tone made him jump, but he was pleased to hear Gill's voice.

"I'm going up tomorrow. It's market day so the farmer will be away. Should give me a chance to get the wife talking."

"Sound affair. Let me know when you're back. Perhaps we could meet up somewhere?"

He made some more notes, but decided it was too late to check the rest of the detail that evening.

The morning was frustrating and Dennis felt he was in one of those momentum time warps. Nothing connected immediately. People were out or not available. Wrong numbers kept coming up, and by lunchtime there were large gaps on the screen where there should have been answers. Maybe it was the cold beer or maybe the end of the storm that had raged on into the morning, but suddenly his luck changed and the calls came in fast and furious.

"Mr Hopkins, Darell Brown regarding your query on Echo Tango."

Dennis smoothed the way by indicating that his enquiry was routine but necessary in order to tidy his files. A description of the purchaser noted along with other details, Dennis slipped in a final question. "How much was the sale?"

"...Twenty, as I remember. Would you like me to check? It might take some time."

"If you can find an invoice perhaps you could send me a copy." Dennis thanked him for his help and felt pleased with this start.

Chris wasn't available but his switchboard girl was her usual cheery self. 'Must get round there sometime. Wonder if the looks match the voice?' he thought.

"I need to know if there's any record of the vendor of India Papa. I imagine you might find it on the accident report?" She said she'd do her best and come back, and he rang off just as the doorbell buzzed.

"Personal delivery. Sign here sir."

Dennis opened the Jiffy bag to find a photograph and a short note. "Tout de suite" he'd said, and he'd delivered. Struggling with the scrawly handwriting and the French/English script Dennis gathered that the lunch had been *"formidable"* and the wine *"parfait"*, and here he was holding his celluloid reward as promised.

Good as gold she was back with the answer. "Gloucester. Private owner. That's all that's on the file."

"Remind me I owe you a favour." Dennis could hear a giggle as he thanked her. "Any contact name?"

There wasn't, so a bit more detective work was required. He needed three calls before getting the answers in a round about way. Apparently a Tony Hastings had registered interest at a couple of sales outlets on the airfield, and had been directed to India Papa by one of the salesmen who knew the owner. The sales guy remembered a price around the fifteen grand mark because he'd had some banter with the owner about the VAT. The owner was apparently not well-liked; the shady dealings didn't go too well with the reputation that the other bona fide professional boys were trying to build. 'Lucky about the aggro' Dennis thought, 'otherwise I'd have never squeezed out the information.'

"Ordinary," was the answer to Mr Hastings appearance, and he noted a blank on the screen layout.

He'd finished the tea when Gill called. "Phone box with a couple waiting and no change. Meet you at Mario's, eight o'clock."

"Right." 'Where do I go now?' He thumbed through the list of insurers leaving out the major players, and isolated the list down to seven, excluding Francis Aviation and Medway Services.

Blank, blank again... After several phonecalls he crossed off all seven with no luck. One interesting common factor was established however, and that was in reply to his question on valuation.

"So you don't require an independent inspection?" He was talking to the Blair-Lloyd underwriters.

"Not for the low cover required for general popular small aircraft. Yes for the larger craft, or maybe specials."

She rang again with her chirpy manner. "Second favour, Mr Hopkins. Mr Alton asked me to let you know that he's seeing Mr Hastings tomorrow morning."

"Great. Can you tell him I'd like to visit tomorrow also. Maybe I can repay you those favours." He played her along for fun, thinking 'this lass is way ahead of me on the teasing stakes'.

"That would be nice." She said it with kindness. Dennis was flattered and felt a little foolish with his chatty approach. But then he was getting psyched up with his investigations, and the adrenalin was pumping blood into special places. Gill tonight. Hope she's got some interesting information.

Mario's was a smart bistro in a cul-de-sac off the main Richmond Road. It was a favourite of Gill's and her father, and they were special customers to Paco who headwaited the busy restaurant.

"Your favourite window?" Paco held Gill's chair for her to be seated.

"The lobster's very fresh tonight, and for you sir, I recommend the calf's liver with Chef's special mustard sauce."

They ordered as suggested for Dennis was anxious to catch up on Gill's visit. Her eyes were shining brightly under the candlelight and the Chanel blended well with the aromas emanating from Mario's famous kitchen. Her beige suit and candy shirt matched the natural decor of the small room, and Dennis felt rather smug as he sipped his wine and watched diners nodding toward his attractive escort.

"Go on then, stop keeping me in suspense."

"That Sandy's a clever women you know. She effectively runs the farm. Well certainly the financial side, the books and all that."

"Christ Gill! What did you find out?"

"Wait on. I needed to get her confidence to probe as you wanted. Couldn't just barge in with both feet. She asked me all about the insurance business and was very knowledgeable on many aspects. I found out she'd been to college and also spent a short stint as a casual nurse in one of the big London hospitals."

The food arrived, and Dennis gave in to Gill's soliloquy and the flambé serving with its "ohs" and "ahs" with an increasingly irritated patience. He had to listen to the family gossip: how the kids were doing, prospects for the farm, and even some bedroom pieces that bored him silly. 'I suppose that's why she's good at her job. Very thorough. But so am I, and maybe not so long-winded'.

"You're not listening are you?" Before he could answer her, this delightful creature in a black cashmere rollneck with matching corduroy trousers and buckled shoes, brushed past their table and then turned back with deliberate effect, raising his hands to his brushed-back hair.

"Gilly darling, how 'luveley' to see you. Who's this gorgeous man. Do introduce me. How's the insurance business doing? Daddy still..." He rambled on without so much as taking a breath, and Gill listened and smiled her replies although she could see that Dennis was getting crosser and crosser.

"No coffee, thank you." He was already on his feet having passed on the sweets, and got rid of their suave acquaintance who was still 'darling it' around the tables.

"You're quiet. Sulking?"

"What a woofter. Where on earth did you meet him – or is it her?"

"Sorry darling." She emphasised the second word. "My roots are from here and I know a lot of people and have a lot of friends. You don't have to be rude to them. Just be tolerant and amusing. That's all they ask."

"I'm sorry. I've got engrossed in these crashes and I was looking forward to seeing you again for my own selfish pleasures. Pax."

"You baby. Just like a kid with a new toy. You know how I feel. Take me to your place and I'll show you again, then we can talk business."

They made love to the small hours with more tenderness than before, both trying hard to apologise for the earlier mistakes of the evening. Dennis reproached himself over the hint of jealousy he'd felt and decided to cool off from letting the relationship get too close. Their backgrounds were different and it wouldn't help his career if his clients knew he was getting too entrenched in the Francis Aviation camp. They hadn't talked shop, both agreeing to leave it till breakfast.

The coffee smelt great and they settled down to the latest healthy oats special offer. Dennis crunched away as he waited for her to start.

"Phial..." She cleared her throat. "Phial, how would you spell it?"

"Quiz time is it? She was obviously enjoying the suspense he reckoned.

"Serious. Spell it."

"File. I'd say – F-i-l-e."

"Another try?"

"Bugger this, my turn now. How d'you spell..." He swallowed as he nearly said something stupid. "Forget it, play your little game. Tell me, how do you spell file?" he replied emphasising the words.

"P-h-i-a-l. Phial, got it? Not file." She let the words sink in. "Do you know I racked my brains on the way back with you the other day as to what this file was all about. I thought it was a suggestion that someone had fiddled about with parts of the aircraft, filed something which had made it go wrong. Then I thought there might have been a file. You know, a file of papers with some evidence or something. Never dreamt of phial."

"So phial. What does that mean?"

She filled in the gaps and related the story of John the farmer finding the plastic tube and the suspicion that Sandy had had when trying to clean up Tony Hastings's head wound, and the fact that there was a healed scar from which the blood had seemingly appeared.

"This phial. Was there any evidence of blood in it?"

"Apparently so. Judy's nursing experience. She smelt blood and also the container was the type used by hospitals she said."

Dennis soaked up this latest finding and filled her in: "I'm getting nearer you know, and with a bit of luck should be able to complete the picture today after I've seen Chris, and looked at the photos. I reckon we're on to a con or sting if you like. Quite a clever sting due to a loophole in your procedures."

"My procedures. What d'you mean?"

"Not yours specifically, but your industry's." He went on to explain that from discussions with the air insurance market there was a deal of casualness in accepting the hull value for light aeroplanes, and the figure stated on the proposal form was taken as gospel in most cases.

"But the insured can ask for what he likes. That doesn't mean we'll pay it all."

"On minor accidents maybe, but on a write-off, usually the maximum. Is that so?" Gill reluctantly had to agree.

"You said photos. What are they?"

"Well I've a photo of the pilot in the French case and Chris is interviewing our friend Hastings today on the premise of some clearing up paperwork, and has agreed to take a concealed snap. I'm going to pop in to see if I'm right and whether we can read Johnston for Hastings and vice-versa. By the way, can you dig out your files on Echo Tango, they may hold other keys?"

Dennis fidgeted about as he waited for the taxi to take him over to Medway services who were based near Rochester. He hadn't got the Jaguar back from the crash episode, which had unfortunately damaged

126

the front suspension. Gill had gone with a "Love you soon, must fly" exit and left him twiddling his thumbs.

The call came from the blue and was perfect for the scenario.

"Blair-Lloyd. We spoke yesterday. You were enquiring about recent business which might involve small planes in the forty grand bracket with a low-houred applicant answering to Johnston or Hastings."

Dennis listened intently without answering.

"You there?" Dennis confirmed.

"I was in the City yesterday evening and talking to a broker who's just started in the aviation field. Taken on one small cover in the last month with us he tells me. Name of Simon Fury. Didn't recall the hours. Told you it's a quiet market at this time. Main reason he remembered the name was the wife who came in with the proposals. Apparently she was stunning. Dark-haired and tanned, very sexy, with a teasing short skirt. Gave him a photo of her with the aeroplane. Guy thought it was almost obscene and wondered whether it was a come on. Don't know whether this info's of value, but you're welcome for what it's worth."

"Who do I contact?"

"Robert Lewis, likes Bob." He gave him the phone and fax numbers.

Dennis thanked the caller and heard the taxi from the lounge window.

"I'll give him a call later."

Barry was concerned. Why had he been asked for more paperwork after the pay-out? "Routine," the girl had said. "Can't you post it?" he'd asked. "Mr Alton wishes to see you personally on this matter."

Barry hadn't got time to grow a stubble again but decided to play that one by ear. He felt a nervous niggle that the farmer might be behind this. 'Very inquisitive that John, I hope he won't be there.' He walked into the Rochester office hardly glancing at the man chatting to the very attractive reception girl.

"Excuse me I have an appointment with your Mr Alton."

'That's it – got you my friend.' Dennis matched the face with his French photo and even got a quick glance at the facial scar.

"Tell Chris I'll be back shortly. Wait till he's finished with the chap who's just with him though."

He nipped round the corner into the nearest local and congratulated himself with a large scotch and soda. 'Got him. No problem. But have I enough proof? Same man yes, but there's no law against changing your name, and both crashes have been accidental by verdict – my verdict. What's he up to? I know he's made out on the insurance uplift but maybe that was just luck. Surely he's not crashing deliberately. Bloody risky. But then the unanswered doubts from the Norfolk enquiry. Looks very much like it might be deliberate. I need to find out more of this guy's background. He's obviously not a novice, and there's the opinion of the farmer who said that the pilot had seemed very experienced.'

He wandered back to Medway Services and checked that Johnston/Hastings had gone before he made it to Chris's office.

"Taken them?" Chris pulled out the mini camera in answer. "Problems?"

"Don't think so. He seemed a bit edgy. What's this all about?"

"Later Chris. You've got my written assurance and you'll have to live with that for the time being."

Chris shrugged and organised some coffee and biscuits. "I might as well give you the negatives to develop. Yes?"

"Fine. One other favour, who handled the cover on India Papa?"

"Oh. let me think, who was he?... Clive... D'you know I've forgotten his surname. Smart lad. Bit too fond of himself. Tried it on with my lass out there."

Not the only one, Dennis wondered. "You wouldn't know if the insurance was proposed by a woman?"

"Probably. That would be the only interest in that boy's mind." 'Chris can be moody, but he obviously doesn't like this Clive,' Dennis thought.

"You want me to check?"

"Please, if it's not too much trouble."

They swapped the latest gossip in the industry and moaned at Government policies, the cricket and others, whilst they waited for the details to be found.

"I think this is all we've got." Chris opened the papers and it fell like a leaf onto the floor. Dennis picked up the photograph to find himself staring at a stunning black-haired gypsy-like girl, posing in a short skirt in front of a smart little aeroplane.

"Checkmate."

Chapter Twenty-Two

Only the crass inefficiency of the place allowed him to seize the moment and give his escorts the slip. He'd noticed the construction workers and thought the confusion might help. He entered the toilets and chose a cabin to give himself time to think, only to find the workmen had knocked the back out, giving access to the women's toilets. Without a further thought he slipped past the wash basins and out to the domestic terminal. He glanced back to see the ugly face of Kobaf guarding the 'men's' like an Alsatian.

Hogan smiled without a further look and hurried to the phone booths before they realised he was missing. For once luck was on his side and the connection clicked straight into the Mitchell office.

"Who, the line's very faint?" Tim was back in favour since the Dallas exercise and Patrick had sorted out a smart new office with some of the latest gadgetry, and a smart secretary to operate it. "I still can't catch your name, can you speak up?"

Hogan twisted nervously. There were no signs of opposition at the moment, but he didn't want to draw attention by shouting down the line.

"Hogan for Christ's sake! You remember me? Hogan, your favourite investigator. You with me?"

The penny dropped and Tim gestured the secretary to the outside office.

"Hogan, damn you! Were the hell are you? What have you been doing?"

"You may well ask but I haven't got time. I'm stuck in the outskirts of Lagunda. Sort of prisoner to the bloody Iraqis! Got to go to South Africa! It's a long story, but I think I've got your evidence. That's if these jokers don't get me killed," he explained as quickly as he could.

"So when will you be back?"

"No idea, but I need money. Can you transfer some to the Standard Bank in Durban, otherwise I may never make it back."

"What... Azif... how can..." The connection was breaking down and Hogan wasn't about to risk it any further. He left the box and calmly walked over to the bar and bought a large baguette-type roll stuffed with soft grated cheese and mayonnaise. He spotted Kobaf and watched him dodging around like a waterfly boatman on a pond. He stood behind a column awaiting his chance then slipped in behind him and coughed loudly. Ugly spun on his foot as Hogan stuffed the cheese roll into his open mouth.

"Thought you might be hungry, all this waiting. Don't offer to share, I've had mine." The sloppy filling ran down Kobaf's face and over the smart peach shirt, dripped onto his white trousers and finally came to rest on the highly polished moccasins.

"Sorry they didn't have any knives or plates. Still I'll wait for you at the gate while you tidy up. Boarding's been called I see."

Hogan thumbed the other two henchmen to follow him to Gate Three and amused himself with the look of disbelief on their faces. They turned to their boss for guidance, but he was too busy trying to clear the mess off his clothes with an inadequate silk handkerchief.

"Farewell to you clowns and your steaming cesspit of a country." Slumped in a tight seat with his bad leg in an uncomfortable position his sympathies were expressed with limited vocabulary, but he hadn't realised that they'd come out aloud.

His fellow passenger smiled in acknowledgement. "You're not the first to say that, but I wouldn't recommend more, not if you want any service."

"I was promised club class but it never works out."

"All the same seats on this heap, let me give you some tips."

"Hogan by the way." They shook hands.

"Michael Webber. Now drinks first. You going to Gabaronne?" Hogan nodded. "Right, well it's a nine-hour flight and they should come round twice. Once for drinks and once for food. Forget the food, my advice. Drinks, decide what you want and order it first round otherwise you'll find they've deliberately run out next time." Hogan worked that equation as one and a bit an hour so he ordered twelve whiskies. With Michael's share the fold-down tables looked set for a party.

Hogan ran his mind over the next phase and his instructions. He was on his own with two passports. One to get him into Botswana and another to Jo'burg because of the apartheid situation. He had to hole up in Gabaronne for five days and then move to Durban where he was to check with Azif before he was cleared back to the UK. If all was well and good, the electronic report would arrive at his Southampton office a week later. Lot of ifs but he'd little choice. That was the good news. The bad was that Azif's enemies where to be primed to trail him, thinking that he would be making tracks to Tehran, only to find the game stops at Durban. By that time the real equipment should have reached its destination, and Azif would be off the hook.

"You'll be perfectly safe. They wouldn't harm you until you reached their sacred soil and of course you'll never set foot in their country. Simple." It had sounded very convincing. At least to him, not Hogan.

"I hear what you say, but when they realise it's a hoax they're just as likely to blast me away."

"I should be extremely surprised if that was so, for they wouldn't wish to risk publicity."

"Bugger your eloquent analysis. It's my body I'm worried about."

"Relax! Treat it as a refresher course for your profession. You can use all the tricks of your trade and be paid for the privilege. In fact you're on double pay."

Hogan grunted. "As if that matters if I'm six foot below."

"Worked it out?" Michael enquired. He saw his companion was thinking.

"Sort of," Hogan replied.

He decided to check out this man. 'Could be my first tail,' he thought. 'Unlikely disguise though.'

Michael Webber was of medium height, although that was difficult to tell from a sitting position. His greying hair gave him a distinguished look which was further set off by a lightweight safari jacket and slacks, and lizard sandals. He was wearing a gold neckchain and gold bracelet which suggested the support of a healthy bank balance.

"On business?" Michael asked.

"Not really. I'm doing a post office job for a friend. Delivering some electronic parts for him." Hogan felt it might not be a bad thing to admit to his luggage. Never know they might be on the plane and question whether his goods were bona fide before he got to Durban, and that would cock-up Azif's scheme. If he went for a cover story it could seem odd. After all he wasn't supposed to know he was being trailed. Spy stuff this with double double crosses. Never could understand how those spies knew who was who?

"How about you?"

"I'm in the shoe trade. Saw you admiring my sandals. Italian and Portuguese mainly."

"Is that good business?"

"Very good. The well-off African classes have an expensive dress code and they'll pay fancy prices for the right goods."

"How much?"

"Italian light leather specials. One sixty."

"Dollars?"

"Pounds." Hogan raised his eyebrows.

"Good business you say. What's the mark-up?"

"You're not revenue?"

"That's a laugh. I owe them a fortune."

"Enough. It buys me three homes and a few fancy toys and privileges. Yacht, cars... you understand."

They continued in conversation with Hogan having some difficulty in manufacturing a cover without giving away his true occupation. The drinks both hindered and helped and finally he was able to feign tiredness and dropped off into a half-dozing sleep.

The old 707 dragged itself through clear skies and Hogan was woken by the call for safety belts pending a descent into Gabaronne. He said farewell to Michael, and booked into a small downtown hotel in the mainly Afrikaans area which was recommended to be a quiet community.

He showered away the travel sweat and took the names of a couple of restaurants from the deskman. The flight down had been early and he was feeling somewhat peckish after Michael's advice on the in-flight food.

The week passed quietly and Hogan relaxed in a boring sort of way. There wasn't much to do although he did take a short safari to pass the time. Animals weren't his favourite, too predictable. He preferred the megalomaniac humans and their complicated lives.

'Funny creatures humans. Totally incapable of living life in peace and harmony with their fellow beings. Must interfere with other people's lives. Suppose animals are the same really, only they do it by nature. Humans achieve it by rhetoric or other verbal persuasion, or just by force.' Put two people in a railway carriage alone for any length of time, and at the end of the journey one will have dominated the other. That was the psychologist's view he'd read.

He researched the addresses of some electrical firms and called in with some vague enquiries to appear active, and let it drop that he had contacts in the Middle East. His bar chat was similar and he started to feel more comfortable.

'Bet Azif's conning me. Sent me on this wild-goose trail while he sorts out his problems. Bet I never receive that report.' He reconfirmed the flight to Jo'burg and decided to visit the Anchor Inn again for his last night.

He spotted him twenty yards from the door and instinctively turned to one side before sliding behind a parked car. It was Michael of that he was sure but why the darkened hair and the rough bush-bum appearance of his clothing, and the backpack? Perhaps he'd been on a camping trip? He watched the shadowy figure of the man as he sussed out the people in the Anchor and then moved down the road to the corner bar that Hogan had used on occasions.

"He's checking out someone," he hissed under his breath.

Michael walked on slowly, turning his head as if watching for something and Hogan saw that he was making his way to the hotel. He followed at a discreet distance until he was able to hide close to an outside window which was side on to the reception desk.

"Mr Hogan, is he around?" Michael casually enquired from the boy manning the teak carved counter.

"I've not seen him tonight, maybe in his room." He searched on the board behind him. "He's got the key. Room twenty-one."

'You're a safe bet for security – my aunt Fanny.' Hogan was not pleased with the young lad's slackness.

He waited until he heard Michael reach the stairs and then slipped past the boy into the small hotel bar opposite the main entrance. As usual there was no barman. The hotel rules allowed you in such circumstances to help yourself, noting your purchase on a special ticket. Hogan fixed himself a quick brandy and positioned himself where he could see the bottom of the stairs through the reflection of the bar mirror. Michael was not long and Hogan waited for him go before he bounded up to his room.

It was gone. It wasn't a large package and Hogan guessed that Michael had tucked it away into his back pack. 'Jesus, if they find out it's fake gear I'm for the chop.' He hurriedly stuffed a few essentials into his hand holdall and placed most of his clothes in the case which he left open as if half packed. He dumped one of the passports no longer needed and quietly walked to reception keeping the holdall out of sight. "I'm off early tomorrow. Like to settle my bill now, if that's okay?"

"Sure thing Mr Hogan. By the way, some guy was after you earlier, did you see him?"

"Yes thanks. Old colleague of mine. I'm meeting him for a drink shortly, probably be late back."

"That's all right. You've got the main door key. Where you off to?"

Hogan thought quickly. "Victoria Falls. Never been there. Looking forward to it. See you again sometime."

Walking towards the town he thumbed a taxi for the airport. "Any chance of getting out tonight, I've had some bad news and I need to get to Jo'burg as soon as possible."

The smart uniformed check-in lass punched the keyboard whilst Hogan paced around drumming his fingers on the counter. She worked away for quite a time and then got up and walked off. He gazed around for any problems but the check-in lounge was virtually empty.

She returned. "I can fit you on SAA 237 twenty-one thirty, but only first class. We're very full tonight."

"I'll take it." 'Sod it, Tim can pay.' "Can I connect to Durban tonight?"

"Hold on." Her fingers rattled the keys again and Hogan wondered whether computer operators would make good pianists. "That's booked. Economy on that leg sir, arrives six in the morning."

Hogan collected the tickets and moved through international customs, giving himself enough time to gulp down another brandy.

He collected the news from an early kiosk as he was making his way to the taxi rank at Durban. *Bomb Attack in Gabaronne* was scrawled on a blackboard. He bought the morning issue and slumped into the back of a cab. "Elangani mate." The front page featured an explosion in an hotel – four dead and several seriously injured. Motive unknown but racial tension suspected. Maybe to do with pending elections.

He wiped the perspiration from the back of his neck and felt the tension aggravating his leg. "Out – definitely out this time."

"What time do the banks open?" he asked the Zulu driver.

"Ten thirty boss."

His watch showed eight and he cursed Azif for the bloody mess so far. 'Out I said. But first out of this country.'

Chapter Twenty-Three

Patrick paced the room as he waited for the fax to arrive. He was really regretting the task ahead and the pressure from his old buddy in Texas. The weekend had been a lot of fun, fooling around with Dianne and the grandchildren in the pool, and later they'd barbecued and wined in the sunshine. The past never goes away, and it catches up with you eventually. He was feeling jaded – 'burn-out' was the buzz word – and he wondered whether it was time to off-load the company and retire from the hassle of running the show. Who'd buy? Small airlines were struggling against a price war and were unlikely to want to take on more investment. The bigger boys might be interested if only to take out the competition. But they can do that anyway by selling cheap fares. Marvel Air – he was proud of the achievement and he didn't want to see the name disappear. It would though. 'I go, and within seven days the company will go or at least change. Nothing's for ever.' It depressed him.

The fax machine rang and then started to cough out its entrails. He smoothed out the sheet and devoured the information.

"Heathrow. Terminal Three. Contact Comet handling. Parcel coded Ocean. Pass authority Redwing Engineering (48)." Patrick could hear Chuck dictating the message and knew he'd be enjoying the kick as much as Patrick was dreading it.

"You wanted me?" Tim came into the office.

"Tim, yes... will you hold on a moment?" Patrick rubbed his eyes and walked over to the window to watch a military jet taxiing for practice. He turned around and put his hands in his back pockets.

"I'll be asking another favour." Tim had guessed as much.

"Niger or near. Can the One-Elevens make that?"

"Not in one go." Tim wondered what was on his mind. Surely not thinking of opening up over there. Wrong economy, wrong planes.

"I want you to take some goods to an old airfield north of Lagunda."

"This anything to do with your friend Chuck?"

"Indirectly, you might say."

It was on the tip of his tongue to take Patrick into his confidence and bring him up to date on the information he'd pieced together already, but somehow it was still too early. Besides if Pat was party to his suspicions then that would hardly help Barry in any re-examination of the evidence. He decided to carry on questioning in order to have a hold on the situation.

"How long have we known each other?" Tim posed.

Patrick didn't answer and stared past Tim's eyes with that vacant expression of someone who's mind was miles away. "I – you were asking?"

"You all right?"

"To be sure Tim. I have some problems. Not a big deal."

"I've always supported you. The Johnston trial, your servicing problems, the salary negotiations... Am I right?"

"You're right Tim, I don't doubt it."

"Then why d'you not trust me more?"

Patrick sighed and then placed a hand on Tim's shoulder. He moved away and produced a bottle of Irish Mist from a cabinet in the corner. The two glasses charged, he replied: "Me father, curse his being, said one thing to me, or maybe it was me marm using Father's words. Any rate, he said you're best off knowing enough, but you're safer not knowing it all."

"Maybe your Irish logic makes sense of that to you Pat, but my British education taught me a situation is better handled if one knows the facts."

"Is that so? Well what'll you need to know?"

"In Dallas, I got some vibes from a colleague of Chucks, Hal... I never got his surname. Got the impression that you're all involved in some Middle East deal."

He could see the hammer had hit dead centre by the way Patrick turned away to refill his glass with some deliberation. He waited as Pat drank thoughtfully before refilling it again. "If I level with you, have I got your silence?" Tim nodded his agreement.

"Terrorism – it's a price we pay." He went on to explain that Chuck had negotiated the assistance of the Iranian government to put pressure on other international terrorist organisations to boycott the IRA by freezing their source of funds and supply of arms and other devices. "It's costing a lot for sure. Chuck's providing some harmless electronic equipment but the real input's diamonds. There was a shipment that went astray. I'm supplying simple replacement transport help on the Lagunda leg. There's no risk."

He knew it was lies. Even though it was told in that convincing Irish tongue. Diamonds probably but for whom. Not the Government for sure. And then there was the equipment. The little he'd had from Hogan and his own investigations told him there was more to it than that. Chuck didn't strike him as a philanthropist. He'd enjoyed the comfort of the Dallas homestead but you needed money and lots of it for that lifestyle. Whatever Chuck was selling, and he suspected it was a prototype, there had to be a potential fortune at the end of it. Bribe in with diamonds yes, but cash out in return. Wonder what Patrick's share is? Not that it mattered. All he was trying was to get enough evidence to reopen the case for Barry.

'Why am I doing that?' Barry'll never thank me? He knew a large part of his concern was to clear his own position because there'd been some stigma on the professionalism of his aircrew training programmes, which would be a black mark on any future career.

"So that's all?"

"There's no more to tell."

"And Azif, where's he fit in?"

"Enough Tim. You've enough to run this trip. You'll be on special bonus. You can offer that to be fair, to the rest of the crew."

"Azif, you didn't answer?"

"Not on my list at all. That's my lot."

At least the lying was consistent and told Tim he was on the right track. He left the office without further questions, satisfied with the interrogation of his slippery boss although he was worried that he might be skating on thin ice. 'I'll make the trip, maybe even see Azif. Hogan should surface soon with his findings.'

Patrick finished the bottle with a feeling of anger and annoyance. He wanted out but that Texan Chuck had called in his card and there was nothing Pat could do. He paced the floor like a caged tiger, trying to come to terms with events... "Jesus fuck!" The glass flew from his hand and smashed into the cabinet shattering the glass door and dislodging the models of his prized aircraft fleet. He watched broken pieces fall on to the floor, and the remaining liquid dribble down the woodwork and stain itself into the carpet.

He stormed out telling the girl to sort out the mess if she wanted to sit her arse at her desk tomorrow.

Chapter Twenty-Four

"You'll be careful."

"I bet she never said that."

"Who?"

"Bonnie. That girl was as hard as nails. Mercenary for sure."

"She loved in her way. She must have. She did it for him."

"Fifty-fifty I expect. Rubbed off on each other."

"Anyhow you will be, won't you?"

"Careful. Of course."

He wrapped his arms around and hugged her more like a doting father than a lover. "Don't worry. In a couple of months we'll be sailing in the Grenadines."

"No fancies this time, we agree?" He signalled consent. "No imitation injuries?"

"Maybe a limp or two, and I'll need a wig."

"Why?"

"The last two were my age. Need to put on twenty odd years. I can't do that just with make up."

"All right." She sounded reluctant in agreement, and Barry knew she was nervous this time.

"D'you want me to call it off?"

"Yes... Oh no... I just want you safe."

"Remember the reaction. We're good yes? And the money?"

Judy shivered at the thought as she recalled the excitement they both got from being scared. Bonnie must have been the same.

"When will it be ready?"

"Not long now, a week maybe."

"Where will it happen?"

"Too many questions Judy. I told you it's better you don't know."

"I'm frightened."

"So am I."

"No more after this. You promise?"

"No more in this country, I promise." He lent forward to kiss her cheek. "I'd better go now."

She put on an anorak and walked with him to the car. She watched the vehicle until she could see and hear it no more, and then turned back with a heavy heart to climb the gang plank of her small houseboat. She was not a gypsy in spite of her looks, but some sixth sense or Romany vision made her suddenly feel cold, and she shook for a moment before shrugging off any forebodings which might try to enter her head.

Chapter Twenty-Five

"Robert Lewis please."

"One moment sir."

Dennis listened to a hubbub of background noise through the earpiece and a distant voice calling: "Bob, telephone!" He waited a while and then the switchboard girl came on. "Just putting you through."

Dennis introduced himself to the broker and explained his position as that of a loss adjuster. "I gather you're new in the market and in that respect I'd like to offer my services. However, there's a specific problem that might involve both of us and I wondered how you were fixed for a chat. Lunch possible?"

Bob couldn't make lunch so they agreed to meet later in a wine bar not far from the Lloyd's centre. "Five thirty, that's a date. You'll recognise me carrying a copy of *Flight International* and drinking Chianti."

There was now to be a lull in proceedings until the afternoon, so Dennis decided to take lunch at his local on the Thamesside. Forking the lasagne and washing it down with a dry cider he tried to focus on the checks that remained to be done to cement any weakness in his evidence. He used the mobile and rang Gill from the table:

"Just polishing the finer points."

"Isn't this Hastings thing becoming an obsession love. You seem to be spending all your time on it. What about the Farnborough Fokker? That's still not resolved and I'm being pressed by the owners for a settlement?"

"You're right. Hope to have something to you on that shortly, apologies for the delay. Bear with me on the other, I'm nearly there. It's slotting together nicely."

"So why the call?"

"Just a thought. Can you remember how you got the business on Echo Tango?"

"You're joking. I do have other things on my mind than an index on all contacts."

"No need to be stroppy. Okay forget your memory. D'you have any file notes?"

"I'll come back. Where are you?"

Dennis gave her the mobile number and chased up another cider with a death by chocolate pudding, which he knew he'd regret later.

"How's it going?" George ran a good pub, but like a lot in the trade was not the discreetest with other people's private matters. Dennis had proved that it was best to keep conversation light and insubstantial.

"So so. Mustn't grumble. Quiet at the moment. You?"

"Same. Trade's down a bit. Weekends not very busy at all. VAT man's on my back. Something to do with profit on food."

"You buggers are always grumbling, but I haven't met a poor publican yet. How's the Rolls?"

George ignored the innuendo and poured a pint for another customer. He returned and said, "This chap asking for you. Did he find you?"

"What chap?" Dennis enquired with curiosity.

"Dark-skinned guy. Foreign features. Wanted your address. Told him I didn't know. Said he'd come back. Not seen him?"

"When was this?"

"Couple of weeks ago."

"Did he say why?"

"No, nothing. Didn't even buy a drink."

I wonder what that was about. Dennis puzzled with it but secured no ideas. Then the mobile rang. "International Enquiry Services returning your call sir. Your command is our duty. No stone unturned. This is your personal manager speaking. Mavis Cocksure. I'm available from..."

"Stop pissing around Gill. This is serious."

"So where's your sense of humour, lover boy?"

"All right, but another time. Got a few things on my mind."

"Tom Goff."

"Tom who?"

"You wanted our contact. Tom Goff I'm telling you. Some small-time broker not normally into the aviation business I gather."

"Address?"

"Of course. And the telephone number." Gill fed him the details. "You're a brick. I'll sort you out later when I've softened up. Sorry for damping your jokes."

"Okay misery. Sod off and write your mystery story. Might be a scenario for a novel?" She left the line before he could reply.

"Change to a whisky, if that's okay. Thanks." He was obliged to accept the publican's offer. "Those gassy ciders fill me up."

He punched in the digits and pressed send. "Mr Goff's not available at this time but he'll be back this afternoon. Shall I get him to return your call?"

"No. I'll call him. I'll be on a different number."

Dennis finished his drink and walked back to the flat overlooking the Thames.

The Fokker file lay open and Dennis fiddled with the papers in an aimless way picking them up and reading bits, studying the photographs and the technical plans of the foreign manufacturer. Somehow he found it difficult to concentrate on this one and his mind kept flitting back and forth. He glanced through Jim's latest findings but they led him nowhere.

'I need more clues or a breakthrough of some sort,' he worried, and continued to thumb through the file for conclusions. He noted the list of those on board that Gill had provided and ran a finger down the page for some inspiration. He crossed off the crew because of their statements, which didn't amount to much. What was left? Four 'diplomats' and two 'broads'. 'Alphabetical is logical so who's first? Azif. Might as well start there.' He made some notes for reference and then, bored again, moved over to the lounge window and the panoramic picture of the Thames; the view was forever changing, and never ceased to please. He idly watched the slim rowing boats and recalled from his college days the difficulty of getting the rhythm together in the fours.

He spotted the figure more by chance than from observation, and then only because the man was moving with uncertainty. He seemed to be noting the house numbers and Dennis watched as he stopped outside the flat. Dark in appearance, he guessed this might be the mystery man from George's place. Nothing happened and Dennis decided to go down and confront the intruder in some way or another. He reached the pavement but the person had disappeared. He wandered each way but the figure had vanished like a ghost, so Dennis returned to the house. 'Strange, I wonder what that's about?'

Noting the time he made the connection with the Goff office and was pleased to speak directly to the owner. "I'm the investigating assessor for a light aeroplane which crashed in France. I understand from the insurers, Francis Aviation, that the original business was placed by your company on behalf of the owner, a Mr Johnston. Can you help me on this one?"

"Well... your information is correct, but how can I help?"

"Although the insurance has been settled I've been asked to check on a couple of facts and one relates to the pilot's experience."

"In what way?"

"There appear to be some conflicting figures on the number of hours flown. One statement talks of eleven thousand hours, and another one hundred and forty. I think there may be some confusion on totals flown, against experience on type, and I just wondered if you had any records that might help?"

"Hold on a minute my other line's buzzing."

Dennis crossed his legs, tapping his pencil on his teeth while he waited.

"You there?"

"Go ahead."

"I can certainly help you in that Barry Johnston is a personal friend of mine, but I don't have any precise details of hours flown. Eleven thousand sounds right with his experience, I should've thought."

"So what's his flying background?"

"Services. Instructor. Commercial pilot."

"I see. So is he flying commercially at this time?"

"I think not." Tom decided to hold back on the Marvel Air period and be somewhat vague. He wasn't quite sure why this background was being required, and he didn't want to foul things for Barry in any way. "I believe he's semi-retired, decided to get out of the rat race.

"Very wise. Feel that way myself some days."

"Is there anything else?"

"No, that's fine. You've been most helpful."

Dennis contacted directory enquiries and was soon talking to a rather pompous official in the records office at the Civil Aviation Authority.

"I am sorry Mr Hoskice."

"Hopkins."

"Hopshins... I cannot give that information over the telephone. I shall require your request in writing, and any authorisation or legal basis for your request as backup."

"But surely you can tell me the name of Mr Johnston's last employer?"

"I've made the position quite clear to you Mr Hospel and you have my considered decision on this matter. Please write and include a stamped addressed envelope with your letter."

'Nasty little bureaucratic man. Bet he's got a mean wife who's kept him starved for ages. Either that or he's as queer as a coot.' Dennis was annoyed with the conversation. 'Maybe there's another way. Wonder if he's got a secretary?'

"CAA?"

"Which department sir."

"Records please."

A different voice came through and Dennis decided to give it a go.

"Just a quickie. I was speaking to your department earlier. Forgotten who with. Was given the name of a Captain B Johnston's last employer. Wrote it down, but I've somehow misplaced my note."

"Hold on sir, I'll just type that into the data base. What's your name?"

"Crook." It came out by chance and Dennis smiled at the metaphorical reaction. He hung in wondering whether she'd check with her boss and he'd be caught out.

"Marvel Air, Bournemouth Airport."

"Of course I recall it now. Thanks a lot."

"My pleasure." He rubbed his hands like a clever schoolboy as he rang directory enquiries again.

Armed with the telephone number and address, he decided that was enough detective stuff for one day, and in any case it was time to meet Bob Lewis.

Chapter Twenty-Six

The commotion in the outer office sounded like the champion had lost at Madison Square Gardens, and the crunches as if the loser was smashing the place to pieces. He heard the yelling and his secretary's attempt to calm someone down, and decided to investigate the source of the fray. As he reached the door it was flung open abruptly and the full force of the coat hook, fixed on the inside, sliced into Tim's face and threw him onto the floor.

"I'm calling the police!" He heard her frightened voice, but the blow to his head was not helping to make any sense of the situation.

"I am the flaming police." The voice sounded familiar but slurred and he couldn't place it.

"Mr Mitchell, my God..." Her voice trailed off and he heard the window open and his secretary Anne shouting for someone to help, "... or this madman will commit a murder!"

"Mitchell – I could murder you. Bloody near got murdered meself, and it's all your flaming fault. Sodding planes, sodding Arabs. You can all go screw yourselves."

Hogan thought he'd given them the slip by jiggling his flights back from South Africa, to muddy the trail. He probably had or they hadn't given a damn, for they were two jumps ahead of him. He arrived back to find the office had been ceremonially dismantled, such that he was finished. His equipment was totally destroyed and his records torn to shreds. The glass door had been carefully smashed and the pieces embossed with his name dug into the desk with the ultimate threat gouged out on the top.

He'd grabbed a taxi, grabbed a bottle from the supermarket and arrived two parts cut and fighting furious at Tim's office, determined to take his anger out on someone.

The two security guards dragged Hogan away and Tim struggled to the toilet to sort out his injury. It looked bad with a nasty black bruise spreading around the deep cut. He went back to his room and Anne patched him as best she could from the first aid kit.

"It needs stitching."

"Who the hell was that?" It had all happened so fast that Tim still hadn't taken in the picture.

"He said he was the law, but I never got his name. He was just swearing and waving a bottle like a maniac, and demanding to see you. He couldn't stand very well and kept crashing into the furniture. It was awful..." She blurted out the words and Tim could see she was shivering with fright.

"Sit down. Let's organise some tea. I reckon I may know who that was, but I'm surprised, if it's who I think it was?"

One of the guards returned. "We're holding him downstairs. D'you want the police?"

"No, just hold him and get some tea for us. I'll be with you in a minute."

It wasn't a minute because his head was still bleeding badly and his secretary persuaded him to visit casualty before anything else. The place was packed and it was over two hours before he returned.

"We couldn't keep him, not without police help. He knows his rights." The young guard was apologetic and worried whether he'd done the right thing.

"Don't worry. He's an ex-cop. You wouldn't credit it, eh?"

Tim was struggling with a thumping headache and was in no mood to continue arguing. "Thanks for your help. You did okay." He let them go: "Anne. I suggest you slip off home. I'm going. We can sort this out in the morning."

Tim drove home gingerly, wondering if he should drop the issue with Barry. Something heavy must have happened to Hogan for him to react like this. 'Jesus, the guy's a professional isn't he? Maybe he's flipped. God, my head hurts.'

"And you." He raised his fingers to the flashy Ford driver, who chased his tail lights through the roundabout with full horn blasting and the appropriate gesture of an impatient thug. Cornering the car wasn't helping and he was anxious for home and a soft pillow.

The unwelcome doorbell broke his slumber and for a time he thought to let it ring. Whoever it was, was persistent, and Tim dragged himself off the sofa and drifted to the door. He nearly shut it, but the boot jammed his action. Hogan looked rough but not dangerous, and Tim reluctantly let him come in.

"Got a Rye or something?"

"You've got a cheek, you crazy idiot."

"Bad news. That's me. Take it out of my fees. I'll make it right for your secretary tomorrow... Look I'm sorry. Blew my top. Past it probably. I'm sorry. Christ! What do you want me to do? Kiss your feet?" Tim sat staring at Hogan letting his words soak into a cotton-wool emptiness.

"What's a fellow s'posed to do? For God's sake they tried to kill me. I reckon you'd get grumpy in those circumstances." Tim raised his hands and protected his ears as Hogan rambled on.

"They blew up a hotel. Killed some innocent guys to get me. You got that? You listening? Now they're back here. Done my office."

Tim rose to the last comment. "Your offices?"

"Yes. You dummy. This is a serious scene you've gotten into, and you're going to get your fingers burnt unless we start to cooperate."

"Go on." Tim's head was hurting unhelpfully.

"Whisky first. And lots of it."

Hogan gave him the full story from the wild-goose chase in Lagunda to Azif's 'hospitality' and the decoy flight to Durban, with the horrific touch at Gabaronne which he missed narrowly, by instinct. He made it sound rough and he emphasised the treatment by Azif's heavies and the terror he'd experienced on reading about the hotel bomb and now the destruction of his offices.

"When I took this assignment I thought it was a bit more exciting than the normal routine stuff, but I didn't bargain for the show so far. Where does it end?"

"You make your point Hogan, but that doesn't give you a licence to break into my offices and frighten the pants off my secretary."

"Okay... okay. I've said I'm sorry." He tried to sound genuine. "Give me the score, you must know more?" He shrugged at the rhyme. "I apologise about your secretary, that was not meant, just happened. You sure you're all right. Can I get you anything?"

Tim chewed on his teeth and massaged his eyes to try and release the pressure inside his head. "Paracetemol. There's some in the bathroom. Get me some water as well."

He took the tablets and indicated to Hogan that he could help himself to another from the bottle standing on the side table. "I think we've stumbled on to something by mistake and are being warned off."

"Warned off. Shit, I don't call bombs 'warned off'."

"Maybe. But that was a set-up by Azif. They really thought you had the goods. They must know by now that you were a hoax to knock them off the real trail. Your office touch is probably a reminder to keep your nose clean from now on."

"You can say that again. I'm out anyhow, they've seen to that. But I want out. This trip has shown me the light and I'm away abroad for a quiet life from now on."

"Same for Barry." Tim was thinking aloud and not listening to Hogan's future plans and solutions.

"What do you mean, the same for Barry?"

"They killed a cat. Sort of frightener. Stop poking your nose in type frightener."

"When was this?"

"Can't remember, didn't I mention it?"

"No you didn't. You never indicated the job might attract any nasty bugs and certainly no violence."

"Well, I wasn't sure. Thought it might have been Barry's boss."

They rambled on at each other wondering where the situation was leading them. Hogan asked for his money and some compensation for his smashed gear, and they argued about the damage inflicted on Tim's office.

"Payment equals service provided." Tim was standing with his hands in his jacket pockets as he delivered the profound statement. "D'you agree?"

"Either you're crackers or that blow to your head is sending you that way. What's this political stance. You practising for parliament?"

Tim started to laugh and then grimaced as the movement grabbed at the nerves in his head which made him sit down smartly. "Phew, I was trying to look on the funny side, but the body's not for it at the moment."

"What's funny?"

"Come on Hogan, I can see the headlines: *Tough Ex-Policeman Investigator Cracks Under Pressure...* you deserve better than that."

"S'pose you're right. Don't normally take things so seriously. You win for the moment. What's with this payment crack?"

"When I get the dummy report from Azif."

"You reckon that's still on?"

"It better be with all you've gone through."

"So you pay on completion?"

"Right on."

"And no completion?"

"You return the compliments to Azif."

Hogan studied his client and the bloodstained plaster on his forehead with an improving respect. "You're a tough old cookie deep down. I'll give you that."

"Flying prepares you for a lot of eventualities. Sort of grown-up boy scouting. If this report is kosher then our troubles are over."

"You'd run it through a court of law?"

"Why not? We now know the genuine article probably affected the navigation instruments, but we also know that we cannot produce that evidence without having our heads blown off." Hogan raised his eyebrows to catch Tim smirking slightly. "So we produce some alternative safer evidence. We're not exactly cheating just substituting the absolute facts."

"Why're you doing this and perjuring yourself at the same time?"

"I ask myself that question often. Barry is (or was) a friend, and one should support your friends. But more, he's a fellow pilot and a good one at that. I suppose it's a bit of – but for the grace of God go I."

"Azif conned me, you do realise? He sent me off with decoy gear knowing that the replacement wasn't ready. I reckon he hoped they'd blow me and the false Wasp together, so that he could slip the real equipment in later without hassle. I'll have him on that."

"You may well get a chance – I'm ready for food. How goes it with you?"

They agreed and made tracks for the hotel where they'd first met.

"So we wait for delivery. Any idea where?"

"Now the office is blown, I haven't a clue."

"Azif's still in the mire. They may get him first?"

Tim chewed the halibut steak, ruminating on the events of the day. He wasn't out of the woods yet, remembering that he'd agreed with

Patrick's trip to Lagunda on which he would be carrying the real
McCoy. Hogan's run was concerning and frightening, but the real
worry was that they, whoever they were, knew that the first package
was a decoy, and also they were still on Azif's back over here.

He kept lifting his eyes to where the detective was demolishing an
overdone wild duck and watched him wash it down with plenty of red
wine. Perhaps Hogan was right. This thing was getting too
complicated for his liking. It had seemed simple at first, but how was
he to know that his initial probings would lead to international
skulduggery. He couldn't care a monkey's about world politics but
here he was wrapped up simply to help a friend and colleague. Silly
idiot. Trouble was his boss was also implicated and he would require
his assistance come a re-trial.

"Off your food?"

"Just thinking."

"You should have done that some time ago. Too late now. Better
eat up like a good boy. Might be your last with these terrorists
amok."

"I need one more favour?"

Hogan nearly spat on his food as he listened to the innocence of
Tim's voice. "I'm not hearing this am I?"

"I think you should know something else."

"Go on. Surprise me."

He went on to outline the Dallas scene and its cast, with the
ambitions of the players, the favours sought, Azif's part, and more
sinister and difficult, Act Three, which required his participation in
flying the replacement electronics back to Niger.

"Are we part of a farce or a tragedy?" Hogan slipped in the
metaphor as he finished his glass of wine. "It gets worse."

"It's no joke, that's for sure."

"So what's the favour?"

"Come with me."

Hogan let it sink in before he replied. "Dangerous, isn't it?
They're on to me which will put you in danger also. One plane's
gone down already. You're putting yourself directly in the firing
line."

"I think not. I think the danger is after Lagunda, and by then we'll
be irrelevant."

"Irrelevant and probably eliminated. So why d'you need me?"

"Straight swaps. One Wasp 200 equals one report, equals one payment to Hogan, equals peace of mind for both of us, equals new trial for Barry, equals you can retire, equals we can all sleep soundly again."

"Surely you can handle that yourself?"

"Possible, yes. But remember I've never met Azif." He paused.

"Okay. But then that's it." Tim nodded his assurance.

Chapter Twenty-Seven

He kicked so hard that he became entangled with the bedclothes and in trying to release himself, fell in a heap onto the floor. Judy woke as the sheet was pulled away to see a ghostly figure struggling in a white cloak, cursing under its breath.

"What are you doing?" She rubbed the sleep from her eyes.

"Making a cup of tea. What d'you think I'm doing?" He disengaged himself from the sheet and stumbled into the bathroom to wash the perspiration off his body.

She waited, saying nothing, and when he returned offered the comfort of her arms, stroking his hair to relax his tensed body. It was happening more frequently, and she was becoming more concerned. Eventually she felt the tension easing and he slowly drew away and reached for his dressing gown.

"I think I'll make that cup of tea." The cups rattled on their saucers as he crept back to the bedroom, and they drank in silence with Barry uncomfortably perched on the end of the bed.

"The same?" She couldn't wait any longer for him to speak, although she knew he would be reluctant to talk.

"Worse."

"In what way?"

"Death. I was being lowered into a grave with the others standing around drinking champagne. I reached for help and Mike handed me some secateurs to cut the ropes. Patrick was undressing you with one hand, and laughing and waving an insurance policy with his other. I kicked out in desperation and found myself on the floor."

"Scrap it. It's not worth your health."

"I can't! They put me in this position! They're guilty, not me! It's the only way I can fight back. The only way I can justify myself. They destroyed my career, what else can I do?" He spoke with so much anger.

She felt his hurt as if it was hers, but with a hopelessness that the help she could offer was running out. The sex had been great to start with. A release I suppose. Then the dining out, finding the in-places, boozing, more wild sex, and the quieter moments. They'd spent many evenings at home listening to their favourite music and sipping expensive chilled wines. The long walks, the lazy lovemaking on the moors. This was the best her life had produced so far, and she wanted it to last. Oh, how she wanted it to last! Deep down however she'd been fooling herself that this was for ever, and that the Bonnie and Clyde fun would see them through. But it wouldn't. It didn't in the film. She knew it was escapism for Barry, and that the insurance fiddles were not the real man. No wonder the nightmares were getting worse. Conscience, self-esteem. It would kill him if they weren't careful.

Halfpenny Green was an old RAF base not far from Bridgnorth and a short flight from Welshpool where Barry had based his latest purchase.

He'd sorted out a small operator who'd done a very smart job on November Whisky and it really looked the part. Barry produced a bundle of false invoices for work done with some fancy spare parts and an avionics fix. All in all he now had paper work to the tune of some twenty thousand pounds and he stuffed badly-copied versions in the side cockpit pockets, to be found by the insurers, hopefully.

He wasn't happy this time and the nightmares back at his bungalow a few nights ago had been too real for comfort. He'd sent Judy home to her houseboat and promised he'd see her again after this was over, "I need some space." She was hurt but understood.

He mooched around for a couple of days trying to choose the right moment and fiddled around with the wig and some scratchy make-up. He was just about to leave that morning when the telephone rang.

"Barry. Tom Goff."

"Tom. Haven't seen you for some time. How is it?"

"Mustn't grumble. Making a crust."

"Why this honour?" Tom usually only rang if he wanted something. He remembered the old card playing days when Tom subtly reminded him to bring the wine.

"Your insurers on Echo Tango were on to me the other day. Queries to do with your experience. I had to tell them something.

They were after your last employer, but I put them off there. Thought it might be important. This one's settled isn't it?"

"Yes. No problems. Probably due to a new quote I was after. Don't worry, but thanks for the call."

"Don't forget that lunch offer."

"I won't." He replaced the receiver gently, unhappy with this latest twist. I wonder? The extension rang again before he could give further thought to Tom's conversation. He recognised Tim's voice with some concern. 'Why now? Was someone trying to send a message?'

"Barry. Remiss of me not to contact you earlier. Been pretty busy but that's no excuse for not making the time. How are you? Miss the banter and the training sessions, apart from your cheerful self."

"Not bad Tim. I still get low sometimes. The facts still hurt. It's hard to forget."

"Look I've some news that might please you. Not over the air. Let's meet after my next trip. Going to Niger." They arranged a date and Barry decided to get out of the house now before he experienced any further interruptions. He put the remaining false documents in his flight bag and drove out to Welshpool for his calculated flight to Halfpenny Green.

Chapter Twenty-Eight

The monitor bleeped its monotonous rhythm with a clinical efficiency as if to say everything is working this end. In the controlled chaos and bustle of hospital life, the silent body hooked up to the machines with drips and pipes connected to various parts could have been anyone. The nurse worked her way down the intensive care ward lifting the cards hooked on the bed ends and quietly read out the details to herself.

She stopped by the machine and registered it counting a steady heartbeat. Having checked the rest of the plumbing she studied the face for any signs of recognition. The patient was still unconscious and breathing with the help of a mask, so she busied herself by reading the prognosis from the doctor's notes. She notice a charred hairpiece on the table.

Simon Fury. Male. Fractures to the right elbow and femur. Suspected rupture of the spleen. Suspected fracture of the skull. Burns to face and hands. Multiple cuts and bruises. Serious concussion on admittance.

Wonder what had happened there? It was a passing thought. She'd seen it all before. Probably some jerk on a motorbike. It was difficult to feel any sympathy for many of the patients, who seemed to heap trouble on their own backs. Her feelings were influenced by the fact that her boyfriend had recently hospitalised two girls in a car accident, driving too fast on a country road. I was all right for him, he only got the remorse. They saw the results of their carelessness, and had to do the mending. It was enough to put her off boys. She knew that was stupid because she loved them really, especially when they worked her body.

The coughing made her turn, and she saw that the man's eyes were open with a rather wild look as he tried to see around the room.

"Careful now. You've had a bad accident. Lie still for the moment. Can you hear me?" He grunted a reply which she assumed was yes, and pointed to the mask with his free hand.

The duty doctor breezed through the swinging doors and the nurse grabbed his arm before he disappeared through the next doors. "Is it okay to take this patient off the air?"

"If he's breathing sound, use your judgement."

She unhooked the gadget and checked that he was coping normally before cooling his face with a wet towel.

"Wher'm I?" The words were slurred and he was having difficulty speaking.

"Birmingham General. What happened?"

His eyes went starry again as he drifted back to unconsciousness. She replaced the air mask and, making sure he was comfortable, left the ward.

"Guy in six is knocked about. How'd it happen?" she asked the matron.

"I believe it was a flying accident. We haven't got much info."

Neither of them realised it at the time, but they both received the news simultaneously and both by the same media. One received it with curiosity and the other with fear in the heart, for both had vested interests but both for totally different reasons. It had come at the end of the news as a throwaway item.

"We're getting reports of a light aeroplane crash in the Midlands. No details are available at present other than that the plane apparently caught fire after landing. There's no information regarding the pilot or passengers. We'll report any further findings in our next bulletin at..."

She froze with the remote control unit held tightly in her hand and sat gazing into the empty space behind the television set. She became aware of a spider which was idly weaving a web in the corner and watched it mesmerised as it swung between the wall and a flower pot.

The Midlands he'd said. It was the Midlands wasn't it. But where? Barry wouldn't tell her his full plans this time, and they hadn't parted on the best of terms. It would be around that area. She gripped her stomach to hold off the sickening feeling. It could be anyone. Why Barry? There were hundreds of planes flying on any day, surely. Somehow she couldn't convince herself and she

experienced a horrible sinking feeling. 'Come on Bonnie, where's
your go and guts?' But she didn't feel the go. All she felt was gutted.

Dennis rationalised the news thinking it was a coincidence that a
small plane should crash at this time. Not unusual though, when his
business was connected with the subject, and of course his current
investigations added some spice to the news item. 'I'll know soon
enough, in any case.,
    The drink with Bob Lewis had been interesting and there was little
doubt left in his mind that Johnston, Hastings and now Fury was the
same man. Bob was alerted and assured Dennis that he'd be the first
to know.
    "Do we involve the police?"
    "Depends. We'd have to prove intent first."
    "Pretty obvious I would have thought."
    "Not necessarily. Could just be coincidence or bad luck."
    "He'd never hang that one. There are the name changes, not to
say the possibility of disguise."
    "No crime in changing your name or dressing up. Maybe he's a
frustrated transvestite?"
    "Seriously, you don't believe that?"
    Dennis sipped the Chianti in amusement, for Bob appeared to show
shock on his young face. 'Not streetwise yet. Still, probably makes
millions on the market by just shifting numbers around while I
struggle to invest in a pension. Depends on what excitement you're
after. Good luck to him.'
    "We'll see."
    "Yes."
    "Still nothing's happened yet. For all we know you've insured one
happy pilot whose only desire is to scoot around the clouds until his
final hour."
    Bob had to go, so Dennis drifted home with a yen to update Gill on
the latest conclusions but somehow he felt the need for different
stimulation. Someone had told him about a drinking club in the West
End that was very smart, rather expensive, but a bundle of fun. He
racked the memory for a name but all he could recall was some
connection with sweets. It's a sweet place, remember? Then it came,
of course – The Sugar Club.
    "Fifteen for entry. Ten per cent off Lanson up to nine o'clock."

Dennis was shown to a dimly-lit table and straight away started to enjoy the smoky atmosphere, and the soft blues from the piano.

"Who you watching?" The voice startled him. She walked to the table and sat down close. She was dark with a silky skin and sparkling hazel eyes. Beautiful eyes, warm and uninhibited. She wore a white top which showed off her tanned figure, and a silly girdle of string to tease the view of her long legs. She kicked off her shoes and curled her arms around his. "Tell me."

"Nobody, really."

"Where are you from?"

"I live on the Thames. You?"

"Everywhere."

"Thank you." He nodded to the waiter as he poured the Black Lanson into their glasses.

"You like him?" She was watching Dennis as he tapped his fingers to the music coming from the pianist in the corner.

"He's good."

"Give me your favourite and we dance."

They moved to the tiny dance area and she lent over to speak into the pianist's ear.

"Julian. He's the best. Plays anything." She pressed her pelvis into his, watching the smile on his face as Dennis hardened. "Can we play?"

"When can you leave?"

"One thirty. Maybe earlier."

"Jesus! That's another five hours, I'll be paralytic by then."

"Give me a taxi fare and I'll come and see you later."

"You for real? I don't believe you," he said as they danced.

Later she held out her hand with a wicked smile which melted Dennis as he slipped her a twenty pound note. He left suspecting he'd been done but happy with the diversion. 'Must have a slash before I go,' he decided as he made his way to the toilet. Working toward the exit he couldn't miss the Irish lilt coming from the bar and he delayed to have 'one for the road'. Paddy was in full flow and the girls fondling him were in their element.

He tasted his drink and signalled to the barman. "Who's the boss?"

"The Irishman sir?

"You've got it."

"Not sure but I believe he owns an airline. Spends a few bob in here."

"Really? D'you know the name?"

"What his or the airline?"

"Both."

"Hang on." The barman collared his assistant as Dennis waited in anticipation. "Patrick. That's what they call him. Dunno about his business, somewhere down south. Bournemouth I think."

'I wonder,' he thought, "Marvel Air?"

"Don't connect."

"Okay. Thanks. Thought it was someone I knew. Some other time, eh?"

He grabbed the first taxi outside the club, with a reminder that he must check the Marvel Air scene so that he'd got the full CV on Johnston.

The bell woke him from a deep sleep and it took him several minutes to register that it was real and not a dream. He slipped into his dressing gown and walked to the door wondering who was there. He stopped for a minute thinking maybe it's that snooper from the pub.

"What d'you want?"

"Did you think I'd let you down?"

He opened the door to feel her warmth and admire the way she slunk so confidently into his lounge. He closed the door and turned as she slipped off her coat to reveal her body, totally naked and on offer for his pleasure.

The dawn was just breaking as the phone went. "Chertsey 7300." He had to reach over her body to pick up the receiver.

"You sound bushed. Still in bed?" Christ, it was Gill.

"Had a rough night. All this obsession stuff, and your accusations."

"I'll be with you in ten minutes. On the mobile just passing through Wimbledon."

"Shit, get up..." He started to shove her out of the bed, "I don't even know your name."

"Danielle." She tried to chew his nipples.

"Danielle. Leave it. Sorry. My girl's arriving in ten minutes."

"Tonight again maybe? You like to compare." She giggled.

"Ring me. But please get your arse out of here quick, otherwise you'll be witness to a murder."

The doorbell rang and Dennis looked round in panic. She'd gone, vanished. Each to their own skills, he thought, and she's skilled.

Chapter Twenty-Nine

"Six hours door to door. Not bad considering the age." Tim said as he talked to Hogan about the One Eleven's performance. He filled in the paperwork for the flight room of Lagunda Airport. "So far so good."

Patrick had organised the packaging and they were to be met by a courier using a code name, Ocean.

They hovered around whilst the airport authorities rummaged through the documentation asking for passports, medical certificates and other unnecessary papers. Hogan felt nervous and certainly didn't want to meet Azif's lot again or the others. An hour passed and still they were held from passing through customs. Suddenly this enormous figure, well over six foot, was standing behind the desk, waving the paperwork in front of them.

His features where of polished ebony and the sweat was pouring off his face. The hulk of the man was enough, but his odour was awful and Tim wished he could close his nose as well as his mouth.

"These parcels, the documents are not in order, you understand?" Here we go, trouble's starting. Hogan knew he shouldn't have come back. He relived the dross of the roads, and tried not to imagine what the cells were like.

"Your representatives at Heathrow stamped them as correct." The large black face beamed at the naiveté of the statement, and Tim found himself looking down a toothless chasm which stank of stale beer and garlic.

"These parcels. What are they?"

"Engineering parts as far as I know. That's what the papers say."

"You must wait." With that he shuffled them into a back office, leaving himself through a side door.

"I could murder a beer or something." They tried the duty officer lounging in the corner, but he chose not to understand, so they were stuck in this tiny hot room with a ceiling fan which didn't work.

"Nice start to our holiday. Might as well enjoy it Tim – great place."

"Bugger off Hogan. Where do we go from here?"

"If I learnt anything last visit you need two things in this country. One is patience and t'other's cash. He'll be back."

The ebony man let them sweat for another hour and returned with a smart uniformed official with lots of impressive gold braiding. "Mr Mitchell, could I see your passports please."

"You've got them sir." Tim tried to sound calm even though he was getting cross and worried.

"Have we?" He turned to the hulk who shrugged his shoulders. He gestured him to go and look.

Hogan was reaching saturation point and decided the direct approach was needed. This guy was obviously smarter, or not so big, anyhow.

"Your President, you like him?"

"As a good citizen, I must respect his authority."

"Fine." 'Like hell he does. Slit his throat if he got half a chance.'

"Now as a good citizen you need to understand that we're working for your President's office and we have an appointment in one hour from now. If you delay us further I'll have to advise them of your involvement." He took the hand-held transceiver from Tim's flight bag, one of the few items not confiscated, and dialled in a frequency. "That's confirmed Joe. Ten minutes from now. Code name's Ocean. Don't delay."

The official grabbed the portable and screamed abuse at them both.

"You can shout the house down but if we're not out of here in ten minutes, I've just left instructions with a colleague to inform your President's office that we're being held as hostages by yourselves."

He could see the official didn't know whether to believe him or not by the way his eyes rolled about. Hogan decided not to waste any more time. He drew the bundle from his back pocket and stuffed it under the guy's nose.

"If I'm wrong you get the money anyway. If I'm right you get the money but it's no good because you're finished. Understand, comprendi?" He wasn't sure on the logic but waved the bundle again and dumped it on the counter.

It took a moment, as his head darted from the money to the papers, and then suddenly they were being hurried through the concourse and found themselves standing on the broken pavement outside of the building. The courier called the black limousine which slid up to them, and Hogan could just recognise Azif through the smoked window sitting in the back.

"Welcome to Lagunda." He smiled cynically. "It's nice to see you back." They drove to a restaurant out of town and were shown to a private room at the back of the building. Suitably seated and with drinks supplied, Azif produced a bound report from his briefcase and placed it before Tim. "I'm pleased to meet you Captain Mitchell, I believe you require this?"

Tim flicked through the pages and studied the calculations and circuit diagrams which meant little to him. Azif leant forward and turned his attention to the heading, *Conclusion*. He started to read then Hogan butted in, "Out loud Tim?"

"...In my opinion the magnetic field and frequency band of this device could have influenced electronic equipment operating in the same hertz scale up to a radius of two miles from the transmitting aerial. I have been asked for an opinion as to whether such frequencies might tally with the instruments used for navigating aircraft, and my answer to that is yes, for some of the directional navigation equipment."

"What d'you think?" Azif said looking pleased with himself.

"This is technically genuine?"

"I can guarantee it. Gentlemen we must get on. Your merchandise has been checked and is already on way to its destination. I thank you for your help. We'll not meet again."

"Hold on Azif," Hogan said as he stood up. "Last time I was here you nearly got me blown to bits. How come you're so relaxed about that?"

"They've been dealt with. You have my word. I couldn't tell you. We needed you to winkle them out."

"Michael Webber?"

"Eliminated – all. Your bad friends in England also. You may relax." He held out his hand and Hogan realised the party was over.

Hogan settled back to enjoy the flight from the co-pilot's seat sipping a gin and tonic not normally allowed on the flight deck. He stretched his aching leg and glanced contentedly toward Tim. 'So that's it, another satisfied customer for Hogan Investigations. All I want now is my payoff and the insurance on the office and I'm away to foreign parts for good. West Indies I favour. Probably buy myself an orange grove and shack-up with a local girl. Drink and shag myself to an early grave.'

Tim interrupted his thoughts. "Thinking of retiring? You'll be back. Sounds good, but you'll miss the intrigue and the adrenalin, I bet."

"Like a toothache, to be sure."

"I might need you for the enquiry?"

"Forget it Tim. I'm away. You're on your own now."

"But how come I got this report?"

"You commissioned this guy who wrote it. Tough that he's not available, but as long as the conclusions aren't challenged, that's all you need."

Tim adjusted the autopilot to change course for Barcelona which was a waypoint on his return route. "How come I got hold of the electronic equipment referred to in the report, and where's it now?"

"You didn't. You rely on the caretaker's evidence of electrical gear being delivered and the bloody great aerial on the roof."

"Circumstantial surely?"

"Look. As I see it you're only trying to establish that there's positive evidence of radio interference that could have affected the information being displayed to the pilot that evening. You don't have to prove it. Just win on the possibility and create the beyond reasonable doubt argument. Hell I sound like your legal advisor. You get the gist?"

"Reckon I need a bit more." Tim chewed on some imaginary food as he talked. "I need someone else who was affected by this interference. Not necessarily that day, but on and off while Azif was in the flat."

They both pontificated on this point and Hogan looked down over the Sahara Desert finding the same emptiness of inspiration there. Tim concentrated on flying and talking to air traffic control.

"The caretaker. Must watch the box all the time. Flexible isn't he?"

Tim nodded with agreement. "I'll try. Fix yourself another drink."

Chapter Thirty

"Fraud I suppose."

"On all three?"

"Well probably two. You'd have to prove intent on the third. I assume there's no claim at the moment?"

"No. I mean yes. A claim has been made. After all it appears to be a genuine accident and it might be difficult to prove that it was planned but went wrong. Of course the insurers are holding on my advice. That's why I said no at first."

Malcolm Jones had only recently qualified for junior counsel but was already being hailed as an astute lawyer, with the target of QC not far away in the eyes of his colleagues. Dennis had used him on a couple of occasions and found his clear mind very refreshing on legal jargon.

"How long ago was the last accident?"

"Must be three months. He was in hospital for some time, badly concussed I understand."

"So have charges been lodged?"

"I believe they're imminent. The police have only recently been able to finish their enquiries due to Mr Johnston's health."

"And the prosecution?"

"Francis Aviation, Medway Services and Blair-Lloyd."

"Substantial?"

"Yes. First one's run by an astute woman whose father's well heeled. No fears there. Second's been established for many years. Last, he's new in the business, but broking through Lloyds."

"And you want me to run this case?"

"Miss Francis asked me for some names and I put yours forward."

Malcolm nodded and referred to the notes that Dennis had prepared and then lit a small cigar as he started to read.

The lull in their conversation gave Dennis time to survey the small chambers and the scruffy, almost Dickensian surroundings of cracked leather chairs and faded, dark oil paintings. The ceiling was well yellowed and the walls where covered with bookshelves of old and dusty law cases which Dennis doubted had ever been used. The only feature that brought you back to the twentieth century was the sprinkling of Mercedes and BMWs which filled the courtyard spaces, just visible through the leaded-glass windows. 'Fees up front and not to be spent on fancy offices, I'm jealous. Friday afternoon back to the country farm. Not a bad life?'

"So let me get this clear. You wish to bring charges of fraud or intended fraud for three of your clients. I assume you're leading with one of these companies with the intention of having the others taken into consideration?"

"Yes."

"And part of your pleadings are that the accused used false names on his insurance proposals. Also – bear with me – he purposely over-insured with intent to profit from destruction of his aircraft, and then deliberately set out to crash the aeroplanes beyond repair to cash in on the insurance?"

"That's the nuts and bolts of it."

"I must say I find such behaviour most extraordinary. Daring maybe but very foolish. Whatever possessed the man to take such desperate measures to make such small gains." 'Small to you maybe, but thirty grand doesn't come easy to everyone,' Dennis sympathised.

He'd done his homework with Marvel Air after the information obtained from the CAA girl and the chance passing of the owner, Patrick Clancy, at the Sugar Club. He found out about Mr Johnston's background and the High Court case which had resulted in Barry losing his commercial licence. He outlined the facts with his opinion as to why Barry had gone off the rails.

"I see, how unfortunate."

"He may have had a raw deal, I don't know. But that doesn't justify his subsequent actions."

"Of course not. Now what evidence do we have to convict the accused on the accident in France. La Baule was it? Lovely area. Enjoyed some fine sailing in the bay."

"Insurance mark-up."

"But that could have been fortuitous. Luck of the draw. The accused was using his proper name. How can we prove that he deliberately crashed?

"You may be right, but I'm sure that's where he got the idea."

"Not strong material for the court. No... not good at all. We may all have thought of deception or even murder in stressful occasions, but we can't be held liable for our thoughts. We may be able to use the evidence to establish the background to future actions, but I'm doubtful whether your client has any other recall on the information you have logged."

"So what are your recommendations?"

"Number two. I feel the situation in Norfolk has plenty of scope. We have a false name, some evidence of medical hoaxing, and some good reliable witnesses."

"And the other?"

"That was...?" He studied the notes, "Blair-Lloyd. Should be cleared from any payment liability providing we can win on the lead charge."

"Right, what else d'you need?"

"Nothing at this stage. Later I may need to take some statements from our selected witnesses."

Dennis left with an admiring glance at the cars parked outside.

Chapter Thirty-One

Patrick put down the report and searched for any positive signs from Tim. It was hot in the office and small beads of sweat surfaced above his eyebrows.

"Why are you showing me this?" He was feeling unusually tired and weary and in need of a holiday. The call to Chuck hadn't helped, especially as they were both worried about being overheard. At least the cash, which Pat badly needed to pay his backer's dividend, was on the way from Ireland. Dianne was being a pain again and kept ranting about his 'whoring', and how she would 'see him in hell.'

"I think we've an obligation to present this evidence if only for Barry's sake."

"What, reopen the trial?"

"If necessary, yes."

"But the trial's happened and judgement given for sure. Can't go back?"

"It must be possible. Appeal to the Home Secretary or something. If this report's right, Barry may have been found guilty incorrectly."

Patrick wiped the perspiration from his face and confronted Tim over the table. "Let it drop. What's to be done's done. I can't allow a retrial or whatever. Jesus, the company could be taken for negligence in bringing the case at all. I can't afford that."

"We have a duty."

"Sod our duty! Are you going back in the box and say you got it wrong?"

"I don't think my evidence was that positive. Besides, that's not the point."

"So, what's the point?"

"I've told you, duty."

"No."

"Is that your last word?" Before he could answer Pat's secretary breezed in with some letters for posting. He signed them mechanically hardly glancing at the contents. "Mike would like to see you before you leave tonight," she said.

"After I've finished with Mitchell."

Patrick studied the desktop for some time before he spoke to Tim softly. "You've done a great job for me, and believe me I owe you for that. But no, I'm not prepared to run this one." He meant it, that was for sure. "Where did the report come from anyway?"

"I commissioned it."

"You commissioned it," he repeated. "Why?"

Tim didn't answer at first as he stood up and circled round the room." I always believed Barry's evidence – that the instruments were on the blink. He had too much experience to make the mistakes he was accused of."

He paused to check whether Patrick agreed with his view. "Also I always felt there was some stigma attached to me as chief instructor. Some blemish in my training methods, you could say. Not something I want to feature on my career details."

"Your career's safe with me, but it mightn't be if you push for this action."

"I hear your concern Pat, and I understand. But this time I've a slice of the chair. I know about your dealings with Iran. I've met Azif. I've had a private detective checking you all out."

Pat took it well, he gave him that. The tough upbringing might be thinning, but it was yet to show any holes. "We'll need an opinion."

"You agree then?"

"No I damn well don't agree! I'll not put my weight behind this. It'll be run through the lawyers on the basis that it came to hand. No pressure from me." Pat was getting angry and was not enjoying being forced into this unwelcome corner.

"Who will you use?"

"Donald Opperman. No reason to change."

"Fine. Can you let me know the outcome. I'd like to be the first to let Barry know."

"You'll be keeping that mouth of yours shut now until I say." He banged the table, "That's an order."

Tim reckoned he'd got enough and thanked Patrick for his concern and how he'd agonised over the matter as to whether to raise it or not. His integrity, honesty – he laid it as thick as he dared.

172

"Tens for crap. People are expendable. Time you learned that Mitchell. Who was it said the graves of England were full of indispensable people? Remember we're nothing in this universe."

"Thank you Pat for listening, and the lecture. Be warned however that I'm genuinely serious. I have to be."

"I think you've made that quite clear, even to this thick Paddy."

It was over and Tim walked through to the outer office telling Pat's secretary that he was now free to see Mike.

"I'd welcome an audience with Mr Opperman as soon as possible. It's urgent."

"What was the name again?"

Tim was concerned and knew he was taking a gamble. He needed to get in before Patrick persuaded the lawyer otherwise.

"I'm afraid Mr Opperman's tied up till next week. He's in court for the next five days."

'Damn. I must see him.' Tim struggled to find a way to break through.

"Please ma'am can you not find a way? You can have everything I've got. I must talk to him."

"If I took the offers I get each day, Mr Mitchell, I'd be a rich woman. I can make one suggestion. Counsel occasionally meets clients in his club during sessions in London, providing it's nothing to do with the case in question. He sometimes welcomes the distraction from matters he cannot discuss during the trial."

"Great. I can meet him anytime. Tonight if he wants."

"I shan't be able to arrange a meeting until he returns to chambers. Is there somewhere I can contact you?" Tim gave her the lot. The office, home, the car mobile, and his sister's, who had tentatively suggested it was about time he bought her a drink.

She found him on the mobile and fixed him for that night. "Gresham Club. Yes I've got that. Nine thirty. You're a darling, I'll marry you."

"Remember I can take you for fifty per cent of your assets," she joked.

"Now that's not friendly after our loving conversation."

"No, but it's guaranteed to put you off the scent. Good luck with Donald."

She obviously meant it, and Tim thanked her again. 'A sporting girl I reckon, if you got to know her.'

The Gresham Club had all the history and the grace of times past, with a slightly fading opulence which suggested the members might have seen better financial days. Tim signed in and the doorman tannoyed for a Mr Opperman to come to reception.

In fact a smartly dressed usher arrived and showed Tim into a small smoking room. "Mr Opperman will be with you shortly. He asked me to offer you a drink."

"Thank you, but not at this moment. Maybe a glass of water."

Tim paced around to steady a slight nervousness and was admiring an oil painting of a schooner in heavy seas when a voice broke the silence.

"Mr Mitchell." Tim turned to be offered a firm handshake and a gesture to be seated in a large leather-bound chair by the Georgian fireplace. "We've met before." It was said in a flat tone that could make it a statement or a question.

"You remember a High Court action you took for Marvel Air – some two years ago? I was one of the witnesses. We met at briefings and I believe after judgement."

"Of course! I recall the trial. The ubiquitous Patrick Clancy. Is he the subject of our meeting?" Donald beamed at news of the old renegade.

"I need your advice sir. Something has cropped up and I'm unclear on how to handle it."

"Um. So how can I assist?"

The usher returned with a tray of iced water, a bottle of twelve year old Ballantyne whisky and two heavy cut glass tumblers.

"For you?" Donald indicated the malt.

"Small please." He changed his mind hoping that acceptance of the offer would lubricate the informal meeting.

The drinks poured, Donald dismissed the waiter and crossed his legs settling comfortably in the matching fire chair. "I await your discourse."

Tim chose his words carefully and slowly as he picked his way through his findings. He related his concerns regarding the evidence at trial and the nagging questions that had never left him. He recited the detective work he'd carried out, leaving the Hogan escapades untold. He explained his personal reasons for his actions and confirmed that the electronic report had been instigated by himself.

Donald listened intently without interruption, except for the occasional clink of ice as he topped up the tumblers.

Tim continued and finally got to the meeting he'd had with Patrick and his concern that Marvel Air would not be prepared to take any action to clear Barry's name.

"I'm not sure they can. But go on." It was the first comment.

"I asked to see you urgently, because I anticipate that Mr Clancy will be in contact, and I wanted you briefed so that you'd have the whole story. I'm not trying to go behind Patrick's back, or say that he wouldn't give you the whole story. I..." he paused to find the right words, "I'm concerned about any... slant of the facts..., that sounds awful." He gulped down the spirit with a spluttered cough, and realised his hand was shaking as he replaced the glass on the side table.

Donald crossed and recrossed his legs and placed his hands on the back of his head, then massaged his eyes as if to squeeze out an opinion.

"Now I know why I took Law. It never ceases to surprise, it never ceases to interest, and there's rarely an absolute answer."

Tim listened patiently for words of wisdom.

"We have a problem. This was a criminal action and the Crown has decided. There was no appeal?" Tim indicated not. "So we have some new facts, so what?"

Tim didn't want to interrupt but he had to. "Are you saying the trial can't be reopened?".

"In a nutshell yes. Trials can be reopened, but only if new evidence is strong enough, to show there's been a miscarriage of justice. One would also have to prove that the original evidence was incorrect or misleading."

"How d'you do that?"

"With difficulty my friend."

"Can we get a pardon?"

"That's the same course. Compensation, pardon – both require a retrial with the blessing of Government intervention."

"Such as?"

"Home Secretary? – Justice Minister?

"Is that a...?" He dried up as the expression on Donald's face gave him the answer before he could complete the question.

Donald's eyes drifted to the clock over the mantelpiece and he checked this with his watch. "Mr Mitchell, Tim isn't it? I have to leave you now because I have to do some reading for tomorrow's cross-examination. I've got the basis for your concerns and I understand your dilemma. Leave it with me and I'll give it some thought and maybe discuss it with my colleagues. I assume you'd rather I act cautiously with Mr Clancy at this stage, should he contact me?"

Tim indicated that he'd be very grateful if confidences could be held for a while.

"Well done. Thank you for contacting me. You can find your own way out?"

They shook hands and Tim walked down the marble stairs and out to face the noise and bustle of London's West End evening trade.

Chapter Thirty-Two

They sat in silence in the Queen's Head whose emptiness echoed their mood on a cold and windy day. Barry stared at the letter and realised it was blown.

He'd handled the police interview skilfully but he knew that someone must have compiled a dossier on his activities by the depth of some of the questions.

"You say your name's Simon Fury?"

"No. The aeroplane was registered in that name. My name's Johnston."

The officer studied his notes and nodded. "So why Simon Fury?"

"It's a little quirk of mine. One can register under any name. Also I had some bad luck when I was flying commercially and didn't want my real name to come up on the CAA computer. They can be funny sometimes." It sounded plausible, but the officer continued to ask about Barry's past and noted the facts very conscientiously.

"And Tony Hastings?"

"Sorry, I'm not with you."

"You're aware of this name?"

Barry decided to remain silent hoping they were fishing on the Norfolk crash. After all Medway Services had paid out and he assumed this investigation was to determine liability to the latest insurers.

"You seem to have developed a habit of flying planes into the ground."

It was a statement rather than a question.

"I haven't had the best of luck lately."

"These papers. You recognise them?" The sergeant was holding some charred remains in a folder which he passed to Barry.

"Yes."

"Can you enlarge on that?"

"They're bills for work I had done on the aeroplane."

"I see. Perhaps you could tell me what this one's about?"

Barry took the sheet. "Engine gauges, gyros and the like, I had a refit."

"Funny, our investigators were not able to identify this equipment."

"Maybe it was destroyed in the fire."

"You remember a fire then?"

"Well no. I was... told."

"They found some old equipment. Perhaps you didn't throw that away?"

"I'm not sure." But he was sure he was getting into deep water.

"Let me ask..."

Barry interrupted. "Sorry I'm not feeling too well, my bloody leg. Could you get the nurse?"

His injuries allowed him to feign some of the answers and a few months had passed since the police enquiries. Judy chased the insurance company but they'd been vague saying that they hadn't completed their valuation assessment on November Whisky.

The letter said it all and Barry pushed it across the table to Judy.

"...my client has reason to believe that the incident may not have been accidental and is not therefore able to settle your claim at this time. Further investigations are being undertaken and we must advise you that these may result in legal action. We strongly advise you to show the contents of this letter to a solicitor..."

She passed it back and they stared at each other for some inspiration.

Judy broke the silence. "We knew the risk."

"Yes, but we didn't expect to be caught."

"You had your reasons."

"What? Sour grapes because I was found guilty? Hardly gives me rights to fraud."

"What will you get?" He could see her eyes moistening.

"No idea. Fine probably. Maybe prison. Remember I have a record."

They went silent again and Barry didn't even feel like drinking the beer in front of him.

"South America." He broke the silence again.

178

"What d'you mean?"

"We'll go to South America. Others have done it."

"And live on what? – and in hiding. You're talking crazy."

"There's nothing left here for me now. This time I'll lose every licence. No flying again. But that's my life Judy. Don't you understand?" He gripped her arm across the table as he forced her to listen.

"I understand, but you can't keep running. You'll have to bite the bullet and explain why you did it."

"And you. You were my accomplice. Bonnie remember? What if they involve you?"

"I did it for love. I stand by that. Women do you know."

The commotion broke their dialogue as a bunch of young sailing types burst into the pub. The clatter of glasses and laughter drowned out conversation for them as did the din from the music box. Barry managed an envious smile and wished he was blessed with the freedom of these youngsters. Face the music. Judy's advice. Do a bunk... He held his head as the depression hit him again and he felt his legs collapsing with the room swimming around. Then darkness closed in.

Judy was watching the sailing lads as she heard the crunch and turned to see Barry spread-eagled on the floor. She quickly checked his pulse and then called for help.

Chapter Thirty-Three

London was having one of its rare foggy November days, less rare than the old-time smogs, as Donald Opperman hurried along the Kingsway to the CAA building. It was cold for the time of year and he was grateful for the warmth of his thick Crombie coat. 'One of the wife's better presents,' he thought as he felt the coldness of the swirling mist trying to penetrate his body.

At the same hour Malcolm Jones was showing his briefcase to the security guard at the entrance to the Criminal Courts. He walked through and shook hands with Dennis Hopkins who was standing inside and indicated a bench for them both to sit. "Room thirteen. I've checked the board. Judge Pearson. D'you know him?"

"Recent promotion I hear. Very harsh on physical violence they say, but a bit soft on deception type cases."

"How long are we set down for?"

"All week, I believe. Probably half a day for openers and half for Friday, that gives us four days roughly."

"Um. Sufficient I suppose?"

"Depends on Johnston's defence and how long-winded that might be. Our case should be pretty tight providing the witnesses hold up well."

"Who are you calling?"

"The farmer Bakewell, Miss Francis and yourself, and maybe Mr Alton. I've put Tom Goff on notice but I think he'll probably be hostile as he's an old mate of the accused. I've also produced affidavits from the brokers who dealt with the girlfriend who took out the insurances."

"Has she been charged?"

"No. Blair-Lloyd decided not. They felt she might have been an innocent to the fraud, not knowing what was going on. Also she's a very good-looker and I understand Pearson's a ladies man. Only forty-eight. That's young for a judge. A bachelor as well I hear."

180

Heads turned and they saw why, as their defendant was escorted into the building and up the steps to the courtroom. He was blown a kiss by Judy who was extracting as much publicity as she could. The pressman had caught her on camera outside, and she was busy talking to a tousle haired reporter as she followed Barry. She made her way to the public gallery.

They'd talked it over and decided he should plead not guilty to the charges of over-insuring with intent to defraud, but guilty to obtaining insurance using false names. There were two charges for deliberate damage to aircraft with intent to defraud, but he'd decided to plead mitigating circumstances. 'Blackouts or just a bloody bad pilot' – he might use it?

It had to happen.

Judy had decided to dress in her gypsy style, although this time she'd spent heavily and the colours of her bright skirt blended beautifully with the lime green blouse. Although it was winter, she'd chosen a neck cut which showed a hint of smooth brown shoulders and she'd emphasised this by wearing a narrow scarf around her long elegant neck. The gold earrings were distinct, and the gold chain round her ankle discreet. Her black hair had grown long and it nearly reached to the waist.

They almost tripped over each other.

Judge Pearson was hurrying from the robe room as Judy took the first step. She lost her balance and Pearson caught hold to stop her falling. Her shoulders shone brightly in front of his eyes and for a moment he was mesmerised by the beauty of this creature in his arms. She'd no idea who he was, but the smile of thanks on her face was given as part of her act for the day. She regained her balance and the moment passed, but not without the Judge glancing back as he passed through the doorway. The reporter was making notes and Dennis managed a sly grin at the scene. A film star couldn't have done it better.

Two miles away another court of sorts was sitting to determine the future of the same man without any knowledge of the other proceedings.

Donald Opperman had been given an irrational lecture on the law and rights of a company, by a very cross Irishman with a lot of cursing and veiled remarks about loyalty, money and whatever else Patrick could muster to throw into the pot. It didn't amount to much in legal terms so Donald let him vent his feelings.

"I can't ignore the material that your Mr Mitchell has produced just because you don't like it."

"Sure to be sure. What's done's done, but I have an airline to run." They talked round all the angles, but agreed on one point for certain, that Tim wasn't going to let this one die on him.

"I doubt I can reopen in any case Patrick."

"Then don't, that's it."

"You know it isn't. We've just agreed."

"So what can he do?"

"Mitchell? Well, give it to the defence first for starters. He's threatening the press for seconds. Justice of the individual, failure of the courts and the like. They may not bite, but can you afford the publicity?"

"Shit. Just shit! That's all I get these days." He frowned his frustration and took a deep breath. "So what d'you advise?"

"A non-legal approach. Sort of mediation. Marriage counsel ruling. It might work for all parties."

Donald was shown to a sparsely furnished meeting room at the CAA headquarters where others were sipping weak coffee having dealt with the initial formalities. They spread themselves around the oval table and Stephen Oaks opened the proceedings.

"Gentlemen – we're here today at the request of Marvel Air to discuss matters related to an airmiss which was the subject of a High Court action last, um... some two and a half years ago. Before we start I would ask each person present to introduce themselves and who they represent so that there's no confusion to this meeting."

'I remember him now.' Donald whispered to himself. 'Very pedantic. Got a bit of a ruffling by that old fool Newall at the preliminary I was told. Gave good evidence during the trial though.'

"As this is not a legally constituted hearing I've not contacted the subject person, namely Mr Johnston nor have I informed his lawyers. I've been advised on this matter as the facts before us may have ramifications beyond the powers of the CAA which might not be in the interest of other parties. I had hoped that the Director in charge would have been with us today but unfortunately he's otherwise engaged. However, we've discussed the matter fully and he's given me the authority to chair this meeting. 'And you're loving it,' Donald thought. "We're honoured to have the presence of Mr Opperman QC who'll no doubt advise us on points of law should they creep in at all."

They went round the table and Donald noted, apart from Patrick and Tim, a beady-eyed gentleman who was present to take notes, two others, one who was a safety officer, and lastly a very relaxed character in an open-neck shirt, and in need of a haircut, who was introduced as an expert on navigation electronics. Donald saw Tim shuffle a bit at this information but didn't dwell on the observation.

"Mr Opperman sir, you called for this meeting so perhaps you'd like to open the proceedings."

Donald rustled his papers and stuck his thumbs behind the lapels of his suit only to realise he wasn't robed for court. He lowered his arms and picked up a pen to twiddle.

"Yes, surely. May I first thank your director for his indulgence in convening this meeting. In essence, and you'll be aware from the papers at your disposal, some evidence has appeared that could have a strong bearing on the judgement handed to Mr Johnston regarding the near miss action. As you know I prosecuted on that case and you may well ask why I'm raising this matter rather than defence counsel? I'm raising it because my client Marvel Air is a wholly respectable company," he guided their eyes to Patrick, "and they've expressed a wish to amend any wrongs, if proven, that may have occurred to a well respected ex-employee. You'll be aware that it's not easy in British justice to reopen criminal cases and hence I'm here today to suggest a non-legal compromise."

The beady-eyed clerk seemed to be taking notes longhand so Donald paused for all to digest his opening remarks. The electronic expert appeared to be taking no notice at all and was thumbing idly through his papers.

"You have before you a copy of the judgement and I would ask you to turn to page five, paragraph three." The table bustled into activity at this request to do something and Donald watched them adjusting their postures to less nervous positions. He continued: "You will read there that Judge Teal-Jones laid great emphasis on Mr Mitchell's evidence that if the captain, Mr Johnston, had been misled by a faulty autopilot, he still had sufficient back-up aids to make a safe landing. He goes on to review the evidence regarding a divert to another airport, but makes no great point of this option, other than evidence of possible low fuel. It's the former evidence which probably swayed the jury that day, resulting in a heavy fine and ultimately loss of the Captain's commercial licence through the offices of your good selves." He saw that Stephen Oaks was nodding in agreement, and that Tim was fidgeting as if an old wound had been opened.

"I've discussed this matter at length with Mr Mitchell and he tells me that the instruments of Oscar Mike were checked meticulously after the airmiss and no fault was ever found. It was on this basis that he reluctantly came to the conclusion that the Captain was in error on that near-fatal descent. However..." Donald paused to attend to an itch on his nose, "Mr Mitchell also tells me that he'd always considered something was missing and maybe there were other factors not at their disposal. He felt this strongly, partly because of the captain's experience, and partly because the incident reflected badly on his position as chief training captain."

"Therefore Captain Mitchell undertook an investigation of his own and you have before you a summary of his conclusions along with a report which seems to support a theory that Captain Johnston may have been misled by factors out of his control." He went on to outline the points that Tim had given him. Tim had filtered his evidence leaving out the Hogan/Azif connection, but had produced a strong affidavit from the caretaker on the equipment found in the flat and the erection of the aerial on the roof.

They listened intently and Tim was asked to comment on various parts of the reports. The navigation expert contributed very little but Oaks went over all the issues in minute detail such that Donald found his mind wandering to other matters.

The meeting dragged on until it was interrupted by two canteen ladies who breezed into the room with a plate of curled up sandwiches and some more weak coffee.

Donald rose to stretch his legs and collared Stephen Oaks on his own. "I hope we can wrap this up today?"

"I see no reason why not Mr Opperman."

"Donald please. But assuming you have all you need, how long will it be before your decision?"

"I can't give you a positive answer to that. I'll have to make a report – a matter of this importance will require a full board meeting."

"So no quick decision?"

"No less than the machinery of your profession I suspect." Donald suffered the dig. "Let me put it this way. We have a priority system with a sort of star point-scoring system. This case is probably only one star. I wouldn't expect a decision for two or three months."

Patrick returned from the toilets and pulled Donald over to a quiet corner. "Jesus! these boys are long-winded, 'specially that Oaks. What d'you reckon? They gonna play ball?"

"Probably. I think we've sown some doubt. They won't want an in-depth investigation. In the end it will hinge on safety. They can't afford to have dodgy pilots flying about."

The meeting continued until all were satisfied that they'd sucked dry most of the goodness from the pickings tabled. Stephen Oaks looked at his watch and took control again from the chair.

"I suggest we've given this matter a fair hearing and unless there are any more questions I would like Mr Opperman to summarise his request to this meeting." He waited for any comeback. "Mr Opperman?"

"Firstly, thank you again for your time. As I said in opening, the reason for this gathering is that my client does not wish to be party to any injustice that affects the future career of any of its employees. It appears from the evidence before you that Captain Johnston may have had a raw deal due to new evidence which has only just come to light. There are options to justice which could involve reopening the case but that lies strictly with Johnston's lawyers. My client is not anxious to pursue this course, as he'd like to avoid any further publicity which invariably interferes with the daily pressures of running an airline. At the end of the day the stigma that sticks with an accused is perhaps not so much the verdict, but more the fact that one has been found guilty of failing in a skill, when the back of one's mind is saying 'It wasn't my fault; it was out of my control.' We have evidence to support that theory, and if you feel that evidence is strong enough to say that the Captain was genuinely mislead by an autopilot which was picking up false signals, then I ask you to give Mr Johnston the benefit of the doubt and reinstate his commercial rating."

Donald left it at that.

There followed some minor procedural discussion before Stephen Oaks thanked them all for their time and closed the meeting, informing them that a decision would be made as soon as practicable.

They shook hands by the taxi. Patrick thanked Donald and asked to be kept posted.

"If they do reinstate Barry's licence will they have to say why?" Tim asked.

"I suspect not."

"So where do we lie?"

"We'll need to expose our hand to his lawyers. We can't predict their reaction, but we cannot withhold our evidence."

"When?"

"Oh, I think we can stretch a point on that. After all, you haven't quite finished all your investigations have you?" Donald winked knowingly.

"Surely the Captain is entitled to serious compensation for misjustice?"

"You may well be right, but as we've discussed before, we can't predict the decision of a new jury. They may well find that your prognostications aren't adequate."

"And I pick up the costs of a retrial," Pat moaned.

"Let's wait for the CAA's decision, and then review the matter. Some generosity on Patrick's part will I'm sure win the day." Donald smiled at the Irishman as he made his final goodbye.

"Sugar Club?"

"Not tonight Pat, I'm feeling bushed." Tim meant it.

"Perfect reason for going. You owe me one for all this hassle."

"Sorry no. Another time. Anyhow I'm flying tomorrow."

"Okay. Leave your old boss to the temptations of the flesh. I haven't got many years left for this game so I might as well enjoy them before they come to take me away." Patrick screwed a grin from his tired face as he left Tim standing by the kerb.

Chapter Thirty-Four

The bundles were emptied from the trolleys and the ushers arranged them on the front of the benches. Copies were placed for the judge and another set out for the witness box.

There being twenty minutes before the Court assembled, Malcolm Jones sat and studied his notes to the prosecution and the list of witnesses. He noted that a young barrister, one Nigel Waite, was defending but he'd been unsuccessful in finding out any background on his learned colleagues skills or history.

The court became busy and the jury were allocated their places. Barry Johnston was shown to his seat by a junior counsel and looked tired and dejected with little to impress his innocence, if that was to be pleaded.

The jury were mostly middle-aged, the majority female. Perhaps defence might try the body-language technique– it crossed Malcolm's mind, for the defendant was good-looking and clean suited, and might be the type to charm the females.

Judge Pearson wore an expression of keenness on his young, flushed face. He was busy talking to the clerk and even glanced at the few present in the public gallery. He seemed to be making a drawing and Malcolm realised he was sketching out a seating plan with the names noted for reference.

As they settled to await the first session, David turned to Nigel and asked, "Have you decided on tactics?"

"Not really, I shall play it by ear. As we've no witnesses ourselves I've little choice but to try and confuse their evidence. You got any better ideas?"

"No. What about the medical examinations and reports, why not put the doctor on the stand?"

"The reports help, but I hate medics in the box. Too many maybes, 'specially in psychiatric cases."

"And the Bournemouth incident?"

"Of course. You do realise that our only real defence is the Captain's state of mind due to that problem."

"So you're not expecting to win?"

"Unlikely. I'll try to mitigate any sentence or fines due to diminished responsibility."

"D'you think Barry will ride along with that?"

"Dunno. Ask him. He must have been listening."

They both turned for a reaction, but Barry's mind was far away and his eyes were staring vacantly into space.

"Mr Jones, if you please." The Court was in session.

Malcolm was just warming to his introduction when the commotion started. First there were words, then banging, and finally the door swung open as the girl staged an entrance into the gallery. The usher asked her to sit down, and be quiet, "The Court is in session." Pearson recognised her and watched as she adjusted her dress to effect an audience from all the males present. The moment passed and the Judge refocussed the Court's attention:

"Please continue Mr Jones."

Malcolm did a good job. Or a least he thought he'd done a good job. He was conscious of Pearson's glances to the gallery, and he vaguely wondered where the Judge had earned his ruddy complexion.

Nigel Waite was awful. He stuttered and seemed to lose the sequence of his arguments. At one stage he dropped his notes and an assistant had to gather the loose sheets to knock them into some order. Briefing notes in a bound book. It was pretty basic. Malcolm could see that others had the same thoughts. It hadn't seemed long but suddenly they were recessing for lunch.

Barry collared David Jenkins with genuine fury. "Where the hell d'you dig him up?"

"I'm sorry, but you've got to accept that with your limited funds, there's no way you could afford Queen's Counsel."

"Funds? I haven't got anything! Why can't I have legal aid?"

"We've been over this course several times. You know quite well why not."

"You take it. You can do a better job than this amateur."

"I can't. I'm junior for this defence, and in any case Mr Waite will be okay. It's early yet. Come on, let's get a quick bite."

They found a coffee shop and David insisted that Judy was not there. "Now the case has started you'd be wise not to talk to anyone. You know that." Barry nodded.

"I want to talk about Judy."

"What about Judy?"

"Your case is that you became mentally unstable after the Marvel Air trial but you had to get back flying. In the blood you might say. Yes?" Barry was non-committal at the diagnosis. "But due to this instability you crashed three aircraft. You arranged the insurance cover of these aircraft through different companies using pseudonyms, because you didn't want your records to show."

"How else could I have got insured?"

"But on each crash you were well over-insured, and you say that was fortuitous."

"Yes. You believe that?"

"What I believe doesn't matter. What we plead does."

"Why are you going over this ground again?"

"Because later this week you're going to be examined on your testament. That doesn't worry me. What does worry me is your cross-examination by Mr Jones, who is very skilled."

"So what's this got to do with Judy?"

David chewed the dry corned beef sandwich and washed it down with his cappuccino. He studied Barry's eyes before he made his point. "Because your evidence is going to stand or fall on your argument of mental stability... flaunting around with a whore in fancy clothes is not going to impress the jury."

Barry nearly hit him, but as it was held back enough to stuff his roll into the remainder of David's coffee. He breathed hard to control his anger. "Don't you ever – ever use that word again or I'll – I'll break your teeth and – and shove your tongue down your throat."

Faces looked in their direction and David waited for him to calm, before ordering another two coffees. "I said it for your benefit. You must see that. You wouldn't have reacted to a gentle approach. That anger may assist your medical argument, I don't know. But you need to get Judy to back off. I understand what she's trying to do. She wants to court public, and maybe media interest, to sway the jury to mitigating circumstances. I believe her game is dangerous and might have the opposite effect." He waited for his words to be absorbed.

"You're beginning to annoy me Jenkins. You lost my previous defence. Why am I using you?"

"We lost the last one because it was manipulated by your bosses. You were a scapegoat. The trial was a farce. This one's different. You took the risks. You must face the music. If you want my personal view you'll lose again, this time because I don't believe you're being honest with me."

They drifted back to the courtroom and Barry thought about David's advice. 'But I'll fight.' He had a strong sense of his own justification, founded on plain common sense rather than legal merit. He was right that September day. 'God knows, you know when you're right. So I've taken a couple of companies for a few bob. Fraud, they call it. Peanuts, in the real market of fraud. I wouldn't be offered a membership of the Fraud Club (if one existed) on my petty do. Wouldn't comply with the Club's constitution.

'"Now Mr Johnston, how much did you defraud those insurance companies?"

'"Forty thousand." He faced the treasurer.

"Did I hear you say four, forty thousand?"

'"No. Forty thousand." He could see the committee giggling like the Smash potato advert on television. "I'm sorry Mr Johnston, our minimum entry is a quarter of a million."'

Barry scoffed his thoughts as the voice sunk through.

"Mr Bakewell. Would you please take the stand."

Bakewell was in his element. All that service training and duty to your country came bouncing back. "Better invest in a new suit." He'd persuaded Sandy.

"What about the repairs to the tractor and the shed roof? Surely they're more important!"

"Give over love. They need me. Justice. Without it this country's finished."

"Gone to his head." She'd talked it over with the children.

"Let him be Mum. Not a lot of excitement in farming these days. Let him have his day of glory." So the kids had persuaded her, and now she was proud to see him dressed to kill. 'Wish he'd done it for me,' she grumbled. 'Thirty years of worn corduroys. That's my memories.'

"So that the jury may get the complete picture could you just run over that point again?"

"I know my aeroplanes. This one had no fuel left and yet it was routed for Norwich."

"But the pilot had declared an emergency."

"Yes, but not for fuel problems. For a rough-running engine."

"So to be clear, are you saying that had the engine been fine, the pilot didn't have enough fuel in any case, to get to Norwich airport?"

"That is correct my Lord."

"So what interpretation do you put on this fact?" Malcolm asked.

John surveyed the courtroom with the thrill creeping up the back of his neck. 'This is great. They're hanging on my every word. They want my opinion.' He waited a moment... "I do not think the pilot intended to go to Norwich." 'Fantastic.'

"Maybe he was going to refuel somewhere, or maybe his engine problem had required him to divert at the cost of additional fuel burn?"

The hairs dropped and suddenly John didn't feel so confident. "I don't know, but there's no field nearby for fuel and from my checks, and I believe the assessor's findings, there was no evidence of engine failure."

"I see. Well we must await that evidence."

John was feeling hot and beginning to regret the wool suit. A blazer and cotton slacks would have been more comfortable 'Why didn't I take Sandy's advice?'

"I would like to move on to the question of the phial." Malcolm dragged through the facts and the hearsay evidence but was unable to make great input other than to establish that the crash had some bizarre facts which defied explanation.

"Finally Mr Bakewell, would you just confirm the name that the pilot gave?"

"Hastings. Tony Hastings."

"Thank you. Your witness."

"Mr Bakewell. You know your aeroplanes?" Nigel cross examined.

"Yes sir."

"You maintained them in the War. Fitter by trade I believe? You have a current pilot's licence?"

"That is correct my Lord."

"Um, let's see... What type was the plane that crashed?"

"A French design."

"Popular model is it?"

"Well no. I believe it was a prototype for later models but not many were made."

"You've flown one of course?"

"Well eh..., no."

Nigel Waite shifted his papers with an authority which suggested his nervous opening might have been an act. Barry waited for the next question and took a comforting nod from David.

"So you really know little about the capabilities of this type?"

"...I suppose not." John was now feeling very uncomfortable.

"Does that extend to knowledge of fuel consumption?"

"Well not in detail. But most light aeroplanes burn similar quantities."

"Three, seven, thirteen gallons per hour. Is that the range?"

"Of that order, yes."

"And this one?"

"I... I'm not sure."

Nigel paused. "Learned counsel for the prosecution told a story of the pilot being covered in blood from an apparent cut to his head. He also went on to describe a plastic tube found by the aeroplane, a phial as it was described. What significance do you place on this discovery?"

"My wife said..."

"I'm sorry Mr Bakewell," Nigel cut in, "your wife's opinion would be hearsay and not admissible at this time. I require your views."

"I found the tube – that's all."

"And the cut on Hastings' head?"

"...I never saw it."

The defence counsel made some notes and then continued with his cross-examination. "One last question. Your evidence in affidavit suggested strongly that the accident on your airfield was somehow premeditated. In your experience have you ever come across such a happening before?" The silence was damaging, and the Judge raised his head. "Mr Bakewell?"

"No my Lord."

"No further questions."

Malcolm re-examined to ask whether it was possible in the farmer's view for a plane to be deliberately damaged in this way. John said "Yes," but obviously there was a risk.

"Now think carefully about my last question." He turned slightly and waited to make sure the jury were paying attention. "In your opinion do you think the crash was accidental or deliberate?"

John looked toward the bench to where Barry was sitting tight-lipped before he replied. "Deliberate, my Lord."

There was a rustling around the courtroom and one or two murmurs as Mr Bakewell was asked to step down.

"Mr Jones." The Judge peered down to the prosecution bench. "The evidence we've just heard is in fact not evidence relating to the main charges being brought. Am I right?"

"That is not strictly correct my Lord."

"For the benefit of the jury could you please explain the relevance of this evidence, as I understand you intend to provide more witnesses on the matter."

Malcolm addressed the jury.

"The charges of this Court are that the accused did on..." He read them out, "...deliberately destroy an aircraft with the intention to defraud and profit from excess insurance of the property secured using a false name... and on..." he detailed the second incident.

"The purpose of my present examination involving the Accused is to establish a similarity showing intention to defraud for all three cases. The Accused is enjoined in the charges and the prosecution feel that the evidence is material to establish a pattern of development in the Defendant's mind and plans. Does that cover the point?" he addressed Judge Pearson.

"Thank you. At this juncture I suggest a recess until ten thirty tomorrow."

Chapter Thirty-Five

They linked arms as he caught her hurrying toward The Strand to ward off the cold afternoon.

"Hang on Gill, I wanted a word." He hadn't seen her since she'd invaded his flat and although she'd never said anything he guessed she was suspicious. His performance, or more accurately lack of it, must have been obvious, for Danielle had drained off all his lovemaking supplies through that long night. There was also the cheap perfume, an absolute give away. 'I must remember to keep some of Gill's favourite brands in the flat.'

"What d'you want?" Her tone was unfriendly and she hardly glanced at him.

"Stop." He held her arm tightly and swung her around until they were facing each other. The attempted kiss was brushed aside as she turned her face. She drew back from his hold and started walking again.

"Wait."

"Please leave me alone."

They were passing the Warldof Hotel and Dennis grabbed her arm again forcing her through the entrance swing door with a sweet smile for the doorman, as he hurried her into the bar. He settled her with a drink at a window table, where she reluctantly threw her coat on the spare chair.

"Why so frosty?"

She didn't answer at first, but looked long and searchingly into his eyes for sympathy. "Daddy's dying."

The bluntness of her statement hit out of the blue, and left him completely lost for words. She emptied her glass and handed it to him for another. He walked slowly to the bar and saw through the reflection of the glass mirror that she was trying hard not to cry. He gave her the refilled tumbler before asking. "How, why?"

"Leukaemia. I've suspected it for years. The doctor's confirmed," she blurted out the facts.

"How long?"

"Weeks, maybe only days."

"I'm very sorry. Sorry I harassed you."

"That's okay. You couldn't know. I feel rotten. I've been tramping around when I should've been spending time with him. Now it's too late. He gave me everything after Mother's death. I owe him so much." She snuffled and blew her nose. "I won't be giving evidence. It's not my case anyway. You and Chris can handle it."

"But if we win you'll probably be able to bring charges on Echo Tango, and get your money back!"

"I couldn't care less about money. Father's dying! Don't you understand? I've no time, but what I have will be with him. Twenty-four hours a day."

Dennis felt helpless and concerned, as if he'd been the reason for keeping Gill from her father. He knew it was stupid and he wished he could take her and love away the pain she was inflicting on herself. He rationalised the news and decided to take the easy path and keep his distance.

"What do you reckon so far?" He thought a change of subject would help.

"About what?" she seemed bemused.

"The trial love."

"I dunno. I wasn't concentrating that much. I think he's guilty but it's going to be difficult to prove deliberate damage."

"I think I agree but I'm relying on counsel to break him down in the dock. When you weigh it up, the guy's been pretty unprofessional. A poor amateur in the dishonesty world."

"You know I feel sorry for the man. He's having a rough deal. Sometimes your luck runs out."

Dennis put his arm round her shoulder. "Come on, I'll take you home."

Chapter Thirty-Six

The tabloid press mostly gave it fifth page rating and only two used photographs about Judy. Stephen Oaks read it as part of his routine information file which was circulated each day. The Authority used an agency service which pulled out any reference to flight activities or news and these were meticulously boxed away on a central computer index. He was in a hurry to attend another meeting that morning, and skipped through his reading before tossing the papers into an out tray. The name Hastings meant nothing, and he gathered his notes and made way down the corridor.

Dennis was feeling nervous as he walked up the steps to the famous court building. He stopped at the top step and surveyed the busy scenes around him. Clerks were bustling in and out with string-bound bundles clasped to their chests as if they were precious jewels and they were frightened of being mugged. Barristers with wigs already donned hustled through the security check desk, followed by their juniors and assistants. He idly studied the footwear of the female lawyers and noted that most of them favoured a slightly raised heel. Easy on the feet I suppose with all that standing. Some however sported high heels and he wondered if it was possible to gauge any difference in their performance from this fact. Make an interesting survey?

He walked through and watched the busy groups huddled in dark corners as documents were shuffled about and notes were scribbled into exercise books. New findings, discoveries, the paperwork was endless. He passed the large clock and reluctantly made his way to the court. On after lunch? It was precisely eleven thirty when he was asked to take the stand.

"When did you first become suspicious that matters were not straightforward?" Malcolm Jones had waded through preliminaries that morning and most in Court were ready for some activity to keep them from dozing off. Counsel's question caused some bottom-shuffling and the jury perked up a little. There was no one in the public gallery and apparently no press about.

"I suppose it was when we talked to the farmer."

"Could you elaborate on that for the benefit of the Court."

"Apparently Mr Hastings said he was very experienced and yet his records to the insurance company only showed low hour figures."

"Go on."

"He also appeared very cool after the accident. His major concern seeming to be that the wreckage was not touched or looked at until the insurer's investigation."

"You were retained by Medway Services to carry out such an investigation?"

"That is correct."

"And what was your verdict?"

Dennis searched for the right words to summarise his answer but couldn't better a straight statement. "I found no mechanical cause for the accident."

Malcolm let the Judge and jury make their notes before he continued. "Perhaps we could move on." He caught the approval in Judge Pearson's eye and almost read the silent lips urging him to 'do so.' "You recall an incident involving a similar aircraft investigation in France?"

"I do my Lord."

"Perhaps you could describe to this Court the circumstances."

"I can, but I suggest photographs tell the story more positively." The clerk was instructed to pass exhibit seven to the jury and a further copy was given to the judge.

"Is there any similarity in this crash to the one in Norfolk?"

"Well my Lord, there's always some similarity in air disasters but I did find that the damage inflicted was consistent in one respect and that was that the plane probably stalled before impact, and hit the ground with the left wing and wheel, bursting the left undercarriage tyre." The Court was now listening more intently and Dennis noticed that the press had turned up. Barry was making notes but seemed unconcerned.

"So from your inspections could you draw any strong connection between the incidents?"

Dennis swallowed before he answered. "No positive link my Lord." He paused. "Just that they were similar enough to make me ask more questions."

His answer caught Barry's attention: 'He's got something else. I wonder what?' They recessed at this juncture and Barry collared David in the corridor outside the courtroom. "They've got something we don't know. What'll be?"

"Relax Barry. They're going to establish that you were the pilot of both planes. That's no hassle because we're admitting it. They're struggling to pin down why. Only you know that, and I don't want to know."

He met Judy in a wine bar off The Strand having made sure that he wasn't being followed. They kissed briefly and Barry related the morning's session.

"Let's do a bunk. South America. We promised ourselves!" she pleaded.

"That was with some cash. I'm broke or will be after this case. We're trapped and all because of that fateful day. Jesus, I wish I could put the clock back."

"Back with Sybil and your cosy cottage. You men are all the same. Brave with words and deeds but when it doesn't work out you want to run back to Mummy's womb." She snuffled and blew her nose on a pretty lace handkerchief.

"But Mummy hasn't got a spare wroom for me," he taunted her slight lisp, and she cuffed his head at the silly remark. They tried to laugh but it wasn't working for them.

The afternoon session continued with Dennis explaining his suspicions of a connection between the two investigations. He related his request for a photograph of a Mr Johnston from France and how he'd matched it with a photo of Mr Hastings from Norfolk.

"So there's no doubt in your mind that the pilot of both these aeroplanes is the accused sitting in this Court?"

That confirmed, Malcolm Jones turned to the evidence relating to the insurance. "So Mr Hopkins, I would like now to move on to the question of insurance which is the prosecution charge set down for deliberation by this Court of Law. Before submitting your evidence I'd like you to tell this Court why you first became concerned that there might be some misappropriation on this matter."

Counsel examined Dennis on the detail, coming back each time to make sure that the jury were quite clear on the points. He established that Dennis had questioned why the crashes had occurred in the first place. Maybe they were accidental? He decided to check on the Captain's background and discovered that Mr Johnston was a commercial pilot who'd been involved in a near-miss incident some two and a half years ago and had been found guilty of endangering the passengers. The Court buzzed with this information and several pressmen left rapidly. Dennis was puzzled as to why the pilot had 'piled-up' as he described it, two more aircraft. Maybe he'd lost his nerve, but Dennis doubted that with such an experienced airman.

So he'd done some investigation and found out that Francis Aviation had paid out forty thousand pounds on an aircraft which had been purchased for twenty thousand. Further investigation revealed that Medway Services had paid out a similar sum for the crash at Norfolk. This plane had been bought for fourteen and a half thousand. Dennis had checked with the insurance companies in question and in the second case the details for the brokers had been supplied by a female.

"Have you been able to identify the female in question?"

I have your Honour, and you may recall that the lady made an entrance during yesterday's hearing."

Judge Pearson pricked his ears at this piece of discovery. 'Pretty girl, probably very naughty,' he sighed. Astrid had become pleasantly boring with her social circuit, and he was not anxious to tie the knot yet.

"And the latest incident?"

Dennis enlarged on how he'd discovered that a small plane had been insured for forty-five thousand through a new broker at Lloyds. There was some question on the purchase price, with some evidence that the plane had been refurbished to value it at around this price. Dennis was still investigating this matter but didn't believe that the plane was worth more than fifteen thousand. He was suspicious that the paperwork might have been forged.

"And would I be correct in saying that this aircraft was being flown by a Mr Simon Fury at the time of its crash-landing?"

"That is the name on the insurance claim document."

"And Mr Fury. He is present in this Court?"

"Mr Fury, Mr Hastings, Mr Johnston – they are the same person."

"One final question. Who instructed the broker for insurance cover in this case?"

"The lady as previously identified."

"No further questions." Malcolm Jones sat down and swivelled around to gauge the effect of his examination. The Judge was talking to the clerk and studying his watch and the jury were talking to each other as unobtrusively as they dared.

"Time's moving on. Does my learned Defence wish to cross-examine?"

"Just a few points." Nigel Waite was on his feet.

"Can we call it four thirty then?"

"As your Lordship pleases." Nigel fiddled with his papers and made ready as if to ask a question and then turned round to talk to his junior. The Court waited in silence and the Judge looked irritatingly at his pocket fob watch. Dennis crossed his legs in anticipation.

Nigel faced the witness with a formal stance. "Mr Hopkins. Would you describe yourself as an experienced aviation insurance assessor?"

"I thought that's why I was here?" Dennis regretted the comment as soon as the words left his mouth.

"Just answer the question if you please."

"...Yes." There was little else to say.

"Yes. Experienced or very experienced?"

"... I like to feel the latter."

Nigel refrained from coming back on this half-statement and delayed again to annoy the Judge, and gain his attention. "So Mr Hopkins, in your capacity of a very experienced insurance assessor, have you ever come across payments for totally destroyed aircraft that have – how can I put it – exceeded their strict commercial value?"

"Well – I – actually..."

"Just a simple yes or no will do." Nigel showed some controlled frustration in his tone.

"Well – yes."

"Yes. Thank you Mr Hopkins... One further question." Nigel saw the Judge's eyes brighten. "Have you in all your experience ever come across a pilot deliberately crashing his aircraft?"

"I, eh, I... well no, it's unusual my Lord."

200

"No. Pride wouldn't allow a dedicated pilot to even consider such action, would it Mr Hopkins?" He sat down without inviting an answer.

Chapter Thirty-Seven

The second day was hardly reported and one or two editors decided that there wasn't much juice in this fraud case to warrant time or space. There was reference to the airline case and Hogan picked it up in the early additions with some surprise at the trial. Donald Opperman read it in the *Financial Times* of all places without connecting at all, and turned the pages to see how his shares were faring.

The prosecution dragged it out for another day with confirmation from insurance clerks of Medway Services and Blair-Lloyd that Judy had handled the proposal introductions. Barry took the stand late Thursday but there was only time for his counsel to introduce some preliminaries on Barry's career and some factual matters relating to the substance of the offences under trial.

Barry slept badly that night and the nightmare visited him again. This time the people were blurred and he had difficulty in identifying the characters of a bizarre dinner where the guests were eating what looked like human flesh. He looked down and saw that his body was being sliced away and laid on a plate to be snatched and devoured as if they were hyenas. He screamed for help but the guests just smiled and nodded like puppets, as they drank from a large chalice in the centre of the table. Suddenly he was falling and he savoured relief as waves of water bubbled over him and cooled his burning body. The visions drifted and then something was pulling him. Judy was holding his hand and crying with joy and for a moment he felt her strength as she tugged at his arm. Something exploded and he cried out in pain as he woke from the dream.

It took him a moment to remember were he was. The window of the small hotel room was banging about in the wind and Barry became aware that this had probably woken him. Further sleep wouldn't come and he tossed about, drowsing until dawn. He arrived in Court feeling washed out, with his eyes heavy as if they were attached to lead weights.

Nigel treated him gently and by skilful examination drew a picture for the jury of a man who had dedicated his life to honesty, integrity, and the skilful exercise of his profession. A man who respected his employers –who gave one hundred and ten per cent in effort– but a man who'd been shattered by events whilst trying to land an airliner in atrocious weather conditions with instruments that he considered were giving false readings.

He was stopped at this juncture as Malcolm found his feet to object. "Can my learned friend please explain the relevance of this evidence from a previous trial?"

"My Lord, I'm coming to that point if you will bear with me."

"Please continue."

Nigel persevered moving his defence to Barry's state of mind and brought in written evidence from the doctor to show that he was suffering a type of amnesia which affected him like an epileptic fit, and which could strike at any time. Although he was fit to fly in the general sense, his unconscious mind clearly wandered and this was the cause of the crashes. Nigel pointed out that it was perhaps not a coincidence that the crashes occurred during the landing procedure, because of course it was the aborted landing that fatal day that was muddling the normal operation of the pilot's skill. Clearly Mr Johnston should not control an aircraft in his present state, and he would be wise to seek advice from experts in this field.

"May I, however, remind the members of the jury that the accused is not on trial for piloting an aircraft whilst suffering from mental stress. The accused is on trial for allegedly damaging property in order to benefit from the insurance payment that arose due to this action. From the evidence I've presented, and intend to summarise in my closing remarks, you'll see that the charges before you have no substance."

Judge Pearson stopped it at that moment. He'd planned a long lunch with some of his colleagues and had no intention of coming back that afternoon. He called both counsel to the bench and suggested he'd be grateful if they could produce some argument to recess at this time. He looked them straight in the face whilst offering no reason. Nigel was well onto such Court tricks and told Malcolm he would take the initiative.

Back in action he attended to the Judge's request. "If it pleases my Lord, I would like to request a recess at this time. I have some additional information which has come to hand, and I require to discuss this with my client. I would ask the Court's indulgence for the remainder of this day's session."

"I see." Pearson sounded grumpy. "This is very irritating Mr Waite. Can the Court be assured that this information is significantly material to your defence for me to extend these proceedings?"

"You crafty old codger," Nigel muttered to himself. "Yes, it is of that importance my Lord."

"Oh, very well then. The Court will adjourn until eleven on Monday. May I remind the jury of their duty not to discuss these hearings with any other person whilst this Court is in session." He rose and without looking at either counsel acted an effective bustling and angry exit.

"He doesn't miss a trick." The two barristers exchanged views as they collected their papers. "How long will you want?" Nigel asked the question.

"What Monday? Half morning with your client and then summing up."

"So we could be through by Tuesday?" Malcolm nodded. "Till Monday then. Good day."

Chapter Thirty-Eight

"Bloody fool. I don't believe it."

He put down the paper and rang the Opperman residence with some trepidation, especially as it was Sunday. Still he'd said to call if any news broke so he was only acting on that blessing. Could wait till Monday. He nearly put the phone down, but thought 'I might not get him on Monday, he might be in Court.'

"Tresco House." She sounded like a maid.

"I'm sorry to disturb you but I require to speak to Mr Opperman on a matter of some importance and I wondered if he was available?" He'd not checked on the time but saw that it was nearly noon. 'Damn it, he's probably on the sherries. I'll get a right dressing down for disturbing him.'

"Felicity Opperman. To whom am I speaking?"

"Mitchell. Tim Mitchell ma'am. I must apologise for this intrusion on your Sunday – eh – just wanted a brief word with Donal... your husband – maybe you could leave a message?"

"Not my Sunday. God's they tell me. Never believed in all that nonsense. You want Don? So do I. We've got the relations coming today. Duty you know. Don can't stand them, so he's slipped off and gone shooting with his buddies. You'll probably get him at the Percy Arms or the Shelley. The old renegade's never around when he's wanted."

Tim warmed to this lady, or was it that she sounded the complete opposite to his image of the eminent lawyer's wife. He wondered how she looked. Tweeds with the matronly flat shoes and hair buffed in a tight bun; immaculate with fine free flowing hair, polished nails and wrapped in a silk Dior housecoat; or just plain Jane in a simple classic blouse and skirt?

"Why don't you join us for drinks?" The request hinted at a loneliness hidden with a tinge of sadness.

"I'd love to. But I'm one hundred and eighty miles away." He sighed.

"Pity." He felt she really meant it. "Hang on, talk of the devil. Don's just burst in. I'll hand him over." Tim heard his name spoken and the clatter of wood and metal which he suspected was Donald's shotgun being dumped.

"Tim. To what do I owe this honour?"

"Donald. Thanks for taking my call."

"Delighted my boy. Sundays are pretty boring down here. How can I help?"

"Do you take the *Telegraph*?"

"Sometimes. Never read it. Why?"

"Barry Johnston."

"What about Barry Johnston?"

"He's got himself involved in a fraud case."

"Really, how come?"

"I only know what I've read, but apparently it's something to do with insurance of aircraft."

"In the press?"

"Yes. Trial started last Monday. Same day as our meeting with the CAA."

"Extraordinary. What is this man playing at?"

"I'm lost to know. Thought I ought to inform you."

"Yes. Indeed. You're right – must go shortly, family matters. I'll research the press coverage and find out more detail tomorrow. Are you contactable?"

"I'm in my office until mid-afternoon. Then I have a test flight."

"Sound. I'll try to reach you before midday. Extraordinary." The telephone went dead.

Tim sat back and wondered what to do next. He could ring Patrick but he could guess his reaction. "I told you Tim. The man's a charlatan. There's no good to be true. You're wasting your time. Backing the wrong horse."

What about Stephen Oaks? It's bound to influence his judgement. Maybe not. He's a person who probably pockets his life. Tunnel vision. He's likely to make each decision on the merits of specific findings and not be diverted by other factors.

He decided to re-arrange his programme for the following week and go to the Old Bailey himself.

Monday dawned grey with a cheerless overcast sky, which was reflected on the unsmiling faces of people as they walked grimly to their offices. The Monday blues and Barry felt them badly. The Court seemed unusually full with more faces in the public gallery. The jury reconvened and Barry was asked back to the stand.

Malcolm Jones was feeling good. The weekend had been fun with a Saturday dinner party that had drifted into the small hours. Any Sunday hangover was soon disbursed on the rugby pitch and Malcolm had scored a dramatic try just one minute before full time. Still relaxing from the hot bath and pints at the club, he'd spent the evening rehearsing his cross examination, and now on his feet he was anxious to go.

"Mr Johnston, why did you deliberately write off three aeroplanes?"

The opening attack had Nigel on his feet protesting vigorously, and the press desk buzzing with notes being made. Judge Pearson reminded Malcolm of his duties whilst the remainder of the Court waited for the next ball.

"Let me rephrase my question. You do not deny that since being dismissed from your airline duties, you have in fact been involved in the destruction of three aeroplanes. Is that correct?"

"... Yes." Malcolm smiled at the Judge who was sitting poker faced and expressionless.

"Yes – and were these incidents deliberate or accidental?"

"...Accidental." The answer seemed to lack conviction.

"Mr Johnston may I remind you that you are in a Court of Law and you have sworn to tell the truth and nothing but the truth. I would therefore like you to consider very carefully your last answer and repeat it, if that is your considered reply, for the benefit of my Lordship and the jury."

Barry searched for some sympathy in the faces staring at him, but there was none. He'd always enjoyed the loneliness of flying on his own, the achievement of finding one's way through the clouds, detached from the world below, and arriving with excitement at new destinations. But this loneliness, surrounded with doubting strangers, and the doubt in his own mind was closer to hell. He knew he was at fault, but one part of him was still reasoning that he was justified. The Court's stitched me up and ruined my life, you must see that, you all must see that. The faces didn't see that or anything as they awaited his answer.

"Mr Hastings – sorry Johnston?"

"As I said – accidental."

Malcolm adjusted his robe and placed his hands in the practised barrister's pose, holding the lapels of his gown by thumb and first finger.

"You're an experienced pilot?"

"I like to think so."

"Before the airline problem had you ever been involved in an air crash?"

"No my Lord."

"So we have a situation where a commercially trained pilot with over eleven thousand hours of experience gained over many years, a man who also has an instructor's licence, suddenly in a period of less than five months has three, eh – 'accidents'." Malcolm ridiculed the word. "Is that what you're asking this jury to believe?"

"Yes."

"Um. I personally find that difficult to comprehend. Perhaps Mr Johnston you could enlighten this Court as to the reasons for these – eh – lapses in an otherwise virtually unblemished career." Malcolm raised his eyes in anticipation but was greeted with a stony silence.

Judge Pearson decided to take over and do some questioning himself. "Perhaps I can help. I think Mr Johnston that learned Counsel is entitled to an explanation of these events. I suggest it would be in your interest to try and help the jury and myself to understand matters more clearly."

Barry felt squeezed and frightened. He couldn't remember his rehearsed defence and he felt he was rapidly losing control. He tried to sip some water but his hand shook too much and he gripped the front of the bench hard to try and steady his nerves.

"Since my trial two years ago I haven't been well... I..."

"Go on." Pearson was still in charge.

"I suffer from bad dreams. I've become very depressed... I lost control... I can't explain..." Barry was struggling.

Malcolm snapped back. "Come now Mr Johnston, we all suffer from bad dreams. If I were to ask for a count in this courtroom today, I would expect to find that everyone's had a bad dream. Are you telling this jury that you had bad dreams when you were flying which caused you to crash? I suggest that the only bad dream you're having is now in this room, with the pack of lies that you're telling this Court! You engineered those crashes to gain the insurance surplus. Is that not the truth?" Barry said nothing, with his head lowered.

"You expect the jury to believe that mental illness was the cause. I think it to be much more plausible that your flying skills were enhanced to devise a cunning fraud, and not diminished by depression and illness. A fraud that you planned with the help of a woman friend with the deliberate intention of financial gain. I put it to you that you were bitter with the judgement at the previous trial and you decided to get your own back on the system in some way. Fortunately I do not have to find the motives for your actions. I only have to prove beyond reasonable doubt that you are guilty of the charge. Nothing you have said this morning leads me to believe a word of your evidence so far."

Malcolm paused to let his argument settle. "Does not your silence tell this Court that I am correct?"

"Mr Jones. We'll leave it at that. Until two o'clock then."

Tim hurried to make the afternoon session having cancelled his training flight. He listened in amazement as the prosecution drew out all the evidence relating to the insurance proposals, the overvaluation of the aeroplanes, the use of false names and disguises. There was reference to phials of blood and wigs, which Tim found difficult to believe. Barry was having a rough time, and none of his answers sounded convincing. The session seemed to go quickly and Tim waited outside the Court to try and catch him. Half an hour passed and he was just giving up, when he spotted the forlorn figure of his previous colleague shuffling down the steps as if carrying all the problems of the world on his back. He called but Barry kept walking. "Barry. Hang on. It's Tim." Barry turned to the voice.

"Tim. You were there?"

"Yes. What the hell have you been doing?"

"I'm in a mess Tim. It's all over. Christ what a mess."

"Let me buy you a drink."

"No thanks. I've gotta go."

"I've got some news for you." He wanted to tell Barry about the CAA meeting.

"Sorry Tim. Some other time, 'bye now" and without a chance Barry jumped onto a moving bus which disappeared round the corner.

She was frightened by his appearance. The stubble only helped to age his lined face and she couldn't believe the deterioration in just a few days. He'd asked her to stay away, but she'd sneaked into the hotel and was sitting on the bed waiting for him.

He said nothing and flopped out hiding his eyes with his hands, like a cat trying to block out the world with its paws. She let him sleep and, mother-like, covered him with the quilt from the spare bed. The cheap hotel had no bar and she yearned for the luxury of their holiday in Spain, and thought of how things might have been. Living on the edge: it had been great while it lasted. She slipped out to the off-licence and was back before he woke.

"It's over Judy. I can't go on. I'm going to change my pleadings."

"You can't. What happened to Mr Clyde?"

"You don't believe that. That was all hype and adrenalin. The novelty's gone. It's not the real us. I was hurt and trying to justify my hurt by hitting back. It's over – you must see that!"

"And us?"

"I don't know. I don't know anything."

She half-closed the tatty curtains and turned off the lights allowing the twilight to soften the starkness of the room. She undressed him slowly, as if she needed to use all the experiences learnt through her life of sexual hell and the love for him that still overwhelmed her. He resisted at first and she wondered if she would be able to spark any feelings from his jaded body. Slowly her skills started to work and he reacted to her touch, struggling to empty his tortured mind. She straddled his body and worked to achieve a deep penetration that made them both gasp with excitement. She made him caress her breasts which she offered proudly by arching and throwing back her head. The worn out bed creaked with their straining as if acting like a metronome to match their increasing passion. She came in a rush of tension and love, but was unable to ease as his thrusting almost lifted her off her knees. She held him inside accepting some pain, whilst his grip on her breasts made her gasp for breath. His explosion was so intense that they both lost their balance and rolled off the bed still locked in each other's arms.

They lay there exhausted and she wished that they could have laughed it away like before, but it was not to be. Barry seemed almost embarrassed as she slipped from his grip and made for the bathroom.

They ate burgers in silence in a small corner café but however hard she tried she was unable to draw him from his depression. At last she became tired and cross and told him she could help no more. He hardly acknowledged her kiss as she left and he sat for a long time just staring at a smoke-stained mural painted over one of the café's walls.

The owner finally started locking up and he was forced to walk back aimlessly to the cold hotel.

Chapter Thirty-Nine

It made the second pages with headlines to match.
"...Lawyers were debating what action to take in the insurance fraud case currently being heard at the Central Criminal Court. The accused, Johnston, whose cross-examination by Malcolm Jones QC was due to be completed yesterday, did not appear for the trial continuance in the morning. In a strange twist the Defence Counsel Nigel Waite informed the hearing that he had received a facsimile note from his client instructing a change of pleadings from not guilty to guilty. The note went on to apologise for waste of the Court's time. The police have been informed and are trying to locate Johnston for questioning. Apparently the accused left cash in the hotel room he was using during the trial..."

The dampness crept insidiously across the moors and Barry hunched lower behind the rocks for protection from the wind and impending rain. He'd caught the milk train to Yorkshire and was now deep in the dales having walked for three hours to get away from the populated areas. He knew they wouldn't take long and that it was sensible to keep moving. He was hungry but at least he had cash, having used his card at five bank dispensers before catching the train. Where now though? They'd waived bail, but retained his passport so he couldn't get out of the country. Europe maybe, but the airports and docks would be warned, and anyway it wasn't far enough. Money? His only assets, apart from the bank, were in the bungalow. Maybe he could find a way of getting someone to sell them, he didn't know. They could probably get a court order to prevent that. At least the money from the insurers was in two Jersey accounts, one in his name, unfortunately, but the other as Hastings. Better retrieve these first. No passport required to get to the Channel Isles, but would they twig? They knew his pseudonyms, and they'd talk to Judy. 'Damn,

I'd forgotten about her.' His head was going round in circles. 'No that's okay. I never told her. Safer not to know. We agreed.'

Dawn was breaking and he needed to make some plans. 'Should've taken the car,' but then he remembered it was a giveaway for the police. 'No, better on foot for the moment. Maybe hire a car if necessary.'

He heard the engine labouring on the hill and eased himself from a hidden rock position to check out the vehicle. He was stiff from the cold and slapped his arms across the chest to warm his body. The road was a quarter of a mile away and he could see a heavy goods lorry struggling slowly on the steep twisting fell road. He decided to cut it off on the brow before the driver started the down hill stretch.

At first it seemed as if it wasn't going to stop. Then the airbrakes hissed and he saw the rear lights come on.

He got off in the village having avoided conversation with the lorry driver and kept his head turned away by looking through the side window. As soon as it drove away Barry realised he was making a classic mistake. He wanted to be incognito yet here he was, a stranger in a small community sticking out like a sore thumb. Big cities. You can get lost there for ever. He drew the scarf to his face and entered the village shop. He settled for a couple of Mars bars and bought two tabloid papers. Outside again he noticed the sign for the station and blessed his luck that the train pioneers had seen fit to expand their ambitions to some of the remoter parts of the country. The train went to York with Barry as one of its few passengers reading about complications in a London criminal trial.

Tim was the last person on Hogan's mind when the phone rang. Since the fracas in his office and the chaos of his own life, Hogan had closed shop and taken a much needed holiday in the West Indies. He'd started in a hotel and then rented an apartment with a lovely local girl to cook and clean. The sun worked wonders on his gammy leg and the local rum helped him have some of the best sleeps he'd had in a decade. It was paradise and Hogan soaked it up for two months before he felt the itch. Maybe it was the locals or maybe the ex-pats, but slowly he found himself getting bored with the same conversations down the bars. He took the British papers, but somehow the news didn't seem real so far from home, and he found he couldn't relate any more.

The end came suddenly in the marina clubhouse one lunchtime. Something made him recognise the voice with its brashness and harsh cockiness. He slipped out to look down the membership list and there it was in black and white. The man was so confident he was still using his own name.

He stopped by the table and waited for the host to finish his joke.

"... so this fellow asked for a long-legged bird with a tight pussy, and he got a flamingo and a flaming cat." Hogan had heard it before and so probably had the female guests, but from the rollicking laughter you'd of thought he was a Palladium star.

The laughter abated and Sid Barron turned his overweight frame to be confronted with Hogan's wry smile and sun-cracked face. At first it didn't click and then his eyes opened and narrowed with recognition.

Hogan struck first. "Hello Sid. How's the porn-and-drug King of Soho performing out here? Got it wrapped up? Shouldn't be difficult with this lot." He gestured at the half-dressed girls. "Run in your own stuff as well I suppose?"

"I always said you should have a red-hot poker stuffed up your arse. Piss off Hogan. You're well out of order."

"Don't worry Sid. Now I know you're here to pollute the place I'm off. Sorry to disturb you ladies." Hogan walked away and out of the Caribbean.

Back in England he'd rented new offices and was re-advertising his services. He was still cross that he hadn't had the guts to see Sid off once and for all. Barron's heavies were responsible for his leg and that crook should be behind bars for a least three murders, and not to be forgotten, several GBHs. 'The swine got away with millions, but I bet he can't be touched out there. One day, we'll see.'

The fancy new telephone with its bank of memory buttons suddenly went off with a shrill ring which Hogan didn't recognise at first.

He took the call and listened to the familiar voice at the other end.

"Tim. How's it going? Thought we were through?"

"Same with you. Saw your new advert in some security magazine. I thought you'd packed it in."

"Did for a while. Sun and sea. Got itchy for some action. Very low profile though. The heavy scene's over... you still flying?"

"Still at it. Yes."

"How'd it go with your mate? Johnston wasn't it? I seem to remember. Read a report about it in the papers. Insurance problem or something?"

"Yes, you might have read about that, but it's got nothing to do with the investigation we were doing."

"How come?"

"The electronics business with the CAA is still awaiting a decision. Now we have another problem." Tim explained the criminal court action and brought Hogan up to date on Barry's disappearing act.

"You still acting nursemaid for this guy? Why this time?"

"I want to explain about the CAA meeting and I'm worried for his future."

"Seems to me the idiot's got a death-wish. Best you forget him."

"I want him found before the police do. Will you take it?"

"For you darling – anything," Hogan grinned to himself, "but mostly 'cause you're my first engagement since I got back and the rent's due next week."

"Thanks. Same terms as before?"

"Sure I'm not fussed. Any news on Azif?"

"No. I think we've heard the last from him."

"Wasn't a bad guy really. Different world, eh? Right, I'll get on to this straightaway and report when I have anything. See you – cheerio."

Chapter Forty

The whole place stank of stale fish and his stomach was struggling to cope with the nausea created by the continuing rolling of the stubby trawler. Designed for fishing they may be, but this one was not good for fast ferry-crossings.

The skipper was a typical 'ask no questions' character with beard and whisky bottle to match. Barry had hired him out of Falmouth having doubled back and forth over the country with his idea of keeping moving. They were bound for Jersey in a force five with winds forecast to increase and the small craft creaked and strained as it was pounded through the heavy seas.

"Another four, I reckon."

The way Barry was suffering he didn't care if they arrived at all. He felt like death, not just from the gyrations of this old craft, but from the depression of the last months and the endless nightmares and headaches which never left him. He wondered about brain tumours and his sanity and whether he should end it all now in these boiling waters.

"Take some." The skipper handed the open bottle and Barry gulped the acidic alcohol, feeling it cut into the phlegm in his stomach.

"Keep it. I've got another." He produced a gristly grin as Barry gave him a grateful nod.

The money. I've nothing else. The money. He was almost paranoid about it. These thoughts had never left his head since he'd given them the slip, but now was the time to act. He couldn't wait any longer.

He'd never been on the run before except for the little deceptions with Judy. Now he was experiencing a manic kick along with his depression as he imagined the whole world was chasing him. He had scoured the papers for reports on his movements, but they were empty. 'Aha! They don't want me to know their movements,' he reasoned. He saw plain clothes policemen watching from shadowy corners and he noticed shop assistants glancing at him as they whispered to their superiors. He'd kept altering his outerwear, and he was currently sheltering from the open sea with a dark grey anorak that he'd bought off a stall in Falmouth.

The little trawler battered on its course and soon Barry could see dark shapes emerging from the gloom of the spray-covered waters and the low, rain-filled clouds.

"Alderney." The skipper waved his arm. "Gets worse through the strait then we'll run for the lee shore."

Barry finished the bottle and tossed it to the elements as he concentrated on his plan. Money first, then I'll slip into France. Contact Judy and we'll hole up on the west coast somewhere. Forget the bungalow. The money she'd get for his few possessions wasn't worth the risk of being caught.

The wind was easing and Barry watched the skill of the trawler owner as he worked his way through the marker buoys to the Jersey harbour entrance.

Lloyds Bank was a prominent building proudly displaying its service in a busy precinct off the main shopping centre of St Helier.

"Why didn't I choose a backstreet bank?" he cursed under his breath. He stopped in front of a jeweller's window opposite the bank and surveyed the pedestrian walkway for suspicious persons. The place was busy and he felt sure that the tramp sitting nearby was genuine.

"I'd like to close my account." The teller was young and needed advice.

"One moment sir." How often had he heard those words in a television thriller? He watched with his heartbeat increasing as the young assistant talked to a smart suited gentleman at the back of the counters. 'I'm off. They twigged me.' He started to turn but there was a man behind him in a beige-coloured lapelled raincoat who was blocking his exit.

"Cash or cheque sir?"

"I... um, cash please." Barry heard the man behind breathing heavily and expected at any moment to feel a metal barrel pushed into his kidneys.

"Would you mind going to the securities counter sir? Mr Cross will deal with you personally."

"This way Mr Johnston." Cross was guiding him to a small office and Barry knew this was it. The office was empty as the under manager offered him a seat. "Safer in here sir. Especially when we're dealing in cash. Now what denomination...?"

Easy does it. Barry was sweating as he walked out of the bank with the hundred pound wads filling his anorak pocket. He felt dozens of eyes were on him and dived into the nearest pub to avoid his pursuers.

The Arab bank was easier and he didn't feel the pressure as the richly-clothed punters moved silently over the marbled floor, minding their own business. He collected the cash and purchased a money belt from a nearby shop. He spotted the advertisement for a small hotel out on the headland near the lighthouse and decided to hide away to work out the next move.

The receptionist accepted his booking and he settled back in the taxi with an anxious look to see if he was being followed. There seemed to be one car behind and then it took off on a side road. He kept turning to the rear window, but the recent boat journey and the tension he'd experienced at the banks had made him tired, and his head started nodding as he tried the fight off the desire to sleep.

"Your hotel sir." The taxi driver made him jump from his slumber.

Chapter Forty-One

The official statistics say that there are hundreds of people who suddenly disappear never to be found, and the records go back many years. Hogan had read this somewhere and he was beginning to believe it. Two months had passed since he'd spoken to Tim and he wasn't even off the starting block. He'd informed the law of his interest and the sergeant in charge had been very cooperative. But all routes taken only ended in blind alleys or dead ends. The eagle had flown.

The court hearing was adjourned and the papers went silent being more interested in the latest scandals and political blunders, than in petty crime.

He'd raised half a chance with Barry's girlfriend, but she appeared to know nothing although he didn't entirely trust her. He'd trailed her on several occasions and the police had monitored her calls, but neither had produced any clues.

Tim wanted him to carry on, so he did. No skin off my nose. Easy money. Having drawn more blanks than a soldier in training he succumbed to contacting an old friend who'd run an agency for many years, and now lectured at the Polytechnic on private investigation law and associated arts. He found him in one of north London's scruffy Boroughs, marking papers with the use of a well-thumbed and battered text book.

"Hogan you old rascal. What's brought you out of the woodwork?" They talked of the past and jaunts long forgotten, and Hogan brought his friend up to date with the current assignment.

"Where now Max? I've run the book. What's left?"

"The banks."

"Tried. At least the law have, so they tell me."

"They would. First reaction, but only local."

"Explain?"

"Resources. This is a small case. They can only scratch the surface. They'll have traced his main account but that will lead them nowhere I suspect. After that it's guesswork. Hong Kong? Swiss banks? No chance. Do you know how many banks there are?" Hogan got the point.

"But you still say the banks?"

"I guess so."

"Help me?"

"Think. That's my advice to the students." He tapped the papers on his desk.

"So I'm thinking... nothing."

"Trouble with you Hogan is you've had it too easy. Always reckoned you were a lucky fellow when we were in competition."

"Give me a break Max. So the box is getting addled. Not long off senior citizenship you know."

"Balls. It's that rye that's buggered you."

Hogan eyed the run-down lecture room of the underfunded state learning centre, and smelt the musty air of a student's classroom. "How d'you work in this dump? Why don't you go back on the circuit?"

"Leave it Hogan." He stared solemnly at the blackboard. "I still have something to offer these teenagers, even though it's a young man's game these days. Won't be long before we'll be arming the police."

"Okay. I'll quit. Just tell me what to do."

Max paced the aisle between the old-fashioned wooden desks and returned to the worn out blackboard. He picked up a chalk and headed it with the words *Missing Person*. He then drew a number of lines from the main heading and wrote minor headings under each line. *Last Address, Employer, Hobbies...* Max was filling the board. Finally he got round to *Financial Status* and *Bank*.

"Great. I'm really impressed. Solved it in one." Max ignored his derision and circled the subheading *Bank*.

"Proper investigation, you must explore all these headings." Hogan nodded his approval. "Does that mean you have?"

"Most yes."

"Not Bank though?"

"No."

"Right. What have you gleaned about the character of your missing person from the answers to the other headings?"

Hogan wasn't sure what Max wanted so he tried – "a screwball out of his depth?"

Max laughed. "Never passed your English Literature, did you Hogan? Okay, can I summarise your description as... amateur?"

"I'll live with that."

"Good. Now let's link amateur with bank. What have we got?"

"Go on, terrify me."

"Well we haven't got the Caymans or the like have we?"

"You mean he's not clever enough?"

"Clever yes, no, not experienced enough."

"Which tells me...?"

"The amateur's answer. Halfway house. Not on the doorstep but not four thousand miles away."

"So where?"

"You guess."

Hogan racked his brain for the answer: "...Jersey?"

Max beamed at him. "You can be quite bright sometimes."

So here he was sitting in the harbour pub drinking Max's forbidden Jack Daniels, and who should scramble through the door but the very target of his investigation?

He couldn't believe it. Magic. He watched from the dark corner as Barry rapidly downed two glasses, and then the man was on his way. The trail wasn't long and Hogan found himself outside the Bank of Kuwait in a pedestrianised sidewalk. Barry emerged and hailed a taxi from a nearby rank. Hogan followed suit and the two vehicles made their way to a small hotel on the Corbiere peninsular. Barry disappeared inside and Hogan drove past before he paid off his taxi.

He was wondering about the next move when he spotted his target making for the lighthouse. He followed at a discreet distance picking his way gingerly over the rocks which didn't suit his gammy leg. Holding on to an overhanging ledge he negotiated a narrow path to suddenly come face to face with Barry who was blocking the way.

"Mr Johnst..." His words faded as the body lunged at him causing him to lose his balance on the slippery rocks. Hogan heard it snap before his head hit a large boulder and then the world went blank.

Barry stood there shivering from his thoughtless reaction. 'Who was he? Police for certain,' he reasoned. Then he started to panic. Blood was oozing from the man's head and one of his legs was twisted back underneath his body. 'Supposing he's dead?' Barry wasn't going to check. 'I need to get out.' He backtracked quickly over the rocks and collected his belongings and money from his room. He checked out and was lucky to grab a taxi which had arrived with a new guest.

"Harbour please." He sat nervously, sweating at this latest change in his fortunes.

The trawler was still tied up but there was no sign of the captain. Barry asked around and finally found him in a back lane snug bar sitting at a table littered with empty bottles. The fat female next to him was trying to unzip his trouser flies, but the skipper kept pushing her away and demanding more beer. Barry reached in his back pocket and found a tenner which he gave to the whore. "Piss off and get yourself lost." He pointed to the bar. "Get up. I'm hiring you." Barry waved a fifty pound note in front of the drunken fisherman.

"Wa Hoo. A bloody miracle." The skipper grabbed the note shouting out, "Drinks on me lads, let's have a party."

With a lot of scuffling and crashing, as chairs fell over, Barry managed to guide him out, and holding firmly onto his arm the two made a crazy zigzagged course back to the trawler. He nearly lost him in the water as they struggled aboard. "Wait there and don't move." Barry grabbed his jacket with both hands as he forced the words through the skipper's bleary eyes.

He went ashore and dialled the lighthouse hotel.

"Reception. Can I help you?" She sang the words.

"Yes. Well maybe. See I left your hotel a short while ago and as we rounded the bend up the hill I looked back and noticed someone climbing the rocks out to the lighthouse. When I looked again the person had gone and I thought I heard some shouting. Might have been imagination but I thought I'd tell you."

"Thank you sir." The sing-song voice sounded unconcerned. "I'll ask the porter to have a look. Enjoy your holiday."

Barry felt a little better but he wasn't happy. 'What a mess. It's getting worse.' He could hear the snoring from twenty yards away and that was against the flapping of sail riggings and the general harbour bustle. The old salt seemed deader than the man he'd just pushed over the rocks and Barry could get no response from his constant shaking. Eventually he filled a pail of water from over the side and threw the lot onto the lifeless body. The roar nearly made him fall but the boathook, which came from nowhere, crashed into the woodwork by his head making him leap for the safety of the wheelhouse door.

He stood waiting and watched as the skipper started to come to his senses. He was grunting and shaking his head as he tried to focus the scene. "Where're we going?" The voice was gravelled as he spat the words over the side.

"Alderney."

Barry breathed with relief as the wallowing trawler rounded the end of the quay and settled steadily in the wind-protected calmer waters. The captain hooked to a buoy and then disappeared into his cabin. Barry waited for the harbour taxi boat to collect him and walked the hill to the small village centre where he booked into a bed and breakfast cottage.

He slumped out on the bed and closed his eyes feeling the movement of the boat which made him keep opening them to stop the giddy sensation. His mind wandered and slowly he drifted into a disturbed sleep. The dream was still with him but even more jumbled than before.

Suddenly he was in court and the jury were filing in to take up their seats. He looked to their faces and saw that they were all there. Patrick, Tim, Tom Goff, Sally, the farmer and his wife, the insurance brokers and two people he didn't recognise. One was holding his head with blood running down his face and the other kept adjusting his hair. He stared hard to recognise them and saw that their faces were skeletons. He shivered with fear at the dawning realisation that they were sentencing him. A dark-haired girl was brought in with her hands manacled and the jury were frowning as they studied a paper being passed around.

"Sign." The usher removed her handcuffs and handed her the document.

"Never, never." The girl was crying and searched the court for help, but they all sat immobile as if made of stone.

"Sign."

Still shaking her head violently the usher opened the door and a filthy bed was wheeled into the court with the hideous shape of an old lined and grizzled woman lying on it. She beckoned to the girl and pointed to the paper. "Sign my daughter, please sign." She gestured behind and the girl saw the queue of drunken and unshaven men grinning in anticipation as they waited in the corridor.

The girl grasped herself in torment and cried out for help as she pleaded for escape from this hell. She turned to find the two skeletal figures standing beside her. One took her hand and the other held out the pen. "It's destiny. You must sign."

She cringed at the words and was forced to take the pen being offered. Barry strained to see the writing but he was too far away. As she finished, the paper mysteriously blew to the floor to be trapped by the leg of the bed, and he was just able to make out part of the sombre heading on the black-edged foolscap: *Death Certificate of –*

He turned toward her and their eyes met as she mouthed the words. "Please forgive me. I had no choice."

Chapter Forty-Two

The news came through as Tim was finishing a welcome breakfast of bacon and eggs. He wiped the bread around the greasy plate and drank the dregs of coffee before bothering to open his post. Putting *The Daily Mail* to one side he slit open the half-dozen envelopes. The CAA logo caught his attention and he read this first.

...so the findings of the meeting are that this authority considers that the new evidence is sufficient to question that the actions taken by the Captain, Mr Johnston may have been influenced by factors not within his control.

Tim smiled like a Cheshire cat as he read on:

...the evidence will be forwarded to the Captain's lawyers for their consideration...

Tim scanned through the report to quickly get the remaining gist, and stopped to read carefully a paragraph of the CAA's recommendations:

...providing he satisfies a class one medical and can provide a current flight check and airlaw certificate... the authority will consider an application for reinstatement of the ATPL licence.

"Great!" Tim spurted it out loud. At last they were getting a break.

So where now? He smiled unkindly at the thought of poor old Hogan sitting at home nursing a broken ankle. He'd received the call from Jersey and the ageing investigator did not sound very pleased.

"I thought you'd given up the heavy stuff? Low profile you told me." Tim was enjoying pulling his leg. Both legs now, he chortled to himself.

"It's not funny," Hogan moaned, and I suppose it wasn't.

"Got any ideas?"

"I'm out of action for some time so I can't really help."

"D'you reckon he's still on the island?"

"I doubt it. He probably thought I was the law and panicked. I don't think he'd hang around too long if that's so."

"You could have chosen a smarter location to confront him. Now we're back to square one."

"Damn you Mitchell. You're the clever one, qualified and all that. Why don't you get out there and chase his tail?"

"Okay, sorry. But I haven't got a bottomless pocket."

"What about the media?"

"TV you mean?"

"Could be, or the press?"

"Small fry. Doubt we'd tempt their interest. Not exactly a rapist, murderer or a gold bullion crook."

"Suppose you're right. Anyhow, I've got to go. I'm due a session with the physio in half an hour. At least she's got nice warm hands."

"How long are you out?"

"Dunno, at least a fortnight. Bye for now."

He drove to the airport wondering if there was any way the news could be directed to the press but he suspected that the parties would not agree to that until the lawyers had had their fill.

The morning was crisp with a ground frost which had turned the grass white. Tim felt good and was whistling as he breezed into the office.

"Good news?" His secretary posed the question.

"You could say that. Got some information on the Johnston scenario. I'm off to see Patrick." He shuffled briefly at the paperwork on his desk.

"Coffee before you go?"

"Later Anne. I've just had breakfast."

Pat was in one of his better moods as Tim settled back in a soft leather chair. He passed over the report and Patrick read it pretty fully.

"I suppose we owe him an apology?"

"We?"

"Okay me. He owes you a favour for sure."

"Put it down to duty. I only did what any senior captain should do."

"A mite more I'd say." Pat seemed genuinely pleased. "D'you want him back?"

226

"Barry's a good pilot, but there's this other business to solve."
Patrick asked for an update on the latest situation and Tim explained
how they'd found and lost him again. "The danger is that he's
obviously getting really screwed up and God knows where that will
lead him."

"Um. I don't know what to advise to be sure. If you do find him.
Well, it's the way it is. Check him out..., I'll take him back."

"Thanks Pat. I'm very grateful. I need to find him to break the
news."

"Going soft. Chuck would never believe it."

"What happened there? Is everything okay?"

"It's a complicated story Tim. Chuck and I go back a long time."

"I gathered that when I was over in Texas."

"I'm out now. We've both called in our favours. Chuck's on his
own as far as I'm concerned. He's ambitious. Political, that's his
aim."

"And the maintenance?"

"Sorted that is. Found a good man. Be after a small fortune but
the market's picking up. I'll afford it you'll see."

Tim decided to leave it at that. Patrick in a philosophical mood
was something to be savoured but not for too long in case the taste
suddenly deserted. He enquired with the police and spoke to Judy but
neither were able to help. He told Judy about the CAA findings so
that she might be able to get to Barry if he made contact. She
sounded grateful and distressed and apologised that they'd not talked
to each other before.

Chapter Forty-Three

The gaunt figure struggled through the gorse in an aimless way, its head turning from side to side as if searching for something and then watching furtively as if being followed. To the expert, the staring red eyes and dilated pupils would have signified that the animal was in serious danger or badly hurt, certainly highly distressed. The figure broke free of the overgrowth on to the rocky headland overlooking the sea and stopped to watch the waves crashing with relentless abandon on the rocks below.

Half-crazed, Barry had been wandering aimlessly for three days. Unshaven, he'd been sleeping rough and eating stale bread and cheese which he hadn't bothered to replace. His holdall still supported two bottles of whisky from the half-dozen he'd bought, and he reached for one of them as he gazed, mesmerised by the boiling sea.

It was over he knew that. There was only one solution left but he was scared. How to do it? He wanted to jump but he was frightened of merely injuring himself: he needed to be sure he'd finish the job off properly. He'd prayed for the hurt to go but God was not listening. His unbalanced mind went round relentlessly as he fought to find the solutions to his tortured thoughts. The whisky was useless, its strength not even unbalancing his eyes, and he tossed the nearly empty bottle to the rocks below, and watched it shatter to pieces. He shuddered at the cold in his bones.

He clambered on and soon a path took him away from the sea to more open land. He watched the torn material flapping in the wind and wondered how it had become caught on the pole. His brain struggled for sense and then it started to focus. He looked again and realised that the flapping white material was a windsock. Airfield? He knew he'd been here before but his wanderings had dismissed a lot of memory and he could only recall parts of his life. The noise came suddenly and made him duck involuntary as the aircraft swept over the fence only a few feet from his position. It was coming back and he knew he'd been a pilot. The realisation made him hungry for the sky and the peace he remembered and a solution to his heartache.

Like a wounded animal he improvised a survival plan, and suddenly his whole body was sharpened as the adrenalin flowed again through his blood. He skirted the field to arrive at a point where he could see the control tower. He watched two of the ground staff unloading the recently landed ferry plane and searched around for other signs of help. There it was, an Italian-made Partenavia twin. He remembered training on one and the easy way they flew. His watch missing, he'd lost all sense of time, but it was already getting dark so he decided to wait. He made his way back to the safety of the gorse and opened the final bottle to wash down the mouldy bread.

The last light finally went out and shortly afterwards there was the sound of a car driving away. The headlights became dimmer as the vehicle headed along the winding road to the village and the dark buildings stood ghostly and silent, except for the wind which moaned past the latticed tower supports.

He waited for more than hour until he was satisfied that all activity had died. The short distance across the field was soon covered and Barry worked his way to the outside of the hangar where he could just make out in the darkness the sign 'Aurigny – Island Airway'.

Alderney is a sleepy place where crime is almost unknown, especially in the winter with the tourists gone. Barry was unknowingly relying on this as he gingerly moved to the main door catch of the large hangar doors. His luck was in, no padlock. The doors were heavy but well lubricated and after some exertion he was able to open a gap large enough to slip through. His head hurt from the effort and he cursed the last bottle that was now working after all. He found it where expected, on a hook next to the main switches. The little torch was run down but gave enough of a hazy beam to scan around the building. The works offices were at the back with the door open. Finding the keys was a burglar's paradise for there they were, hanging neatly on hooks, with the aircraft registrations marked below.

He doused the torch and picked his way out to the aeroplane. A quick check satisfied his now active senses and he measured enough fuel for his purpose. Covering the light with a handkerchief he gave the passenger seats a quick reconnoitre and spotted several unmarked boxes. He opened one to find it full of vintage wine. The next was champagne and the others hid various spirits and quality brandies.

'Some unfortunate is going to get a smuggling shock.' He smiled for the first time for days. 'Just the ticket for my trip though.'

Armed with a comforting malt he settled back in the generous cabin to take some well-needed sleep, with a promise to his body to be awake before dawn.

Twenty-four hour manned air traffic got the message at seven thirty-five Zulu time, and the rest got it as their stations opened.

Beryl Stanton had been overseeing traffic movements at Alderney for eight years and she tended to act second-hand nature to most activities even if they boarded on emergency. She'd slept fitfully the night before, and heard the engines out over the bay without questioning why. Probably from Guernsey did just register, and then her attention was diverted as Pierre started to use his sensitive hands in those places she couldn't resist. It was always the same as Christmas neared. The hotels took on extra staff from France and many of them only got to know the islands topography from being buried in Beryl's generous breasts.

'It isn't that I'm a nymphomaniac,' she would justify to herself, 'it's simply that my heart tells me that I should do my best to comfort lonely souls.' And Beryl was proud, that being conscientious, she'd never had any complaints regarding the physical execution of her duties.

She guessed something was wrong as she climbed the spiral steps to the control tower. 'Partenavia's not there.' She instinctively knew, and the empty tie-downs confirmed her fears. Flight planned for an IFR departure at ten thirty, it had obviously gone earlier. 'Something odd about that.' The noises which had disturbed her sleep came back.

She contacted the owner who was half way through a shave, and sounded very bleary. "Your plane's departed. Reckon it went at dawn or just before. Is that in order? Did you re-file?"

The spluttered reply didn't help but she gathered that "I bloody well didn't!" meant 'No!'

"I suggest you get down here as soon as possible, meanwhile I'll inform air traffic of a possible infringement." That done she attacked the land line and set the whole industry on alert. She spoke to the local constabulary who agreed to send someone to the airfield.

The initial suspicion was that the incident was drug-related, and the owner was interviewed with this in mind. His own duty-free gamble with a cabin full of wines didn't help, and he had to choose his words carefully.

Tracing an aircraft that doesn't want to be found is like looking for a needle in a haystack. Without radio contact and any transponder signal the Partenavia could be going anywhere: France, mainland Europe, the Mediterranean, the possibilities were endless. They established that there was only sufficient gas for about three hundred miles which narrowed the field of radius to Southern England, Wales and Northern France. Further than that would require refuelling. It was a laborious task to inform the major air traffic zones and airfields within the circle drawn with its centre at Alderney, but it had to be sorted. They all knew that the stolen craft could put down at any small unmanned grass strip and this left everyone with a feeling that no more could be done at this stage.

The sky lightened very slowly as Barry trimmed the aircraft for its final journey. 'I've always wondered what happens during a ditching, especially with a fixed undercarriage.' His unbalanced mind swung like a pendulum between reality and fantasy as he set course for Land's End and switched in the autopilot before settling back for his final task.

He closed his eyes to review his whole life which seemed so utterly depressing. He relived the bad times again and again, and was incapable of focusing on any of the successes which all seemed so pointless. The side pockets contained some flight pads and he tore off a sheet and started to write for Judy.

He found it difficult to choose the words to describe the pathos and anger eating into his heart. He reached for the bottle and drank heavily to blot out the reality as he tried to finish his epitaph. The bumping of the aircraft made it difficult to write, and a sudden lurch caused the letter to drop on the cabin floor. He looked down at it with distaste and disgust then emptied the remaining wine over the paper to watch in slow motion as the liquid blurred his spiky handwriting.

"Sod'em all. Why should I bloody care? They don't. No one does! Besides, I've got a plane to fly and that's more important."

He grabbed the controls and dived down to fifty feet off the sea to skim through the spray coming from the white tips of the waves. The tanker loomed into view as he turned back from reaching another bottle; he heaved back violently on the yoke controls to roar a few feet over its masts and then barrel-rolled the plane as he climbed.

"Wha hee. Nearly got you that time. Didn't know this Italian crap would do that! And not a drop spilt." He glanced back at the boxes of drink, proud of his remembered flying skills.

Warrant Officer Eddy Edwards was monitoring the screen when the call came through. He was feeling tired from last night's squash tournament, although pleased with the way he'd played. Third prize was better than expected and all he wanted now was an easy day.

"Culdrose Radar. Warrant Officer Edwards speaking."

The duty officer from London information relayed the facts relating to an aircraft apparently stolen from Alderney airfield with a likely duration of three hours. "We've no clues on motive or destination so we're requesting cooperation from a network of radar stations for any infringements or unusual sightings."

"Roger. That's copied. We'll be in touch." Damn, there goes my relaxing day.

The eight o'clock news on both the radio and television included a final report about a missing light aircraft possibly stolen from the Channel Isles. The TV showed a photo of a similar twin and rumbled on about drugs and arms. Hogan saw it and rang Tim. "What d'you think?"

"Highly likely. Makes sense from your Jersey contact. He's mad enough to do anything."

"What d'you reckon he's about?"

"God knows. I think he's blown his mind."

"Shall I contact the girlfriend?"

"Why?"

"I think we may have a disaster on our hands. I think she should know. The authorities may need her help."

They agreed that Tim would pick her up and to rendezvous in Hogan's office. "The ankle can probably make that, but no further," he grumbled. She appeared calm and very pretty that morning and Hogan had to admire her legs as she sat with her skirt hitched in a rather battered low chair in his office. 'Why the hell doesn't he concentrate on servicing that instead of all this daredevil nonsense?'

"Disaster you said. In what way?" asked Tim.

232

"The man's acting crazy. We all agree?" They did.

"You know him well Judy. What d'you think he'll do?"

"I knew him when he was sane. Now... I dunno. He frightens me." She crossed her legs and Hogan swallowed in thought.

"We don't have much time."

"How come?" Tim said. "We don't know where he's going, sure. South of France, Portugal, possible. He's got the range. Surely we have time?"

"I doubt it."

"Explain?"

"He's hurt. Like a wounded animal. The systems hurt him, bureaucracy if you like, but he probably blames the people. He wants revenge. What better way. Up there he can do some damage. Get someone. Hurt them. No, he's not off to Europe. He's on his way here."

They listened to Hogan's hypothesis and Tim walked over to the window before he spoke. "So where's this retribution? Who's he going to hurt?"

"Marvel Air for starters. Could make a mess of your boss's fleet."

There was a stony silence before Tim could muster an answer. "You're not serious? Jesus I hope you're not!" He paused for a reply but Hogan was silent. "You are... Jesus! No way!" Tim paced the small room which he found was becoming claustrophobic.

"I don't believe it." Her voice was very quiet. "I don't believe he would hurt anybody. At least not physically. He's very gentle at heart."

"So how do you see it?"

"Himself. He'll take it out on himself. He's lost his self esteem and he blames himself deep down."

"Okay if we buy that, where does it lead us?"

She took a small handkerchief from her handbag and gently blew her nose before clicking it back in the bag. "Suicide." The word seemed to echo round the small office as if it had never been heard before and needed somewhere to settle.

"Suicide." Tim spoke. "You really believe that?"

"I do. I've been afraid of it for some time. It was just a question of when and how. This way will seem right to Barry. Dying at the controls..." Her voice faltered and Tim put his arm around her shoulders for genuine comfort.

"I need to alert the authorities," Tim said.

"How can that help?"

"Maybe Judy's right but maybe you are also. He could justify hurting others as long as it eliminated himself as well."

"I see. You might have a point. Where do we start?"

"You inform the police. Leave the flying bits to me. Come Judy, I'll run you home."

Tim looked at his watch. Nine o'clock. He must be over the mainland now if he's coming this way. I need to move fast. God! what a mess.

Culdrose got their first break, and Eddy requested a meeting in the briefing room as a matter of urgency.

"Perhaps you'd like to report on the present situation, Warrant Officer." The calm and precise words emanated from Squadron Leader Gus Roberts who was officer IC search and rescue for the south and south-west of the UK. Although still young for his rank, Gus had spent most of his service flying from aircraft carriers and had seen action in many seas around the world. This posting was ideal for his experience, and he was dedicated to its challenges, and the satisfaction it gave in the dual service to military and civilian personnel.

"We've had a radio transmission from a container tanker steaming westerly in mid-channel about thirty minutes ago. Apparently it was 'bombed', for want of another word, by a low flying aircraft. The watch reported that the plane was so low that it nearly took out the main communications mast."

"Did the watch identify the craft?"

"Not specifically, other than it was twin-engined. Apparently it did a roll as it climbed away."

"Brave or mad," was the best Gus could offer. "Seems like it could be our bandit though. Which way did it head out?"

"Westerly we think. That's their best interpretation."

"If that's so, he should be with us now." Flight Lieutenant O'Neal interrupted the discussion having listened to the other views in silence.

"Check with radar," Gus instructed, although Eddy had already picked up the intercom connected to operations.

"They have an unidentified bleep travelling west at about one hundred and fifty knots. Over Land's End at this time. No radio contact, nor have St Mary's. Will infringe Scilly's airspace shortly."

"Roger. I think we've got our man but where the hell's he going?"

"Search me," said Eddy.

"Probably very appropriate words," came the reply.

They quickly scattered to their respective duties to await further information and instructions.

Tim at last connected through London information that there might be some news from the south-west quarter. "Try Culdrose," he was offered.

"I'd like to talk to the operations officer urgently!"

"Please detail the nature of your enquiry sir? We're very busy today."

"So am I, and you're wasting precious time. I'm a senior commercial captain and you have an emergency. So please put me through." The serious approach had its effect and Tim was soon talking to Squadron Leader Roberts. He quickly explained his position and his concern that the stolen plane might be piloted by a Mr Johnston, although no one had any way of confirming that. Roberts informed him that they had a radar contact of an unidentified plane heading out west of Land's End. "Have you any idea where he might be routing?" asked the Squadron Leader.

"No idea sir."

"The authorities have suggested drugs or even arms so it could be Southern Ireland I suppose, if he can make it."

"How do you mean if he can make it?"

"Okay, air traffic Alderney tell us he's only got three hours' fuel and he must have used half of that already."

"I see... How d'you know you're tracking the stolen aircraft?"

"We don't. We're working on a mid-channel siting." The officer told him of the events with the tanker and the coincidence of a radar observation shortly after.

"That's it then, I feel our conclusion is the most likely," Tim said.

"You've lost me."

"Think it through. If the guy was smuggling he'd hardly dive bomb a ship and give away his position. No, he'd try and track outside radar range wouldn't he?"

"It sounds logical. So what's your theory?"

Tim found it necessary to explain some more of Barry's background and his problems over the last two years. "We think that he's got so screwed up that he's decided to call it a day."

The line went quiet as Gus ruminated on his best line of action. There was no declared emergency and no danger to third parties. Instructing a search and rescue was an expensive business and he couldn't make that decision lightly. He had...

"You still there?" Tim was becoming slightly impatient.

"Sorry. I hear what you say but I'm not sure what action to take."

"You have the authority I assume?"

"Yes indeed, but I need to be sure this is an emergency as defined in regulations."

"For Christ's sake! This isn't a time to worry about the book! There's a guy out there who's about to top himself and you're ranting on about regulations!" Tim vented his frustration on the operations officer.

"I'm not in the business of nursemaiding cranks," he snapped back.

"Okay calm down. I apologise. Look, this man's a friend of mine. He's had a tough time, partly self-induced I accept, but stemming from an injustice. He's effectively been pardoned, but he doesn't know that. He deserves another chance. We must try... you must try. Please."

"I'll probably lose my stripes on this one. You and I and that guy out there, I suppose we all owe it to each other in a way. We're all in the same game and something similar could happen at any time. You're convinced you are right?"

"Known him a long time. It's the best I can offer."

"The guts approach eh? Well Mitchell, here goes my training. You've got your request." He replaced the receiver and pushed the red operations button.

The Shackleton was one of the last in service with the RAF but still one of the best-equipped for surveying the open seas. Its pedigree of successful sorties was almost legendary, and the crews knew they would be sad when the old warrior had finally to retire to its resting place.

The counter-rotating engines were already warming as Gus Roberts grabbed his headset and hurried out onto the tarmac. Seeing the beast ready for action always gave him a thrill and he suspected that the crews of the old Lancasters, from which ancestry this plane had developed, must have felt the same. His co-pilot had it rolling before he was belted in and he felt the hairs on his neck rise with the deep throat noise of the engines on full power, and the almost orgasmic sense of adventure that he always got from rescue operations.

"Two six zero!" he snapped the staccato instruction and then moved back to the navigation station with its panels of electronic wizardry and radarscope screens which stretched down both sides of the fuselage.

"How's the weather?"

"Deteriorating."

"Have you got a fix?"

"We did have, but we've lost it."

"How come?"

"I think he's flying low or maybe we're getting some interference from wave effect."

"How far ahead on your last contact?"

The navigator punched in the code numbers. "One hundred and fifty."

Gus nodded. Good as she was, this flying nerve centre was not renowned for speed and he realised they were unlikely to reach the target before it ran out of fuel. 'If only he'd use the radios,' he urged, although he suspected this would be the last thought on one's mind in the mad situation out there.

Gus had them transmitting continuous calls on the local frequencies, and also the Mayday code, for the possibility that the pilot might switch on for any reason. He hoped they would catch the twin and maybe attract attention, but that now seemed unlikely. He debated on scrambling a fighter, but decided it was too late. Besides, there was little chance of finding anyone in this weather.

They were down to thirteen hundred feet with only a couple of miles visibility and he was not feeling confident. He moved back to where Tim and Judy were sitting and asked if they were comfortable.

Against regulations Tim had persuaded the Squadron Leader to take them, and had flown down himself so that they could join in the search. "She knows his state of mind. If we do make contact it could be crucial to talk him out of it." Tim had worked hard and eventually Gus had surrendered.

"Any contact?"

Gus shook his head. "Weather's against us."

Judy sat with hands between her legs, and her head nearly touching her knees, as the plane battled on.

Chapter Forty-Four

The rules say that the pilot in command should not fly within twelve hours of partaking of alcohol. Barry had smiled about that in the past. Although he'd always been conscientious himself, he'd met several who were 'well over' as they took to the flight deck. 'I wonder how they arrived at that rule? Doubt it's ever been tested scientifically,' he pondered as he reached yet again for another bottle. 'Wouldn't they like to test me now!' He tried to unscrew the top before he realised it was wired and he'd picked a champagne. 'What a way to go...! All I need now is a woman.'

The plane was all but skimming the waves and he glanced idly at the fuel gauges as he worked off the cork. The shaken gas blew the wine into his face and he laughed crazily as he forced the bottle neck down his throat. Not long now the gauges were telling him. The sea was beckoning in the same way as when you looked to the ground from a high-rise building.

He knew he was safe. 'They'll never get me now. No more standing in court with those righteous souls telling you what you should or shouldn't have done. Paying themselves fancy fees and then committing the very practices they preach. Parasites – all of them – bloodsuckers!'

He flicked on the radios and picked up the transmit phone. Let's tell 'em shall we? "Bastards, can you hear me? Listen to me will you? You're bent as nine-bob notes the lot of you...! Why don't you all sod off and leave me alone!" He tossed the bottle behind his head and still slandering broke into song as the port engine started to splutter.

The startled message came through loud and clear to all in the Shackleton and overrode the rumblings of the heavy four engines. At first they looked numbly at each other and then Judy jumped from her seat and tumbled her way to the cockpit.

"Let me talk to him." She directed her words to the Squadron Leader.

Gus was already trying to make contact and she heard his formal approach to the lost aeroplane. "To station transmitting on 121.5 this is Shackleton S3, please let me know your position. I repeat, please notify your position."

She grabbed the microphone from him and screamed into it. "Barry! This is Judy! For God's sake what are you doing? I love you, please turn round, please speak to me!"

The singing rambled on in a delirious way interspersed with laughing and swearing. "...baby I love you... and did it my way... Hypocrites! Thought they could get me? No chance!"

"Barry please! It's all over! They've pardoned you! They're giving your licence back!" She started to cry.

Gus took over and tried again.

"They've made contact." Eddy radioed the message to Flight Lieutenant Tony O'Neal who was directing the Wessex helicopter out into the Atlantic winds. Gus Roberts had flight-planned this backup before they were airborne, but the slower craft was still fifty miles behind the rescue plane.

"How is it?"

"Crazy apparently. Guy's off his rocker or well drunk, by the sound of it. Must be on the edge of his fuel."

"Weather's bad. Down to two kilometres with a forty knot headwind. Going to be a haystack job if he ditches in this."

"Have we located him yet?" Gus was staring at the screens.

"Radio fix only. Still no radar. About fifty nautical ahead."

Gus made his way back to the flight cabin where he'd left Judy to her pleadings. Tim tried but neither could get any reply.

"He's probably on transmit all the time with the button held down. Damn maniac. Still, keep trying," he instructed Judy.

"...Red One this is your Leader calling. Make a fast run down the valley. I'll try to cover you from the port side flack..."

"Roger leader going in." '...rat-a-tat-tat... rat-a-tat-tat.' Barry squeezed the handphone button as he played the war games of his childhood. He fumbled as the Partenavia bumped around, and the mike slipped out of his hand and fell to the floor.

The noise in the cabin suddenly changed as the port engine gave its last cough and Barry watched the propeller slowly idle to a stop. It was quieter now and the change of flying conditions sobered him slightly as his training overrode his tortured and fuzzy mind, and he automatically trimmed to fly with one engine.

"It's Judy! Please talk to me..."

The sounds came from the speakers above his head. and startled him. He looked round as if he expected to find her sitting in the aircraft. He couldn't rationalise the voices. Where were they coming from? Voices from heaven maybe? Is she trying to make contact? He shook his head to try and clear it.

He picked the hand phone from the cabin floor. "Judy. Is that you? I'm sorry. I couldn't take it... Please join me soon."

She started to reply but Tim snatched the microphone from her hand and barked his message over the radio. "Barry listen to me! This is Tim. Whatever you're up to scrub it! I've got your licence back! D'you hear? You're in the clear. Turn back and lean the fuel. You must be nearly empty. We're just behind you if you have to ditch. Turn on your transponder."

"Licence back? ... Whad'ya mean? Tim is that you? Where are you?"

"Barry concentrate! Tim Mitchell, your old buddy! You're clear! Don't waste your life! Turn back!"

"My old buddy Tim. That's a joke. You shopped me mate. I'm finished, can't think straight. Come and have some champagne with me, there's a good fellow. Where are you? Thought I heard Judy's voice?"

Tim's frustration grew as he realised he didn't have the training to deal with this situation. Keep talking. Isn't that the advice? Keep it professional and don't treat him like a child. Concentrate on his trained mind. "We're in an air-sea rescue Shackleton, and we've a helicopter in the area."

"Shackleton? Where the hell d'you borrow that?"

"Didn't borrow it Barry. This is for real. You're an emergency. Please try and understand. Put on your life jacket."

"Won't find me. Fuel's gone. Thanks for trying." He was laughing wildly.

"Barry, this is Judy. We've got your licence back! Can't you understand? You're pardoned! Save yourself! I want you... I need you!" She prayed as she sobbed out the words.

"Need you as well." His voice sounded slurred but softer. "Licence? Don't understand. We're going. Engine..." The transmission went silent.

"Barry! Tim here! How d'you read me?" The speakers crackled but gave no further reply. "He must be down." Tim turned to Gus Roberts.

"Okay. We've got a fix. Five miles ahead. We'll set up a search pattern on a ten mile grid at one mile intervals." The Squadron Leader sprang into action. "I need to advise you all that I'm not confident."

Tim knew the odds were against them. If he survived the ditching the plane would not float for long. No life raft and no life jacket. Ten minutes in the cold Atlantic seas, and the aggressive weather out there, kaput. He looked from the side observatory windows and calculated that the co-pilot was down to five hundred feet. The waves were breaking on their tops, which made sightings even more difficult in the black unfriendly sea.

"Wessex to base. We're reading two..." The professional teams were in charge and there was little Judy and he could do but wait.

"D'you think there's any chance?" She seemed so small and frightened that she raised a protective feeling in his body. He wanted to hold her in his arms and take away the anxiety and pain.

"Slim. I wouldn't be honest if I said any different. Have some coffee." Tim gave her the flask and also covered her shoulders with a blanket from the overhead locker. She drank the hot liquid in silence.

The Shackleton's fine-pitched engines thrummed on as the crew rigorously flew their search pattern. They never saw the Wessex in the poor visibility but the radar screen picked out the ghostly dragonfly as it complimented the larger aeroplane's movements.

"Shipping. Is there any to help us?" Gus asked Eddy back at Culdrose.

"Nothing in the immediate area. No salvation there."

"We're in for a long haul," Gus told himself.

The jolt as the twin-engined craft hit the sea was gentler than the book would have you believe, but then the alcohol had deadened all senses and he hardly felt the torn metal as it seared through the skin of his leg, biting hard into the bone. He heard the arm snap and then his head was banging against the windscreen support. The sickly smell of blood filled the cabin with the signature of death. Miraculously the plane hadn't up-ended and was floating on its submerged fuselage with the wings dipping in and out of the water, as though it wished it had been born a seaplane with floats.

The descent from engine failure to the ocean below had only been two minutes but was long enough for Barry to hear and repeat those last words singing in his ears. "Licence back", they'd said "licence back". It wasn't clear what they were trying to tell him, but as his befuddled mind grew clear: he was suddenly very afraid to die. He wanted to feel the warmth of Judy's body again and shuddered in fear as he saw the raging dark sea rapidly filling the whole vista of the windscreen. 'I want to live!'

Fighting the controls he'd pulled off a textbook ditching on the upside of a wave with the strong wind holding the plane in a highly stalled position. The pain started to penetrate the body and he knew there wasn't much time. He reached under the seat with his good arm and somehow managed to find a life jacket and wiggle it over his head.

The pilot's door was jammed and Barry tried to smash it open with the empty bottles but it wouldn't budge. He fought the rocking plane and dragged himself past the seats to the rear door. The bright yellow colour caught his eye and he marvelled to reach up and drag out a neatly packed dinghy bag. Somehow he managed to tie the release rope round his arm. The plane was sinking fast but with luck it was nosing down engine-heavy, to momentarily throw the tail and the rear door clear of the raging sea.

He opened the door to the wind and waves which were howling around the fuselage and threw himself out with the rope from the dinghy firmly wrapped around his arm. He heard the hiss and was almost swamped by the rubber vessel as it expanded alongside his body. There was no time to inflate the life jacket, but this was ignored as he struggled to get into the dinghy which was wallowing violently in the windswept sea.

The pain was agonising as he tried to haul himself aboard using his broken arm to maintain a hold to prevent the vessel floating away. The dinghy was too slippery and again and again he kept falling away and being submerged by the waves. Weakening, Barry made one final effort and managed at last to drag himself out of the water. Once aboard he flopped into the soaking bottom and tightening his lifejacket, drew himself into the semi-protection of the tented canopy.

The effort and concentration drained all energy from his body, and the pain and alcohol slowly took control as he drifted into unconsciousness.

"Culdrose control. This is Shackleton S3. We're returning to base." Gus Roberts left it as long as possible but the light was now fading badly and they'd been patrolling for over seven hours with no success. Not that he'd held out much hope anyway. Crazy man with a death wish and a voice that sounded full of remorse. Probably taken some pills as well. Still, we've a duty to try in case I'm wrong or he changes his mind. The only chance as Gus gauged it was if by some miracle the pilot had been carried by the ocean's flotsam, maybe on a seat or piece of debris floating in the sea. They'd thrown out a dinghy around their calculated ditching point, and watched it inflate before disappearing into the vast seas. Even the fluorescent orange of this vessel was soon lost and they only saw it once again in all those lonely searching hours. Gus had long ago called off the Wessex. "Suggest you stand by on St Mary's," he'd instructed Tom O'Neal.

Tom decided differently and put down at the Tresco heliport on the Scillies and negotiated with the commercial services to supply him with fuel. This way he could make short sorties to the patrol area if required.

She was crying openly and even the hardened crew felt saddened for this slip of a girl. Tim tried to comfort her and explain that it was hopeless, and that the Squadron Leader had probably held on much longer than regulations would have advised. "It was Barry's wish. Everyone has a right to finish their life. He just couldn't hack it. You'll have to come to terms with that and respect his decision."

"I loved him. Why couldn't that be enough? He must have known! His right you say? What about others and the hurt he's leaving behind?"

Tim found it difficult to argue. Barry had no children and that was perhaps a blessing. Maybe if he'd had a family it would have given him something to hold on to. Then, maybe not, for it seemed that Barry had lost his self-esteem and that might have been worse to face

244

within a family. He knew Barry's parents were still alive, although he'd not met them. He also knew of a younger sister whom he'd met once briefly, and gathered she was very proud of her brother. '"The hurt left" she'd said. Is suicide a brave act or a selfish one?' Tim pondered the moral complexities which these fateful events had suddenly brought to the fore.

The landing lights flickered a welcome home as the four-engined senior citizen quietly descended into their warm glow and taxied to the protection of the wide hangar doors. The ground crew took over and Gus and the others made their way to the debriefing room.

"Coffee?" He offered it to Tim and Judy.

"Anything stronger?" Tim pointed to the hunched body walking slowly through the rain that was sweeping across the field.

"I'm sure we can fix something... By the way, thanks for your help. I wish it could've been different."

Chapter Forty-Five

The sun broke through briefly before hiding again behind the drifting sea mist. The short-lived brightness registered on his swollen eyelids as he tried to bring his sore eyes into focus. A few days had passed since the ditching, but the pathetic figure in the yellow dinghy could not know that or why he was there. The seas had taken their toll and the body was numb and wet and nearing the final stages of hypothermia. His hair and bearded face were matted with salt, his lips red with dried and fresh blood congealing together. That he was alive at all was a mystery, and probably only due to the rain falling on to his face and seeping into an unconscious open mouth. His arm lay at a confused angle and the smell from the badly gashed leg was stronger than the natural aromas of the surrounding ocean. The sun tried again and this time was winning. The cold front that had plagued the West Country for days had passed through, and fine weather was forecast for the next forty-eight hours. The morning drifted on and the mist and low cloud lifted to make way for the winter sun to shine brightly in a turquoise blue sky.

Barry felt its warmth soaking into his face and rubbed a frozen hand over his eyes to at last make out some objects. He studied the yellow craft and could see the gentle waves rocking the dinghy. A bird perched briefly, then flew away in the wind. The only recollection was of dreams and people and places that dominated his subconscious mind as he drifted in delirium.

Now it was coming back. He remembered a plane. Who was in it? The smell was causing a deep sickness in his parched throat. Water slopped around in the dinghy, and he wanted to get up and dry his clothes. He made to move, and as the pain from his injuries racked his body, cried out in agony with no sound coming from his mouth. The low drone entered his ears without recognition before he drifted again away to the dreams.

The message was received around noon from St Mary's. "Air traffic here. We've had a pan call from one of the Islanders flying out of Land's End. They spotted what they consider might be a dinghy some ten miles west of the lighthouse."

The Duty officer logged it and Gus received the information ten minutes later. 'Probably the one we dropped,' he thought, for they usually turned up somewhere blown onto rocks or the foreshore, and they hadn't had a report so far on this one

"Any info on colour?" he quizzed the officer.

"Didn't say."

"Can you check?"

St Mary's couldn't help and the Islander crew had disappeared into town to get some breakfast.

"I can't authorise on that." He'd summoned Flight Lieutenant O'Neal to the office for a discussion.

"Ten miles off. Shouldn't be a problem."

"Rules Tom. You know the pressure. They're cutting back everywhere. Waiting for us to make a mistake and then chop."

"You're getting paranoid with this hobby horse of yours."

Gus fiddled with the buttons of his tunic and then rose to study the map on the wall. "About here I'd say. Wonder if there're any vessels in the area?"

"What about the Penzance lifeboat?"

"Slow – if we're going, it's got to be us."

"If it's our man, he's got to be dead by now."

"I agree. All the more reason for not jumping the gun."

"So what's your decision?" Tom joined him by the map.

"We'll alert shipping. Look out for an orange dinghy. Also ask the Land's End boys to keep a watching brief on its drifting course."

"So you don't need me?"

"Nope. You can take lunch."

"See you in the mess then." Tom walked out of the office.

Gus paced around the room, arguing with himself on whether he was making the right decision. He could see the girl's face and her pleading eyes. Any other occasion and he could have taken a fancy to her for himself. A wild, natural looker, he wished that some of the sophisticated women that came his way could ooze a bit more basic sex appeal, instead of their hard to get techniques. The buzzer interrupted his thoughts and he recognised the duty officer on the line.

"Yellow."

"Sorry. Can you repeat that?"

"Yellow, the dinghy. I've just got the confirmation from air traffic."

"Jerusalem! Thanks – I must fly." He rapidly dialled the mess and demanded Tom O'Neal on the phone.

"Gus. I'm just on my roast..."

"Forget your food! Get your butt up here *tout de suite*! We've got an emergency."

Gus was already kitted out when he met Tom hurrying along the corridor.

"Grab two winchmen. I want us airborne immediately."

"What's the rush?"

"It's not ours. It's yellow."

The many-bladed rotors of the Wessex helicopter thumped the air as Tom O'Neal lifted the craft off its pad and set course for the Land's End lighthouse and the unknown findings waiting for them out in the hungry seas. Gus held up his thumbs to the two other crewmen on board in a gesture of 'let's go for it lads.'

The weather was being kind and Gus wished it had been like this a few days ago. 'Still we don't know what's down there. Maybe jumping to conclusions.' He was sitting in the co-pilot's seat and the low winter sun made it difficult to see clearly through the wind-scratched windows.

"Reckon we should approach from the west when we find it. Should be better with the sun behind us."

"My thoughts entirely." Tom had upward of nine thousand hours on helicopters and had been flying them since he joined the RAF at the age of eighteen. He loved this job with air-sea rescue, not only because it brought his skills to the fore, but also because of the sense of satisfaction he got from a successful mission. They weren't always happy endings and he felt in his gut that this one could be a disaster. Still at least they were trying and that's what mattered. He always felt frustrated and low if weather conditions or regulations prevented them from having a go.

The winchman spotted it first. "Ten o'clock." He relayed his findings down the intercom.

"Roger. Got it," came Tom's reply. "I'll circle to the east and then we'll go down for a look."

The life raft looked so small in the empty seas and Tom wondered that they kept floating at all. He lowered the Wessex but could see no bodies or sign of life. "Reckon it's empty," he spoke to Gus.

"Keep circling, and down further. It's got a fairly big canopy."

Gus trained the glasses on the life raft although the juddering of the helicopter and the rolling of the rubber craft made it difficult to focus. He saw what he thought was a foot and some bloodstains before a wave moved the canopy opening from his view. "Someone inside I'm sure. We'll put one of you down," he said to the back-up crew.

The hydraulic motor whined quietly as the winchman lowered his colleague harnessed to the stainless steel winch rope. Tom was hovering as low as he dared to limit the swing of the rope in the wind. The cable inched nearer and they all waited in anticipation of the aircraftsman's findings. Gingerly he reached the raft, and after securing a second rope, ducked under the canopy. The sight that presented itself was frightening as he made out the crunched body, and the smell from his shattered leg made him gasp for air. The man was dead, he was sure of that. He checked the neck pulse and was amazed to feel a weak beat which had slowed to well below the normal rate. His intercom buzzed and he pushed the key. "Take me up." As he was lifted he spat out the foul air that had entered his lungs and braced himself for the job ahead.

"He's alive. Just. In a nasty mess I'd say. We don't have time for any first aid. We'll have to drag him out and hope for the best. Need a mask. The guy's foul. Gangrene."

Chapter Forty-Six

The actions were automatic as she hung the clothes on the worn line tied to the battered wheelhouse of the house boat. Days unaccounted had passed since the fruitless search for Barry and she felt herself returning to the total emptiness that had dominated her life since childhood. She had not eaten properly since the search, and the scruffy jumpsuit hung on her frail body like an unwashed pillowcase. She'd spent wasted hours in the Queen's Head, for company more than anything, to try and deaden the sense of loss of the one man who'd brought some meaning into her existence.

They'd taken advantage and the fat man had forced himself on her after they'd shared a whole bottle of brandy one evening. She'd laid there as he grunted and puffed for his pathetic pleasure, and felt the nausea rising in her stomach as he strained away, as if to satisfy any bodily function. She felt nothing and didn't even notice the smell of his sweaty body and bad breath when he finally belched his orgasm in her ear. Pushing away his revolting body she forced him out of the home and down the gangway, before clutching the rail and retching into the slow flowing waters of the creek.

The vomit stank and she crawled back to bed to curl up, foetus-like, praying for the relief of sleep to blot out this living hell.

The morning breeze played with the clothes line and the freshness of the washing and the watery sun made things seem better. She boiled an egg and nibbled toast over a cup of coffee on the boat deck. The man passed on his way to the pub and stuck up two fingers as she was finishing her drink.

Instinctively she threw the mug, and was lucky to catch the back of his head. He turned in fury toward the boat, but she was quick enough to pick up a boathook with a spear end attached for spiking fish, and wave it at him with menace. Her whole body shook and she mouthed a fusillade of obscenities learnt from her mother, which stopped the fat man full in his tracks.

"Fucking whore," was all he could manage as he walked away, turning once to reinforce his earlier gesture. She shivered at the encounter and returned coldly to the living room.

Hearing the car draw up she looked with curiosity, to see who was visiting whom. Two gentlemen got out and started toward the houseboat before she recognised Tim Mitchell as one of them. Hurrying to the mirror she rapidly brushed back her hair, and was still using the lipstick when the old boat bell rattled an announcement.

"Anybody in?"

"Be with you in a moment." The soft voice was remembered.

She came out on deck and Tim smiled and took her hand. "How are we?"

"So so. I've not been sleeping too well. Feeling a bit tired. I'm pleased to see you again."

He nodded. "Like you to meet Patrick Clancy. He owns the airline Barry – eh – I work for." She studied the clean-suited Irishman not knowing whether to be friendly toward him or not. 'Wasn't he the cause of Barry's problems at the outset? Why's he here?' she wondered.

"I'm awful sorry my dear. That was a good man you had. He'd a rough ride to be sure, and I'd like to help if you'll let me." The lilt in his voice immediately won her over. The voice, she believed, of a genuine man.

"Please sit down. Can I get you anything?"

"Not for me ma'am. Thank you." Tim shook his head also, but they both took the offer of a seat. Judy waited for something to happen.

"I believe Barry had no children," said Pat.

"He has a sister and parents. I've not met them."

"And children?" She shook her head.

"You lived with him, is that right?"

"Not really. He was a friend. You understand?" She turned to Tim.

"Well it's not my business for sure, but I do have a duty to undertake. That I do." He went on to explain that because of Barry's pardon from his company, he had passed the findings over to the solicitors and offered compensation for loss of earnings and damages. Barry's solicitors had agreed a figure which needed ratification from the pilot.

"It's generous you'll find. No problem for me. Insurance pay you see."

She sat and listened before speaking. "What good's that now he's dead?"

"We know how you feel or at least we can guess. You were his girl. He wanted to be with you." Tim asked her to understand. "The relatives will probably inherit his assets, but they don't have to be party to this agreement. Patrick wants it to go to you."

Pat looked into her eyes. "Take it girl. Life must go on."

She looked back at him and sighed. "That's what I said to Barry but he didn't take my advice did he?"

Pat got up from the chair. "Pub back there. Any good?"

"All right. Some of the customers are a touch rough."

He moved over and took her arm. "Let's sort this with a Guinness or two, shall we?" Judy agreed but asked for them to wait while she changed into a dress.

"How much Pat? You never told me."

"A hundred and eighty thousand."

"Phew. Not bad for two years."

"Should make her an attractive catch."

"You mercenary sod..." He stopped his sentence as Pat indicated for him to turn round as she re-entered the room. "Doesn't need money," he hissed.

Tim agreed as they both took in her transformation into the black-haired gypsy girl who had so attracted Barry in the first instance. "Beautiful." It was all he needed to say as he took Judy's arm and walked her to the Queen's Head.

The fat man was there and wouldn't leave it. "Not good enough for yer eh? Prefer your fancy boys? Like it both ends do we?"

Tim was first but Pat was quicker and the man gasped as the ex-rugby player kneed him in the crutch as if taking on the All Blacks entirely on his own. The force of Patrick's charge took them through the bar and on to the veranda, scattering tables and chairs as they went. The fat man, in his efforts to back away from the hand screwing into his face, hit and smashed through the railings with flailing arms, swearing and cursing as he drifted out into space. There was nothing to hinder his fall and Patrick stopped without a care, to watch him splash and disappear below the water before he turned and made his way back to the bar.

252

He dumped some notes on the counter. "That'll pay for the damage. Don't let him – and I mean don't – let him be here when I come next time."

The barman was speechless, and the other customers in the house stayed hard in their seats, talking among themselves to make certain it was nothing to do with them and that they weren't involved.

"Out of this poxy joint," he indicated the door to the others. "Let's find somewhere decent."

The mobile was ringing as they reached the car. Patrick picked it up whilst Tim opened the rear door for Judy. "It's for you Tim."

He took the handset. "Tim Mitchell."

Pat busied himself with the car keys and prised out the one for the ignition, whilst Judy checked her mascara as Tim took the telephone message. Their thoughts were personal as they partly listened to the one way conversation in the car.

"Yellow you say... any identification – alive?"

Patrick pricked his ears and started to take an interest. "Who is it?" Tim's flick of his hand told him to hold it, but that was not in Pat's nature.

"So it could be...?"

"Tim what's going on?" Pat could see that Judy was now starting to listen.

"Shut it Boss."

They had to wait as Tim carried on with the caller with the odd frustrating interruption which was suggesting half a story. "Land's End... ten miles. Penzance you say...?"

"For Christ's sake Tim what's going on?"

"Hold on." Tim put his hand over the speaker and turned to the others. "They've found a dinghy. Man inside and alive. Just a chance it could be Barry. They don't know. Want me to go to Penzance hospital for identification. Bringing him in by helicopter."

"Sorry, I'm still here. Carry on..."

Chapter Forty-Seven

"Take the King Air." They were back at Hurn and Patrick was barking his instructions.

"You sure?"

"Take it I said, and keep me informed."

Tim hurried Judy to the steps of Patrick's private executive turbo and fired the engines for a rapid departure.

"Tell me Tim. Be honest. Is there a chance?"

"I don't know Judy. If there is, he'll be a very ill man."

"Oh please God. Save him for me." She sobbed the words out loud.

Tim set course for Culdrose and trimmed the King Air to maximum cruise speed. 'I can do no more,' he told himself.

The Wessex helicopter danced over the dinghy as the flight lieutenant caressed the controls to keep the aircraft hovering against the wind rising off the waves. The second line holding the frail craft was taut, and the pilot was trying hard to prevent any violent movement from breaking the connection.

The aircraftsman didn't want to go back to cope with the task ahead. This was only his seventh sortie and the others had been tame compared to this. He remembered his training and the simulated operations but somehow they weren't matching up to the reality. As the dinghy got closer he became scared, and would have done anything to turn back. 'I'll tell them he's dead. Stupid. Supposing it was me. Maybe I'm not cut out for this.'

The intercom buzzed. "Don't forget. Inject the morphine before you move him." Okay for them. They're only flying the sodding aircraft. He'd wanted that, but his physical and the aptitude tests had scotched any ambitions in that area.

The sea was closer now and although the weather was still fine, the wind had backed and was blowing a healthy force five. In fact it was easier than he had feared and the training won the day down there. The occupant was unconscious and it was difficult to get the harness around the body with the dead weight and the rocking of the dinghy. Eventually he achieved the task and the winch wound them back to the Wessex. Once on board he was able to relax and hand over to the others.

The flight to Penzance was only twenty minutes and Tom O'Neal obtained a clearance to fly directly to the hospital where Barry was handed over to the emergency team, leaving the RAF crew to fly silently back to base.

Gus carried out a routine debrief and thanked them for their efforts before he made his way down to the mess for a well-earned drink.

Tim threw in the reverse thrust and fast-taxied the King Air to the apron. The ordered taxi was waiting by the gate and he and Judy ran across the tarmac and told the driver to move it. Forty minutes later they stepped out of the lift and hurried the few yards to the intensive care ward. They were asked to wait for Matron who arrived quickly, looking very smart and efficient in her white, starched uniform.

"You're enquiring about Mr Johnston I believe?"

"Please. How is he?" pleaded Judy.

"May I ask for your interest or relationship with the patient?"

"Friends and employer, in my case," Tim told her.

"I see, you're not next of kin then?"

"His wife's dead. He has little connection with his parents and family. I'm his closest friend. Please tell us how he is?"

The matron understood her impatience. "I'm obliged to ask these questions for such a serious situation."

"How serious. Tell us?"

The nurse stalled for a moment. "I doubt he'll pull through. Suffering from intensive hypothermia with a very low body temperature. We've a ruptured lung and internal bleeding. Several bones are broken and one leg is virtually beyond repair. Before we can operate his body heat must recover. On transfusion at this time..."

Judy sat on the hard chair and covered her face. "When will you know?"

"I can't say... I need your help on one matter."

"Fire away," Tim answered.

"The leg. It must come off. Often we can get the patient's permission. This isn't going to happen in this case. Normally I'd ask the next of kin, hence my question. Are you able to sign a permission?"

"Jesus!" He saw the matron cringe slightly at his outburst. "Apologies for the blasphemy ma'am. The man's a pilot. He needs his legs to fly. It's his career. What are you asking us to do?"

"He may not fly again – I'm sorry. Without the amputation he'll not live to fly. Even with it... I can't tell you." She let the words soak in.

"How long have we got?"

"An hour."

Tim pulled Judy to one side. "We can't take this on alone. We must talk to his folks."

"How, d'you know them?"

"You know I don't."

"What about Mr Clancy?"

"Good thinking, I'll go and try."

He was in luck and found them living in Lancashire. They were shocked, but he gathered that there'd been little contact over the years. Something to do with Barry's wife. A family fracas.

"They've left it to me. No comebacks."

"So what's our decision?"

"Do we have a choice?"

Judy shrugged her shoulders in despair. "I want him alive."

As often in life some major decisions are made by fate. Whilst they pondered over their duty, it was taken from them. Tim started to fill in the authorisation form when the matron returned and brought them the news. "It's done. The surgeon had to act. The poison was reaching his lungs. We couldn't wait any longer. I'm sorry. You can relax."

"When can I see him?"

"You'd best go home. It'll be a long battle before we know. Ring for information. Can't let you visit until we've achieved some stabilisation." They flew back to Bournemouth fearing the worst.

The fever raged for days whilst the hospital staff fought for his life.

"He must have been fit, otherwise he'd have never survived this far."

"Seen worse," the registrar retorted.

"Maybe it was the alcohol? The fellow still had traces in his bloodstream when I operated. Apparently they found empty bottles in the dinghy." The surgeon chuckled at the thought.

"I don't believe you."

"Honest! Pretty resourceful if you think about it, to load up with refreshments when you're about to risk drowning."

Judy rang every twelve hours but there was no change. The days dragged on and she began to loose faith. Impatient, she grabbed a train to Penzance and demanded to see her lover. The policeman joined her in the lift on the way out.

"Couldn't help overhearing. Gather you were trying to see Mr Johnston?"

"Yes. Why are you here?"

"Same reason. We need to talk to him."

"You've seen him?"

"No joy. I gather he's pretty ill."

The tunnel suddenly seemed brighter and the blurred images more in focus. He became aware of people talking and large faces appearing in front of his eyes. His head was banging and he wanted to sneeze. He tried to raise a hand to his nose but it seemed to be all tied up with plastic tubes. He smelt the aroma of food and wished for a bacon and egg.

With eyes larger now, he blinked as the white-coated man leant over him and took away his face mask. "Welcome to the land of the living."

"Any chance of a drink. Whisky?"

Chapter Forty-Eight

"Still recuperating I heard."

"Will the case reopen?"

"Up to the Crown prosecution I expect."

"They could drop the charges? I gather there may be some mitigating evidence relating to the previous trial."

"Yes I heard that. Not sure of the facts. Think I'll have a word with their counsel and see if I can dig up the latest."

"Perhaps you could call back?" David Jenkins replaced the receiver and made a note for his secretary to contact him at the Law Society if Nigel Waite rang.

She'd waited for this day and now it was here shivered nervously. Wearing his favourite dress, she'd grown her hair long and combed it carefully in the style that he loved. The battle was not won and Judy knew he'd a long way to go. The medical team had performed wonders and the neurologist had called it a miracle.

Patrick had been true to his word and she squeezed herself with the pleasure of knowing that some money was tucked away. He'd also provided the car for the day and she glanced anxiously out of the window to see if it had arrived.

They were waiting at the main entrance and she hurried the farewells in order to have him to herself. He looked drawn as the porters helped him from the wheelchair to the car. "Give it time", the registrar had advised. "He needs to settle the mind as well as the body. He'll be fine." The journey to Wales seemed endless and Barry spent most of it asleep. Finally they were there, and she busied herself with domestic chores and arranging the flowers before she gave him the envelope marked with the CAA logo.

He read it slowly and the drawn face changed to a grinning smile as he took in the sweet succour of the words. "Pardon. I was right."

258

"Dropping the charges," Nigel informed him.
"Really? On what grounds?"
"Public interest."
"What about the insurance cash?" David asked.
"Writing it off I gather. After all, no case proven."
"Lucky fellow."
"Suppose so. Been through a lot though. Rather him than me."
"What about your fees?"
"The loss adjuster has agreed to settle those. Yours as well I understand."
"Good day all round then. Thanks for your help."

The piano could be heard above the bustle of the port as they sipped the Martinis in the warm Spanish sunshine.
"Tell me again." She gazed at the bronzed body of her man, still afraid that their luck would not hold and someone was waiting to take it away. He was nearly back to full health and talking of flying again and she was pleased to sec the freedom from the tension that had so often featured in his face.
"Tell you what? I love this place. D'you remember the fun we had?"
"Stop changing the subject. You keep losing me." She kissed his cheek and ruffled his hair.
"I feel great. Bouncing around like a kid on a birthday trip."
"Listen. You never really told me the reaction when you first read the letter."
"Yes I did."
"If you did, I don't remember it. Everything was in a haze at that time."
"How d'you think I felt?"
"Pleased, ecstatic?"
"Like an orgasm, just like the one you're going to give me this afternoon."
"You're sex mad Captain Johnston. I give up."
"How can I explain it? My career and reason for living were taken from me, and now I have them back. I'm simply very grateful. What more can I say?"
"Me?"

"Of course, 'me'. What d'you think changed my mind that dreadful day. It was your voice. From heaven I thought at the time, but what does it matter."

They kissed again and he led her away with a wicked smile on his face.

Hogan read it in Reuters as he relaxed in his favourite pub around the corner of his new offices. It was a report from their correspondent in the Middle East.

'News is surfacing from Iraq of a bloody killing involving nationals who have been supplying defence equipment to neighbouring Iran. It has been suggested that they sold devices capable of nullifying the strength of Iraq's latest missiles, making them ineffective, and worse, redirecting them through guidance blocking technology to return and attack the launching sites. It's not clear who unearthed the anti-regime culprits, but it is understood that the Iranian Government were assisted by the CIA, as the missiles in question originated from the USA.'

'Azif, I wonder? Poor bastard, and the family. Something to be said for the British system even with our weak verbal politicians. Better than those crazy Arabs?'

The bistro was quieter than usual and Gill sat in the corner glancing at the report.

"Happy reading?" Dennis asked as he slipped into the opposite chair.

"If you like an unsolved mystery... suppose so."

"I'm not a magician, can't conjure answers from the sand. The Fokker is, and will remain a failure on my part. Satisfied?"

"Grant you do have some probing strengths," she joked. "Maybe you're not using such talents in the right way?"

"Nobody's perfect."

"Come to think about it, the desert crash and the Johnston affair have really been unmitigated financial disasters for my small outfit."

"You can afford it, or more accurately Lloyd's can afford it."

"Okay, but the lunch is on you."

"And the afters?"

She raised her eyes to his. "We'll see, lover boy."

Epilogue

The early morning mist was finally lifting as it gave way to the increasing strength of the spring sunshine. Tim and Judy were sitting outside the clubhouse of the newly resurrected airfield at Old Sarum near Salisbury, watching young students preparing for their training flights.

The car drew up and Patrick found them enjoying a cup of coffee. "Arrived yet?"

"No. Probably waiting for the mist to finally burn off."

Patrick ordered more coffee and chatted to Tim about the latest business venture he'd established in the small executive market. Judy sat comfortably, showing her legs to the sun and enjoying the warmth soaking into her body.

They heard the distinctive buzz of the two-stroke engine before spotting the aircraft in the distance.

"Over there," Judy pointed.

"You know Tim. The eyes are awful suspect these days. To be sure I can't see it."

"He's just on base leg. Should be with us shortly."

The microlight turned onto finals and Barry glided it to land a few yards away from where they were sitting. He hooked himself away from the open seat and limped his artificial leg across to the party.

Tim stood up to assist saying, "If you don't mind me taking the piss Barry, that's got to be one of your best landings for the last three years."

Barry laughed as he kissed Judy, and then shook hands with Patrick. "What d'you think?"

"Looks bloody dangerous to me," the Irishman said.

"They're all right. Pretty twitchy if you don't concentrate. You know of all the craft I've flown this is probably the most demanding, but by far the most enjoyable. I think I'll stick with it. Maybe the boss up there's been trying to tell me something all along."

"I think I'll stay grounded," Judy said. "I've had enough flying scares to last me a lifetime."

"Decided then?" Barry turned to Tim.

"Best man? Of course. Just let me have the date."

"Hang about now you lot. There's got to be a condition." They waited for Patrick as he deliberated, "Only if you'll be letting me give away the bride."